A Place
Called
Zamora

The Zamora Series, Book One

A Place Called Zamora

LB Gschwandtner

SparkPress, a BookSparks imprint
A Division of SparkPoint Studio, LLC

Published by SparkPress, a BookSparks imprint,
A division of SparkPoint Studio, LLC
Phoenix, Arizona, USA, 85007
www.gosparkpress.com

Published 2020
Printed in the United States of America

Print ISBN: 978-1-68463-051-6
E-ISBN: 978-1-68463-052-3
Library of Congress Control Number: 2020908446

Formatting by Katherine Lloyd, The DESK

This is a work of fiction. Names, characters, places, and incidents either
are the product of the author's imagination or are used fictitiously. Any
resemblance to actual persons, living or dead, is entirely coincidental.

For Bob

When you passed from this life on October 9, 2018, I was just finishing this, my seventh work of fiction. Always, Bob, you were there to listen, to teach, to share, to shine. No one was more imperfect than you, Bob, as you showed us in so many of your self-deprecating, funny, charming, enthralling stories, almost all based on your own most human frailties.

How do I miss you? I miss you the way all your students and friends miss you. With all my heart. You loved your family, yes. But you loved the world you inhabited, and that world included all of us who learned more about writing and living for writing because of you.

Be at peace, my teacher, my friend, wherever you've gone. You live in the books you left, the stories you told, the lives you touched, the joys you shared, the gift of loving stories, no matter how they're told. We who are about to write salute you.

Contents

Prologue

Long Before
The Collapse

First there were the endless wars fueled by governments that poured their countries' money into ever more costly and complex technology and machinery for killing each other off. Entire centuries were engulfed by wars until whole populations were wiped out or displaced to camps where the rule of law broke down. Famine and disease followed, killing off more swaths of surviving populations.

Arable lands were ravaged by successive plagues of insects. Animals went extinct and the seas turned too hot for many life forms. The promise of nuclear energy gave way to deadly explosions followed by climate disruptions that rivaled even the fallout from nuclear wars which culminated in a search for life beyond Earth. Those searches devolved into aborted attempts at relocation to other planets and, over time, societies lost much of the technological knowledge they'd developed.

After several centuries colonies of survivors formed into city-states or moved deep into mountain ranges to cut themselves off from the horrors left behind. The natural ecology of climate and vegetation had become so disrupted that near the sea only tropical plants grew, while high in the mountains deciduous trees slowly took root.

One city located at the edge of a hot sea was renamed Infinius. It came under the control of a brutal dictator who installed systems that controlled every aspect of life. The Regime, as it was known, named what had come before The Collapse and made it a priority to "cleanse" the people of memory so they could be re-educated into obedience.

The Cleanse was simple and effective. The Regime divided people into lotteries with identity cards. Each lottery group was assigned three numbers. The Regime decided which numbers to choose for The Cleanse. When a group was announced, their children were sent to Child Holding Centers and the adults were rounded up and delivered to a Cleansing Camp. The moment they arrived, they were stripped of whatever personal belongings and clothing they had and then marched into a great hall. Men and women together naked under blaring lights. And then, a siren sounded and another sound, lower than the siren, a kind of buzzing noise that grew louder as the siren faded. People slumped over as the buzzing continued until it finally ended. After that no one remembered much of anything and they were sent to re-education centers where they were indoctrinated to follow obediently anything and everything that The Regime and Premier Villinkash ordered. Since even The Regime realized the city needed some thinking members, the ones who escaped were watched and reported on by The Cleansed. Thus The Regime maintained maximum control over the population and all its goods and services were owned and operated by The Regime. And The Regime controlled all the wealth except where corruption ruled. And it ruled everywhere.

Part One

The
Race

Niko was twelve when he ran away from Child Holding Center Number Five. It had been a particularly bad day. Two boys sent to solitary with only water and another beaten by a fat guard for not walking fast enough to the exercise square. Still, Niko had managed to hide in the kitchen behind two giant flour sacks. Always hungry, he had stuffed two slices of stale bread into his mouth. Of course just being there was a punishable offense.

A fine powder coated the floor where rats had chewed holes in the sacks. A scattering of tiny paw prints made haphazard patterns like bird tracks in snow. There was no way to avoid leaving footprints. Niko worried if he was caught . . . well, he refused to think about that.

Crap guards, he thought. *Crap feeders. Never give us enough. Sell what's supposed to be for us on the black market. One meal a day for kids is not enough. Bastards.*

A soft, scraping sound interrupted his thoughts. He peeked around the sacks and saw a boy he knew. Younger than Niko and small for his age, the boy was scraping a long, pointed butcher knife against the inside of the vat used to make the putrid soup the feeders served once a week. The boy scraped and then swiped the goo off with his index finger, and sucked what he'd gathered.

As Niko considered some way to approach him so they could both escape, the door swung open. Two large guards caught the boy by his arms and pinned him against the vat.

Niko ducked his head back behind the sacks. He wanted to help the boy and attack the guards, but he couldn't figure out a way to overpower them all by himself. Even if he could, he knew eventually they would beat him. And there were worse punishments. He'd heard about them. His heart pounded and ached at the same time. But, even though he'd grown stronger in the past few months, he knew it was useless. He covered his ears, but the boy's cries would reverberate in his nightmares for years. And always there would be that scraping sound just before he would awake in a cold sweat.

When whatever they had done to the boy was over, the guards laughed, and Niko could hear them swilling something from bottles. Soon they were slurring their words and reeling around where the boy had been pinned. After some time, they opened the back door to an infested alley and threw the bottles onto a rubbish pile. Niko heard shattering glass as the bottles landed. Then, laughing, they tossed the boy's thin, lifeless body on top of the heap. It landed with a thud.

Back in the kitchen, they clapped each other on the back and soon stumbled around until both of them slid to the floor right next to the flour sacks.

Niko slipped from his hiding place and passed the snuffling, snoring guards. He found the knife the boy had used. It was cold and sticky with his blood. Niko approached the first guard, whose head was tilted to one side, drool dripping to his chin.

He contemplated the guard for a moment, remembering him from the yard where the boys were allowed to run around each day for fifteen minutes. A feeling of hate welled up in Niko. Hate of the guard, the hunger, the whole place, and everyone in it.

When he stuck the pointed end of that knife hard into the side of the guard's neck, blood spurted out like a fountain and Niko jumped back. The guard moaned for a second and then was still.

Niko moved to the other guard but decided to simply leave the knife in his open palm. No one would miss Niko, he thought. And they would blame the guard for what had happened there because Niko knew that, in this system, no one was safe from blame.

After he was done, he moved swiftly to the door, pushed it open, and glanced at the poor boy's body lying like a dead leaf on top of the rubbish heap. Then Niko ran for his life. Ran past the open gates that allowed delivery trucks to enter, past the spindly pine trees, past piles of gravel and broken fences. Ran as far as he could without stopping. He had no plan, but was sure no one would bother to find him. He'd be just another boy lost forever.

He didn't stop running until long after darkness had enveloped the city. And he never knew that his disappearance back at Child Holding Center Number Five had, indeed, been noted by someone.

Six years later, Niko spotted his name on one of the InCom kiosks scattered like scarecrows throughout the city. You couldn't avoid them, always blasting lists at you. Lists telling you what to think, what to do, what not to do, the latest threat to the city, who to report, ways the Regime was so very good for you. That day, exactly halfway down, number seven of thirteen, *his* name was on a list.

He had known, when he moved to The Ring, this day might come. Now he had turned eighteen and that day was here.

The mechanical voice barked lists day and night.

These five citizens have reported neighbors for the List of Hoarders.

(Lists of names were always displayed on the screens so everyone would know just who had been singled out.)

Hoarders will be punished and re-cleansed.

Our beloved Premier Villinkash will post a list of people to be carefully watched for the next month.

Look for that list tomorrow. Your neighbors may be on it. You may be on it.

The voice droned on and on as the words scrolled across the screen until . . .

And now, today's Special List, which appears only once a year. Thirteen names have been chosen. One from each building in The Ring. These are the very courageous young men honored to represent our city in The Race. Remember: the families of these boys should rejoice and give thanks to our beloved Premier for this chance to participate in this year's Race.

Every year since The Collapse, a list of thirteen names had showed up six months before the day of The Race. No one could know which number would be the year's winner, but Niko understood the odds were against him. They were against everyone. Unless you had an edge. In this city, if you wanted to survive, you needed an edge for just about everything.

As he stood in front of the screen, staring at the list of names, he tried to think who he could call on to get that edge.

There's not one damned thing in this city that isn't fixed, so why not The Race? Question is, how far up would I have to go to fix it in my favor—and what would I have to give up in return?

Niko had learned ways to beat the system. Always in small ways. That was best because the small scams usually went unnoticed, or if they were discovered, they were easy to bribe your way out of. Then someone else had something to hide.

After he'd run away from Center Number Five, no one looked for him. He'd fallen in with one gang after another, grown tough, learned how to survive, made his way. Now this.

There was something about Niko, though. Some quality that none of the other street kids had. People listened to him, hung around him, did what he told them to do. He was confident. Not arrogant. Not a blowhard. Not a bully or a braggart. He was the guy everyone picked to lead the team, even though, in the streets of Infinius, there were only gangs for survival.

Even the older guys who lived in The Hovels and the roamers who never stayed anywhere more than a few nights looked up to Niko. So, as he stopped outside The Hovels to study the lottery list, a group of young men gathered and waited for his reaction to the news. If he'd told them to tear it off its base and crush it against a concrete wall, they would have done it for him, knowing the Detainers would round them up and beat them senseless.

"Number seven," one of them said. He was a powerfully built youth, older than Niko, sporting a stubby black mustache and wearing spiked boots that protruded below black denims. "That's a good number, man. You're gonna crush it out there. Crush them all, man."

The others mumbled and nodded.

"Last year, number eleven won it," Niko said with characteristic calm. He poked the curb softly with the toe of a scuffed boot, as if kicking off dried mud. "Seven *could* be it," he added.

All they knew for sure was out of thirteen starters, there would be only one survivor. The Race was stacked against the others from the start.

Up in The Globe, Watchers sat in shifts. The Globe used to be the place where they'd guided airplanes in and out before The Cleanse. Now there was no need. No one except the Overseers and Protectors were allowed to travel. The Watchers observed people scurrying here and there, searching, working, wandering with nowhere to go.

It was said they saw everything, everywhere, all the time. From inside the glass bubble, screens monitored the scarred and crumbling high-rises. The monitors watched the one- and two-story Prefabs, constructed after The Collapse, and The Hovels where Scroungers scraped by on whatever they could steal or pillage.

One of these was named Gruen. He lived at the very edge between The Hovels and The Shanty Alleys where the most unfortunate, known as the Leftovers, barely survived. Gruen didn't spend much time in The Hovels since he was always on the move, scrambling for a score of any kind he could turn into a barter for something bigger or more valuable.

After Niko left the Holding Center, he'd fallen in as Gruen's runner for a time, but he'd moved on when Gruen asked him to be his bagman.

"It's the best you can hope for," Gruen had said. "And I'll protect you. As far as I can."

"Hey, man, you know I trust you," Niko had told him. (Of course he didn't. Not entirely. You couldn't trust anyone a hundred percent.) "But I got my sights on running my own operation, you know? And, anyway, bagman is not my style. I'd get stuck somewhere on a bottom rung with nowhere to go."

Gruen was a lumbering, oafish sort of guy with only one good eye and one milky-blue one that seemed to have a will of its own without focus or direction. Niko never asked him about it, assuming something must have happened to Gruen during The Collapse. After that, The Cleanse would have wiped out his memory of whatever had caused it, so what would be the use of asking?

"That's okay, man," Gruen had said with a shrug. What did it matter to him? He could get a bagman any day. But the kid was an asset. He was smart. And not afraid of the street.

So Niko had kept up with Gruen, and their alliance had turned into a kind of street gang with tentacles that led as high as the Watchers, who eventually got a piece of whatever game Niko and Gruen were running on any given day. Niko ran the gang while Gruen dealt with the street people and the Watchers. He also passed the proceeds back up the chain.

But life was not easy in The Hovels, an endless sea of huts with dirt paths where Scroungers attempted to survive in row upon row of dwellings. Cobbled together from whatever could be found from day to day, the huts would be blown to bits by hard rains and blistering winds, and Scroungers would rebuild using whatever they could gather until another storm rained down on them.

So, although new dangers would confront him even there, Niko had been determined somehow to move to The Ring.

El was twelve when she first met Niko. She had no birth record. Even her name—Elenora—had been given to her by The Sisters of Mercy the day they'd discovered her after The Cleanse, left in a sack at their convent, which had been set up in a spacious, abandoned garage that had once been a major hub for taxis near high-rise number six. A note hidden in bunting made of old paper bags begged the nuns to harbor this precious baby and keep her safe. The sisters took her in and cared for her and other babies as best they could. There was no medicine, little food, and only black-market baby formula.

Furtive Scroungers would appear at the garage with bundles of torn cloth tied around cans and small bottles. The sisters provided refuge for a few nights, cleaned and fed the Scroungers before they left to search farther and farther out for whatever scraps were left. Many babies died in their first months. But El was strong. She wailed for food louder than the others, lifted her head before the others, crawled and stood and grabbed at what she wanted.

When one of the sisters held her, she rested her head and hummed as if satisfied just to be alive. The sisters doted on El.

They gave her goat's milk that had come from somewhere beyond The Perimeter, where only night Scavengers dared to go during The Collapse and The Cleanse that came after it, when few adults over twenty remembered anything outside the city limits. Anyway, by then, you weren't allowed to venture past the walls, gates, barbed wire, and electric fences that were known as The Protections. No one ever said what they protected against.

By the time she was ten, El roamed the streets outside the convent to find fresh food like eggs and fruit. The nuns raised chickens for a while, but with all the children to feed, that didn't last long. Other kids who'd lived at the garage convent left when they were old enough and never came back, but El always returned.

On one of these foraging trips she passed Niko on a street corner and saw he held a flat box battered around the corners. She figured it could have eggs inside, so she stopped to ask about it.

"Do you have eggs to trade?" she asked him.

"What do you offer in return?"

He looked her over carefully. Certainly nothing threatening there. And she had a lovely oval face with big, greenish-gray eyes, the kind of eyes that pulled you in. Her hair, with glints of red in shiny dark curls, held back with a plain piece of torn red cloth, fell gracefully down beyond her shoulders. What he could see of her legs looked like two slender sticks beneath a skirt that came just below her knees. Only fifteen himself at that time, he could see she would soon be a beauty. She was too young for artifice and was obviously not offering herself. And there was something else about her that attracted him in a way he'd never felt before. He would think about that much later.

"I have this." She reached into a pocket and pulled out a very small rectangular object. She waited to see if he showed any interest before divulging what it was. He looked unlike the others she usually encountered when bartering. He wore a loose, long-sleeved shirt, untucked from worn denims so faded it was impossible to tell what color they had been. His mop of hair curled around his ears, but it was his mouth that she found arresting. His lips curled slightly up at the corners as if he were holding himself back from laughing. No one laughed. Except, every once in a while, the sisters joked with each other and the children, especially when they read books aloud.

She almost smiled at him, but not quite. He reached out for the object, but she pulled it back.

"Are those eggs in the box?"

Then he did smile. A broad smile that crinkled his dark eyes.

"Yes. Fresh this morning. How many do you need?"

"How many are in there?"

"I'm not sure. Suppose we go over there and count them." He pointed to an old bus stop with a crooked wooden bench.

El looked around. This wasn't one of the more populated streets, so they were alone. She hesitated since you never knew who might be dangerous or even a spy for the Regime. But she needed eggs, had promised the sisters she would come back with some, and he seemed harmless. She followed him to the bench.

He pushed aside some dust and sticks. "Here, sit down."

Except for the nuns, El had never been treated kindly. She hesitated.

"Go on, sit down. I won't bite."

She sat a little farther away than he had suggested. He placed the box carefully between them on the bench and lifted the sides to reveal a whole batch of eggs.

"Where did you get them?" she asked. Her eyes grew wide with wonder, and she looked up at him as if he'd just shown her a jeweled crown.

He chuckled and said, "They're only eggs."

"But so many. I bet they were laid by . . ."—she stopped to calculate in her head—"thirty chickens?" She looked at him and he smiled.

"I suppose so."

"They'll have to be kept cold," she said almost to herself, thinking about where they could be stored at the convent. She still held the small rectangular object in her hands. "Or we could hard-boil them."

"Well, you've seen the eggs. Now what is that?" He pointed to the little thing.

"Oh, no. I don't think you'll want it for so many eggs." El shook her head.

He laughed out loud at that. She jumped up. "Maybe you think I'm not old enough to bargain."

"I'm sorry," he said, and patted the bench. "Sit back down. I didn't mean to offend you. It's just that no one ever traded in that particular way before, and it made me happy for a minute."

"Oh," she said, and sat down again. "Well, here it is."

She opened her palms to show a tiny picture of Jesus. The frame and the corona around Jesus's head were both done in gold leaf. The painting was delicate and detailed, showing Jesus washing his disciples' feet.

Niko studied it carefully, bending over to see it clearly, placing his hand above it to shield it from the sun. "What is it a picture of?"

When she explained it to Niko, he asked, "But why would he do that?"

"To show that he is their servant."

Niko pondered this. *What does this mean that he is their servant? A servant brings rich people their food and cleans their house. A servant? Why would anyone want to be a servant? And why would anyone paint a picture of a servant?*

He stared at it for many minutes, mesmerized by its careful

brushstrokes and the gold around the subject's head. *This wasn't just any servant. And the look on the servant's face . . . why is he looking up at the sky?*

Niko wanted to ask these questions, but he didn't want this girl to think him an idiot, so he just asked, "What's your name?"

"El. What's yours?"

He told her and then said, "I'll trade with you. The eggs for the picture. I think it's fair."

Later he would unwrap the tiny picture and stare at it for hours, puzzling over its meaning. This was the first of what would be many encounters with El. They would trade or talk. Sometimes Niko would just gaze at her until she reddened and turned away. El asked him questions about his life but he never told her about how he'd run away. Niko also asked her about her life in the convent and what the nuns had taught her. And so they became close in a way that was rare in that city at that time.

By the time Niko was fifteen he was already running his own street operations. This often involved brawls, which Niko made sure to end quickly before the Watchers showed up. Although it was well known they didn't care if the Leftovers wanted to kill each other, Niko was careful about protecting his loot and made sure to control every situation.

On that day the fight had begun when someone grabbed the bag of loot Gruen was carrying. He'd just made a score—bruyaha or something else smuggled through The Protections from outside the city. Smuggling went on all the time. There were regular trade routes that illicit go-betweens used, all paid off through the Protectors. They smuggled by underground tunnels the Watchers couldn't detect from up in The Globe. Burrowers were in high demand and spent their whole lives half-buried in earth, digging new mazes of tunnels so intricate there were stories of people getting lost and dying in far-off dark corners. When the stench of their corpses reached into the main tunnels, the Collectors were called in for extra duty. They hated having to work underground. Still, they were paid underground extra so they did it, but not without much complaining.

The Collectors worked for more than wages. When someone died in a living unit, before hauling the body onto their ghoul wagon, they were entitled to whatever had been left behind with the corpse. Scroungers followed them on their rounds, ready to make deals for old furniture, clothing, jewelry, kitchen appliances, fans, shoes, hats, coats, telephones. They even traded InCom screens if they could yank them off the wall from inside a unit. These were encoded for each person in the city, so once a person died, it was useful only for parts. After everything had been looted, the living unit went into listings for a new resident. Again, there was graft involved through an elaborate system run by the Protectors.

On that day, Niko happened to round a corner in time to see Gruen's fist connect with the nose of a burly Scavenger. It was a well-known street fighting tactic to temporarily stun an opponent by smacking his nose so badly blood would spurt out, giving you a moment's edge to land a knockdown to finish it quickly. Niko knew the Scavenger only by his street name, TMan, and had traded a few items with him in the past. He also knew TMan wouldn't let a bloodied nose stop him. And Gruen wasn't much of a fighter with that one weird eye.

Niko always carried a heavy iron pipe. He walked toward the gathering crowd slowly, the way a guy walks when he knows he can overpower the situation. He didn't want to kill anyone. It was crucial to end a fight before the Detainers got wind of it and everyone was hauled away to the camps. Some of the bag of loot Gruen carried was his, too, so he had a financial motive. Still, Niko liked to keep his sectors as clean as possible. Which is to say his unofficial sectors. He patrolled them as diligently as any Protector. Of course, he paid off the uniformed thugs on a schedule as regular as any mortgage.

Niko circled behind TMan as his arm went back, fist clenched, to take a swing at Gruen. *Whack.* He clubbed him a solid one on the back of the head. Still holding the pipe as TMan wheeled around to see what had hit him, Niko was ready to flatten him full in the face. But the guy's knees buckled, and he went down in a heap at Niko's feet.

"Stomp him!" yelled the others. "Kill him. He's a rat anyway. Destroy the rat."

Niko held up a hand to shut them up before the Detainers showed up. He knelt down and felt for a pulse. Feeling the slight throbbing, he stood again.

"Get out of here before you get hauled away for an illegal gathering," he said in a low, authoritative voice. They hurried off, leaving TMan on the ground where he was beginning to moan softly as he came back to life. He would crawl away soon enough, back to his hovel to nurse his wounds and prepare for the next street fight.

As soon as they were gone, Niko led Gruen into the doorway of a nearby one-story building with no windows left and a door hanging on bent hinges. There they divided what Gruen had been protecting in the bag hanging from his belt.

"You had a good day," Niko told him.

"Unit ten raided a warehouse outside The Perimeter. They paid off the guards. Cost them plenty, but it was worth it. Look here. I got a watch."

Gruen showed off the watch on his wrist. Niko whistled softly. "Nice one too," he said.

"Hey," Gruen whispered, "you notice anyone following you? I got this creepy feeling of someone dogging me every time I meet up with you."

Niko shook his head. "No, man. No one's watching me. I'm real careful about that. Anyway, who would care about me?"

Gruen shrugged and tied the bag onto his belt. He stuffed his take into a flat pouch he kept in a kind of holster he'd created inside his faded jacket.

"You never know," he cautioned Niko. "But I got a definite feeling about this. Just watch out. Might be we're not paying off the right people. Or spreading enough around."

He sneaked a look outside the doorway before stepping back into the street, which was empty except for a scrawny cat sniffing at a drain.

"Got a bead on something that could be big. I'm not saying it is, but it could be. Only getting it is risky. Nothing I could handle. But you . . . Meet me in the third quadrant over by that big pile of old bricks. It's near where those same Scavengers hang around."

"Okay." Niko nodded. "But I doubt they'll try this again. They're a bunch of low-life cowards most of the time."

He waited until Gruen was out of sight before he also left the shadowy doorway and turned toward the Tower of David over in The Ring. He never walked on the streets without being aware of his surroundings. The faint scent of meskitta smoke came to him as he passed an alleyway where a scrawny dog pawed a piece of garbage. Niko glanced at the dog and then saw the toes of highly polished black shoes that looked new and expensive protruding from a corner.

Darkness would envelop the city soon, and Niko wanted to get home. But he thought about what Gruen had said. Was someone following him? If so, he had to know who and, more important, why. So he veered into the alley, fingers clenched around the iron pipe, eyeing the dog that now pawed a crumpled cardboard box.

Meskitta scent was heavy now, sweet and musty. He held the

pipe firmly in case he had to strike fast. And then, as he advanced deeper into the alley where anything might happen, from the shadows a man appeared, his hands up, two fingers holding the meskitta cigarette, a bemused smile on his face, an expensive-looking, carefully pressed suit that matched the shined shoes covering his trim frame.

Niko sized him up quickly. He looked—how did Niko think of it?—pampered.

"I give up." The man stepped forward. He was grinning broadly now.

There wasn't much to joke about in Niko's daily life. So he didn't respond to the teasing. And the man kept coming toward him, his hands raised, his face in shadow, the meskitta trailing a slender stream of smoke above his head.

"Here." The man opened his jacket with one hand. "Have at it. Whatever I've got. It's yours. Go ahead."

"I'm not a thief," Niko said, but he kept hold of the pipe.

"Of course you are," the man said, and dropped his arms. He took a last puff on the meskitta. "We're all thieves at the right price. I have nothing against stealing." He shrugged and dropped the stub to crush it underfoot, then looked up and smiled at Niko. "What's your price?"

"What do you want?" Niko relaxed a bit. He looked down at the pipe as if considering whether to let it drop.

"You can keep hold of it, if it makes you feel safer," the man smiled again. "Although, if you decided to slam my head in, you'd find yourself in trouble like you can't imagine. But we all take chances, don't we?"

"Why are you tailing me?"

"Am I? Or did you just happen to find me in this alley?"

"You don't look like the kind of guy who hangs around in alleys. Especially in this part of town. So, yeah, you're following me." Niko wondered if he was one of those older men. The ones who like teenage boys. And when the man reached into his jacket pocket and pulled out a slim wallet, Niko backed up.

"Not interested," Niko said. "Go on back to your mansion and leave the streets to the rest of us. You've got enough already."

Niko turned to go, but the man was on him like a hungry wolf. He took hold of Niko's shoulders, pressing him to turn back so they'd be facing each other. And then he grabbed the pipe before Niko realized what was happening. He tossed it far back into the alley and spun Niko around, and the grin was gone. The man had a tight grip, a weight trainer's grip, the kind of grip that was foolish to resist.

"Listen, I know who you are and how you live. I'm on your side. I won't tell you why or how, but I'll be around. And one day, you'll come to me and I'll help you."

With that, the man let go of Niko with a little shove. He handed Niko a card and said, "Come see me here," and walked quickly out of the alley.

Too stunned to react quickly, Niko exited the alley just in time to catch a glimpse of the man sliding gracefully into the back seat of a long, black car. Niko had never seen one like it before. The door slammed, and the car pulled away rather fast. Niko marveled at the car and wondered about the man. He looked at the card which read simply *Huston*. There was also a number with an address in The Compound.

One night, not long after Niko's encounter with Huston, Miriam happened to be at the newspaper office after hours when she first met Niko.

Once an investigative journalist, Miriam was now an elderly woman with a weak heart who'd been relegated to compiling old newspaper articles and rewriting them from the new slant. Which is to say, propagandizing them and changing history to reflect the Regime's post-Collapse directives.

She hated doing this, so she secretly transcribed all the old stories onto a computer no one used. One day she planned to write an honest account of what it had been like before The Collapse. She intended to tell the truth of how the shift had been engineered. For now, safeguarding the history was all she could do.

That night Miriam had come back for her clandestine work and stumbled upon Niko crouched beside the desk next to hers. Every night the office lights went out automatically just before dark, so she nearly fell over him in the roomful of closely packed desks. The maintenance crew was supposed to be there much later when it was pitch dark outside, after all the streetlights had gone out with curfew. She'd sneaked in so quietly he hadn't heard her as he riffled through a lower file drawer.

Watching her in the dim light, his young face was a mix of terror and bravado. Had he been sent by the Protectors to spy on her? They circled each other like a couple of cats. Miriam considered grabbing the sharp scissors from the cup on her desk. But before either of them made a move, they heard something, and she placed a finger to her lips.

He nodded, and they both knelt behind the desks like two supplicants. He held some papers, which rattled a little in his shaky hands. Realizing he was nervous and that she was in no position to question him right then, Miriam kept her distance. There were no other sounds except the blood thumping in her ears. After the noise ceased, she relaxed a bit.

"What are you doing in here?" she whispered.

He looked so young, while she was already old. Her gray hair wispy around her face, she wore thick glasses all the time now and relied on comfortable shoes with rubber soles. She should have quit the paper after The Collapse, but she felt an obligation to the truth of history. It may have seemed anemic by then, as if she alone could do anything to avert what had happened or change what had been like an avalanche: unstoppable and catastrophic, burying everything they'd known. But journalists' tools were not powerful enough to hold it back.

Also, she still needed the salary. They had done away with old-age pensions. And Miriam was alone. The boy, who was a handsome, sinewy teen, stared at her intensely, his dark eyes still narrowed with mistrust and caution.

"Who are you?" he asked back.

She told him her name. "I was a reporter. Before The Collapse."

She tried to calm herself, taking a deep breath, thinking how she must treat her heart with care. It was an anachronism, still thinking of herself as a reporter. They'd taken over all media long ago, relegating everyone to churning out the most despicable lies glorifying the Regime. That was what made her sick, she reasoned. Living day after day with dishonesty was as deadly as any virus.

"I know that name," he whispered. "Are you the one who wrote that story 'Horror of Life in The Hovels?'"

It was her turn to nod, and she thought he must have read that when he was very young. This interested her. Many children could barely read these days. The reporter in her wanted to ask him about it. Instead, she said, "But that was before. I can't do that now. Too dangerous."

His expression changed suddenly. He, too, relaxed a bit and glanced around, squinting at the semi-dark room. Some electric light from the streets outside filtered in vague shafts through the windows.

He came into focus now: a mop of dark, curly hair, piercing brown eyes under steady brows, thick dark lashes, and a muscular frame. It was hard to tell, from his crouched position, how tall he was. But one thing she noted . . . he was dressed in black down to his sneakers, the kind climbers used to wear back when people got out of the city on weekends and such.

"What do you have there?" she asked again, and pointed to the papers stuffed under his arm.

He stood up then. "I have to go," he said, almost to himself.

Now she could see he was tall. Over six feet, she estimated. And graceful, moving in the tight space with the ease of a stalking cat.

"Be careful," she whispered, feeling protective toward him. She pulled open the top drawer of her desk to retrieve the backup drive with her notes. Bags were inspected, and everyone who worked in the building was patted down every day coming into the building and leaving it. This was the only way she could take out what she needed.

"You go ahead," she told him. "I'll follow in a few minutes. No sense making a target of two people. How did you get in?"

He opened his jacket, revealing a coiled rope and a hook. It was climbing gear, Miriam realized, and she wondered how he had come to own such things these days. So he had come in from the roof or a drainpipe. Had he scaled the outside wall?

She'd managed, a few days earlier, to get a counterfeit keypad card and instructions on how to wipe out the memory it had used. It was more than she could afford. Everything on the black market was overpriced, but what choice did she have? It was rumored they would be installing eye readers soon. Rumors were like eddies in a stream, endlessly churning. She figured it was now or never to steal her own backup drive, although according to the Regime, it all belonged to them.

Niko crept toward an open window. Although neither of them knew it then, they would be spending considerable time together in the months before The Race. And it wasn't until later that night that she realized he'd never told her what he was doing there.

Niko made the climb out of the window and down to the dark street. He walked with the papers still tucked into his belt. It was dangerous because of curfew. But he also had a pocketful of

bribes in case he was stopped. Keeping to alleys, hiding in abandoned doorways and flattening himself against crumbling walls if
he heard anything, he set off to find Gruen. Periodically a siren
would wail as someone was nabbed and hauled away to a work
camp. But Niko kept moving until he passed through The Prefabs
and came to the outskirts of The Hovels.

In the daylight he recognized the maze of shacks and crumbling walls, dirt paths and trash-strewn walkways. But at night it
was more difficult. And the Nabbers didn't patrol out here unless
they needed to fill a work camp quota; then they would appear
with searchlights and chains.

Niko hadn't told Gruen he'd look for him that particular
night. He had no way to know exactly when he'd be able to get
into the newspaper office. Gruen was the one who'd heard about
the papers. But he couldn't make a climb like that down from the
roof and across the ledges. So Niko said he'd go. But now he had
no place to hide them. Hoping Gruen had found somewhere, he
fumbled on in the dark, feeling his way by instinct until he came to
an open area he recognized. This was where there had once been
a school with a playground, someone said, but the Overseers had
it blasted away since the only schools they approved were now
indoctrination centers. Yes, Gruen's hut was nearby.

Niko crossed the lot and headed down a dirt pathway until he
came to Gruen's place. He was about to enter through the sheet
of loose cardboard that subbed for a door but stopped when he
heard muffled noises. A woman's voice. And then gasping. Then
the woman again and the sounds of moving around, thumping,
and then a long groan from a man. Then nothing.

"You done?" It was Gruen's voice. "You oughta be done after
wearing me down like that."

Niko heard a slap.

"Ow." The woman's voice. "You hadn't got to do me like that."

"You know you like it." Gruen again.

"Yeah, you're right. It's better than some. Better than a lot of 'em."

Niko heard a deep sigh. He wondered when he could break this up. He wanted to get on with it.

"You better get out now." Gruen's deep voice.

"Why you wanta push me out right away? You don't wanta go again? I could go again. Couldn't you?" The woman laughed.

"Shut up." Gruen. "Just shut the shit up and get out now. You had enough for one night. You got what you came for. Go back to what's-his-name."

Now Niko started getting nervous. If they had a fight, he'd have to wait even longer. If the shack had a door, he would have knocked. But it didn't. And he couldn't let whoever she was see him. She'd start asking questions, and that would leave them open to a ratting out. So he waited behind the shack in the dark. His stomach growled, and he remembered he hadn't eaten in a long time.

Then he heard a commotion inside: Gruen telling her to get dressed, her complaining about him, and they went back and forth until Gruen finally pushed her out onto the path.

"I'm tired," said Gruen.

"Yeah, you're always tired after. But not before. I think I oughta tell someone about how tired you are."

"Here." Gruen's voice. "Take this."

"Wow." The woman. "You musta liked what you got tonight. I'm gonna buy me a real pretty something for the next time. When's that?"

"I don't know. I'll find you sometime soon. Now you go on back to him, and don't tell him nothing or there won't be nothing for you next time. Understand?"

Niko heard some more fumbling and then footsteps fading into the night. Carefully, in case she was hanging around, he slid along the hut wall until he could see Gruen standing there, scratching his head in the dim light that came from his hut.

"Pssst, Gruen," Niko whispered.

Gruen spun around, his fists ready to pound whoever was there. He couldn't see well in daylight with only the one good eye, but at night it was even worse.

"Hey, it's me," Niko said.

"Man, what're you doing out here? I almost thumped your head in."

"I got it," Niko told him.

"What?"

"The plans. You know. What we talked about."

"Shh, come inside." He pulled Niko by the arm. "Shit, that woman don't know when to stop. Insatiable, that's what she is. And that man of hers ain't worth shit for nothing. Keeps a roof over her head but never fucks her. So she comes around here every night almost. I can't get rid of her."

"Got you a regular beauty queen?" Niko joked.

"She must be one ugly bitch to come around here every night and want me. You get a look at her?"

"Sorry, I was hiding in case . . . well, you should be careful," Niko said. "Maybe she's on the payroll. She could be a ratter."

"Naw, she's not. Good for what she is, though. Keeps a man's head on straight. You know what I mean? So, what've you got?"

"We better go in." Niko had lowered his voice. He figured Gruen bragged about women because he was disfigured, just to prove he was still in the game. But Niko also thought it made Gruen vulnerable. That made him a possible danger too.

The huts in the section were packed pretty tightly together, with laundry lines and electric poles and InCom screens everywhere. He could hear snoring from nearby and a baby wailing farther off.

Gruen's hut was dark except for light from a streetlamp outside the back window. Not actually a window, it was just an opening that let in dust and rain and bugs. Niko walked the few steps to switch on a small lamp on a box next to what Gruen used for a bed. Just a thin pad on the floor, sheets all rumpled and kind of gray looking, as if they hadn't been washed in a long time. There was a musty smell of sweat and dirty laundry. Niko opened his shirt and pulled the rolled papers out of his belt, then unrolled them under the light.

"Those the plans?" Gruen asked. He stood next to Niko and looked down at the papers with his head tilted toward his good eye.

"I think so. You were right. I don't know why they were stashed in that newspaper office, though. Seems odd to leave them there. Think it's a plant?"

"The guy who gave me that piece of info used to work over there. It was a payoff for something I let him have, that he needed really bad. He's no ratter. Did some computer stuff for them before he got sick. A fucking tech genius, he is. Told me one day he saw some reporter come in real hush-hush and stash some papers in his files. So this guy, name's Fuller, when no one was lookin', opens the drawer and takes a look. And secs these papers he thinks must be plans for the whole of Infinius. You know, the underground stuff and all the walls and The Perimeters. He let it go at the time, but when he told me about the medicine he needed and how I could get it for him outside the city, well, that's when he told me he'd have some info that could be useful for that kind of operation. Because, you know the higher-ups, they get past The Perimeters all the time. So there must be ways."

They spread the papers on the floor and held the small lamp down to cast light directly on the lines and symbols.

"Yeah, look, there's The Ring. And the Tower. And all the roads." Niko was breathing hard. This was a goldmine. He followed the plan with his finger. All the roads. And The Perimeter. And there, up in the northeast corner, what looked like a huge park and low buildings.

"So there really is a compound where The Overseers live." He pointed to an outlined area that was marked *Area C*.

"You said it, brother." Gruen whistled. "I wonder what it's like in there."

"A lot better than here or The Ring, or the Tower, or anywhere *we* know." Niko traced around The Compound and down along the edge of the drawing like he was studying a treasure map. "Probably where the rat Villinkash hides out, too."

"What about the other papers?" Gruen reached down and slid out papers under the master plan. "I can't tell what they say." He squinted at one, his head cocked to one side to look with his good eye.

Niko laid them all out and moved the small lamp from one to the other.

"They're details of everything," he breathed. "It's the whole city right here in front of us. Perimeters and even down to details of walls and barbed wire. And look," he said, pulling over another sheet. "This one seems to show the InCom wiring system."

He looked up at Gruen. "Do you know what we could do with this? If we had someone who knew about electronics and computers?"

Soon after that night, El hurried along a street early in the afternoon. She carried a large package wrapped in yellowed newspaper.

"What have you got there?" Niko called out from the shadow of a doorway.

She stopped abruptly, ready to fight. She'd grown more womanly by then, looking older than her almost sixteen years, and had learned to protect herself.

Niko stepped out and smiled at her. "Something to trade?"

"Oh, it's you. You shouldn't creep up on me like that."

El, too, had begun to hope they would meet like this or maybe in some more private place, although she couldn't imagine where that might be. Usually El confided all of her daily experiences to the nuns but these she kept private, thinking about Niko as she fell asleep at night, sometimes even dreaming about him. She wondered what it would feel like to be kissed by Niko. It was there her daydreams stopped.

"I was just standing here and happened to see you. There was no creeping up at all." He was still smiling. "Come over in the shade. I want to talk to you."

El followed him to the doorway. As they reached it, the shade felt good, and she looked around at the street. No one was out. The lunch hour was over. Everyone was back where they were supposed to be. The closest InCom screen was telling people about the value of working for the Regime, about the rewards their work would yield. Of course the rewards would go to the Regime, but the announcer didn't say that. On the screen there were shots of happy people at clean, bright factories and in Regime greenhouses. They waved and saluted.

"What do you want?"

As she asked, Niko reached behind her and slid a thin piece of metal along the edge of the doorway, and she heard a click. He pushed the door open and took her hand. Once inside, he closed the door behind her.

"Cooler in here," he said.

The building had once been a shoe factory. There were skylights in the roof. Light bathed the old wood floor and the long tables, pitted from decades of use, now abandoned like so much of what had once been alive in the city.

El wandered away from him, glancing around in wonder.

"The sisters have told me that there used to be so many factories before. And . . ." she was afraid to tell him more.

"And what?" He waited, but El didn't say anything else. "You can trust me, El. What else did they say?"

El shrugged and moved away from him to look over the tables.

"I wonder how many people used to work in here," she said. "I wonder about all those people and what happened to them. What happened to the way things used to be?"

"What do you know about the way things used to be?"

El shrugged again and leaned her back against a table.

"No, you said the sisters told you. Then you said, 'and.' And what, El?"

She stared at Niko, thinking about the sisters and their warnings. Could she trust him? Should she?

"Tell me. I wonder about what happened too. About who my parents were. If they're even alive. Don't you wonder about things like that, El?"

She moved back to where Niko stood and nodded.

"Yes. I wonder about things. But that's dangerous. You never know what you might find out."

"But you did find something out, right? What was it?"

El's shoulders slumped and she curled her fingers over the edge of the table, almost as if she felt she might fall and need to hang onto something.

"They have a place where they store things," she whispered. "A secret pit. I found it one day by accident. I've watched things and read things. Things that tell what happened."

"A secret place?" He walked over to where she stood and put his hands on her shoulders, nodding down at the newspaper-wrapped package. "Did this come from there?"

She backed away. "No. This is just . . ." El laid the package on one of the big tables. She unwrapped it and pointed to two jars lying next to each other. "See, this is just honey that I use to barter. We collect it at the convent."

He came to her side again. "Can I taste some?"

She looked up at him with clear eyes framed by thick lashes. "I guess." She took one and opened it. Lifting the lid, she wiped her finger on her shirt and dipped it into the honey, swirling her finger so it wouldn't drip off. "Quick," she said, and he leaned in and took her finger into his mouth.

He sucked it like a baby bird, and when all the sweetness had transferred down his throat, he let go of her finger, then dipped his into the jar and said, "Your turn."

She was too surprised to refuse, and besides, the sisters had taught her not to waste food. Their admonitions had become part of her instincts. She, too, sucked at the sweet, thick liquid. Before she knew what was happening, Niko pulled his hand away and leaned into her so close she could feel his warm breath and smell the honey still on it. It was like one of her dreams, as if she had willed this to happen. And when he took her finger and pressed it to his lips, it created a delicious thrill that ran through her body, down below her stomach, down, down farther, and she didn't pull away or make a sound.

In the next minutes, El lost track of time as Niko explored her body with his hands and pressed his fingers to her breast until she felt like crumbling. When she felt his fingers between her legs, something changed. She tried to back away, but his other arm was around her and his lips were on her neck.

"Niko," she said, and her voice was so throaty she wasn't sure any sound had emerged.

He was lifting her skirt, and she felt dizzy. "Niko," she said again, this time with more strength.

He pulled away from her face to gaze at her, his eyes heavy, a determined look about him.

"Niko, stop." She said it with certainty this time. "I can't. We can't."

"Why not?" He stroked her arm.

"Because we just can't. Not now. Not here."

Could she guess what he was thinking, feeling? That she wasn't like those other girls, or the women who worked at the clubs? That she was fresh and new? That he felt something but couldn't have said what? That he wanted her but also he wanted something else. What was it? What else *was* there? Even if he had told her his thoughts, she couldn't have understood them because she had been protected by the old nuns.

"There's no place for us, El. Not ever. And soon I may be . . ." He couldn't say it out loud.

She placed her fingers against his lips. "Don't."

"Why won't you let us be happy while we can?"

"I don't know. I just can't. Not yet. Please understand."

"Then will you do something for me?"

"What?" She eyed him, wondering what else there could be.

"Will you hide something for me? Trade the honey for it, if you like."

He let her go and walked to a dark corner of the big room. He picked up a bunch of papers and brought them back. After unwrapping the honey, he folded the newspapers over the maps of Infinius. "Take this back to the convent. Hide it in your secret place. One day, if things go all right, I'll ask for them. If things don't go all right, burn them."

"But . . ."

Niko placed his fingers on her lips. "No questions. It's better if you don't know anything. Just hide them for me. Okay?"

She nodded and he let his hand drop, but he leaned into her as if it might be goodbye forever. El folded against him, and suddenly she wanted what he'd wanted just a few minutes earlier. But this time, he pulled away and, with a rueful smile, said, "I have to go now. But when we meet again, then you'll be ready?"

He took the jars and left El there to exit the building a few minutes later. When she shut the door behind her, the lock clicked. With the newspaper bundled under her arm, she hurried back to the convent.

No one was sure exactly the day or time when reporters realized their way of life was about to crumble or that a new order would take its place. Miriam, like other journalists, certainly saw disturbing signs, but whatever they reported was like a cork trying to stop a bursting dam. By the time she met Niko that first night, they had all lived through late-night raids and house-to-house searches. The Protectors never said what they were looking for, and if they found something of value, they often conscripted it under some vague rule of *threat to the state.*

Miriam hoped enough clues would remain to accurately reconstruct what had happened. She knew that history is always being rewritten, and eventually, although it can take many generations, truth emerges grudgingly from behind curtains shut by those who seek to hide it. So she kept on, even after salvaging scattered folders from the wreckage of her office desk after the Protectors had it ransacked by thugs who could not discern waste paper from important records. So they made a great show of scattering everything while never examining anything.

Notes she had smuggled out of her office the night she met Niko showed what had happened before her investigative pieces had ended with a thud when the Regime began to use reporters either as weaponized dirt collectors or propaganda spreaders who were expected to shovel and spread the Regime's shit.

It began when a small group managed to take control of the great wealth beyond the city by exploiting abundant oil and other mineral reserves. They took advantage of starvation wages, and over time, a small faction led by a vicious but seemingly affable man named Villinkash, who had given himself first the title of General and later, Premier, came to dominate the country's largest and wealthiest city, which was also its financial center.

Back when he first had been circulating his credentials for office, she and her colleagues referred to him with a smirk as "General Villin." He made speeches about his service to the country and wore a military jacket studded with medals, although he had never served in any capacity. In the newsroom they used to joke that he got one medal every month when he opened a new cereal box for breakfast.

By pitting group against group, he and his followers drew out the most aggressive and easily controlled factions of the city. These were the ones who felt as if they had been particularly wronged, although they never really articulated who had wronged them or how. Still, Villinkash used a standard playbook on how to divide a country against itself.

His faction took over the banks, co-opting the country's wealth to hold within a tightly controlled circle. They came to be known as the Overseers. They rallied around Villinkash, who held a strange sway over his followers, so that no terrible act could dispel their worship of him. In addition, he tapped into the belief among enough ordinary people that he could—and would—improve their lives. By the time they realized that they had been duped, it was too late. Whatever self-governing power they'd had was gone like a puff of smoke.

With these two groups behind him, he took control of all the levers of government. He turned the city's police into a paramilitary force and expanded their numbers by the thousands. With the Overseers' backing, he took over all businesses, schools, trades, and everything else that had once operated privately and peacefully. Of course he took over all media and reinvented it as a propaganda tool. As this happened, his reputation began to change from affable and charismatic to ruthless and determined. His speeches became more fiery. They ended with salutes and cheers. And always he pointed to the "others" who would take away the rights of his followers.

With the help of the Overseers and the Protectors who ran the practical, day-to-day operations of the new order, he'd seized all government functions and placed them under his control. He had renamed the city "Infinius." And then the electronic "cleansing" began.

At the same time a glittering high-rise, designed as the height of luxury to house and glorify the people of wealth and influence, rose above all the others at the center of what was called The Ring.

But something went wrong before the dazzling tower was completed.

An ambitious young developer who had visions of a grand future for an influential city looking outward beyond the sea named the skyscraper after himself. The Tower of David, at forty-five stories, had been designed as the tallest of all the high-rises and could be seen from anywhere in the city. Built in stages, the top floors had never been finished, and on the twenty-third floor, a huge flat, cantilevered roof jutted far out, like a bird's wing over the wide avenue below. The narrower unfinished skeleton led to a second, smaller roof twenty more floors above.

Even its name, emblazoned in two-story golden letters above the entrance, was designed to show the world the importance of its builder. But the handsome, well-toned former athlete, David, became too wealthy and popular. It was rumored that his tower was deeply in debt to the Overseers, who controlled the banks. His bravado and brash public persona made enemies of the wrong people, and one summer solstice before his tower was to have been completed, a tragic fall from its roof ended his life in a heap on the concrete below. The tower was never finished, and with electricity, plumbing, and other necessities never installed, it began to deteriorate.

Almost immediately rumors swirled like a bouillabaisse through the city. One story said David had been eliminated by the relentless Villinkash. It was just the sort of could-be- or might-be-real story Villinkash relished. So he embraced and fostered it. And why not? It enhanced his reputation and encouraged people to fear him.

Was it true? No one ever knew, and by that time, reporters were having a hard time getting anyone to talk. Miriam knew because she'd tried. She'd even had a brief interview with one of the Overseers, a man named Huston, a smooth operator whose own rise was something of a mystery. She'd never found out if he actually knew anything, but by the end of the interview, he had taken her hand in his and looked searchingly into her eyes and asked:

"What do you lack, my dear? I can help you if you need something."

Too stunned to answer, she stammered some nonsense, and he withdrew his hand. It was amazingly soft, she'd reflect later, and his nails were carefully manicured. He simply smiled benignly at her.

"Here is my card," he'd said. "Feel free to call on me."

By then they were living through what later came to be known as The Collapse. It was orchestrated by the Overseers, the Protectors (its generals), the Watchers (its informants), and the Detainers (its armed enforcement). Above them all was Villinkash, well on his way to consolidating his power with one more scheme.

By co-opting the name of his victim, he declared a holiday in David's *honor* and established a great and terrifying motorcycle race to honor the city's favorite son and commemorate his passing. The Race would be held every year on the summer solstice. It would celebrate the glorious rise to power of Villinkash and his Overseers and turn David into a martyr for his cause. His building was left unfinished, and the people took that as both a warning and an invitation. Slowly at first, people with few resources and nowhere to live began to inhabit it. They came first as squatters and then became tenants with no landlord. The Overseers looked the other way, and the Tower of David became a sub-community of its own at the center of The Ring.

The motorcycles had been polished to a glossy shine. Numbered from one to thirteen, they reflected orange and gold gleaming in the sunset. They had been placed to the millimeter as if machined to each spot. The Race would be visible to all the people of Infinius. Attendance was obligatory. The long summer solstice provided sunlight until the very last moment.

Official betting started a month before The Race, giving the Overseers a long lead for their vig on every bet placed. Regime bookmakers stood on street corners, writing in small black books. They were easy to spot: disheveled men in suits with bulging pockets that held all their pieces of betting scrip. Their tout sheets stuck out of side pockets, and their greasy fingertips were black from counting out coins and bills.

They hawked from designated street corners. "Hey, I got a lead on number eight. A sure winner. Who'll make big money on number eight?"

"I'll take two." A fat woman raised her hand and held up wadded bills.

The bookie grabbed her money and tallied it in a thick notebook he had pulled from his pocket.

"Name," he barked at her.

"Juanita O'Brien," she whispered back. "He better win, too."

The bookie stared at her, his head tilted down so he could see over his grimy glasses.

"Yeah, sure. I guarantee it. That's why they call it 'betting.'" He snorted and slipped her money into a fat pouch hanging from his belt loop.

Everything was tabulated, regulated, notated, stored, and audited. The bookmakers changed the odds from day to day, but there were certainly favorites. It was said that the entrant from Building Six was as close to a sure thing as you could get. Odds were he had an in with one of the Overseers.

Now the day had arrived, with crowds wild in anticipation. Under the crushing weight of the Regime, they'd waited for this day all year. It was a festival of epic grandeur. No expense had been spared on visual technology. Free food and liquor helped stir excitement. Bruyaha in all its forms was everywhere, even though the Regime had outlawed private sales years before. Still, like everything else, if there was money to be made, it was a commodity to be traded. And if you had to pay off the Watchers, well . . . it was just a cost of doing business.

Thirteen boys, each eighteen years old, stood by a preassigned bike. Some were solemn, some arrogant with raised fists. These were the crowd favorites. When a fist went up, a deafening roar erupted from all the rooftops surrounding the Tower. The boy would beam and puff out his chest in defiance of his probable fate. Some pumped both fists into the air and twirled for the crowd. There was foot stomping and tossed confetti. Rolled-up newspaper sheets were also a crowd favorite. Lit at one end, they rained down from the rooftops like a meteoric shower of fire to the streets below.

Although the Tower at its highest was the tallest in The Ring, its jutting lower roof was two floors below the others, so when crowds gathered on the twelve roofs of The Ring, they could look down and see The Race from all angles. The Race. Captivating in its gruesome theater in the round.

From huge hovering jumbo screens on the high-rise rooftops to small window-sized units all over the city, screens of all sizes kept track of the betting and profiled the racers in an endlessly looping hype.

Miriam spotted Niko on one of those giant screens, his face set and grim. So young. So determined. And she wished she could stand next to him and take his hand in hers at that moment.

As she stared at his image, she thought there was something about the set of his jaw or the look in his eyes that told her he felt different from the other boys. It was such a subtle distinction that it wasn't until later that she realized she had caught it at all.

Last-minute betting continued in a frenzy. People cast whatever meager savings they had into the pot. They may as well have rolled it into the flaming papers and tossed it away in the hot solstice wind. Debts piled up with the ashes and the Regime took its piece of every bet.

The winner would be showered with gifts and money, of course. But beyond that, he would have a seat at the Protectors' table. A novice's seat, yes, but a place from which to start building his own empire within the system. And since even the Protectors were not safe from Villinkash, periodically there was a purge, which created room for more junior-level hopefuls to move up closer to the head of the table.

That wasn't all, however, in this system of rewards and punishments. If a young man from one of the thirteen buildings was chosen to be a rider and refused the *honor,* his choices were dismal to downright deadly. He could be shipped off to a forced labor camp, working in mines where he would never see the sun again, and would probably die within the first year. Or he could simply disappear. There were certainly occasional escapes from one of these fates. One year, an eighteen-year-old named Garret from Building Four escaped to The Shanty Alleys to melt into the vast melee of people who lived like rats in endless warrens. With a price on his head, he was soon handed over for the reward.

Rewards and punishments began long before The Race. Once the thirteen riders were identified, the Regime brought them to a replica of the rooftop track where they were each presented with a motorcycle and ordered to practice, which seemed like a benign request until they started the bikes and began to ride. Each boy quickly discovered that applying either the front or rear brake resulted in an electric current that shocked the rider. If a rider applied the front brake, the shock ran through his hand and up his arm to his neck. Pressing the foot pedal brake sent a shock through his leg. The first shocks were mild but the more a boy applied either brake the stronger the shocks and the more severe the pain. The same was true of throttling down. And so the boys learned, like race horses on a track, to ride full throttle as fast as they could. But the training didn't end there. The Regime took no chances on The Race. A sniper was assigned to each boy. Should a boy fail to perform at the last minute or anytime during The Race, his assigned sniper would shoot to kill.

But this was not the final treachery of The Race. Each year riders were chosen from families who had been allowed to keep their sons at birth. And now after raising them for eighteen years, the spoils would be doled out in the order that the riders reached—and went over—the roof edge. The faster the rider, the bigger slice of the winning pie his family would get. Speed, agility, and sheer bravado were at a premium and were rewarded by The Regime. Niko, having no family, had no such incentive, yet everyone knew there was also no percentage in holding back. Punishments would be doled out as often as rewards.

The track that year began straight, then curved slightly, leading to a straightaway toward the edge. Racers had to throttle up and gather speed as they advanced, leading to the straight run at the end. The rider who came to a hard stop at the edge of the roof would win.

Everyone knew there was no way to escape, and only one boy would survive The Race. The rest would catapult over the edge as David had done because only one of the motorcycles had brakes. And everyone knew it.

At one time the stairs El climbed had solid concrete walls, intended only for a fire emergency, but now she could see through to the blight that had once been a thriving metropolis. She was too young to remember the time before everything changed. She'd heard stories from the nuns. Rather, she'd heard them speaking in hushed tones as they went about their chores, looking furtively around as if afraid (or, El thought as she got older and more curious, ashamed). But of what, El never asked.

It was dawn on the day of The Race. El made the climb up steel steps that clanged and swayed as if from a slight breeze. Her fingers rested lightly on a dangling handrail too unstable to trust anymore. Going slowly took too much effort. So she no longer stopped at each landing as she used to in those first months after she'd left the nuns, before her leg muscles were taut and firm, when she'd had to stop to catch her breath and her legs ached with each ascent.

She'd had it easy with the nuns, who had doted on her, but then the oldest ones had died and gone to Heaven. At least that's what the two who were left told El. She wasn't sure about Heaven. Their descriptions were so specific. There was a gate and St. Peter was waiting there. And angels. All the nuns who had died were angels now, they told her. Now there was only one left: Sister Catarina.

El had been protected by the nuns until she was fifteen. But when Sister Catarina was too ill to care for herself or anyone else she was taken away by the Retrievers in their white overalls and face masks and rubber gloves. Then El was told to leave. The Retrievers boarded up the garage the nuns had turned into their sanctuary. The city was rife with such boarded and abandoned properties. El had been given an envelope full of enough cash to buy some canned goods and pay two months for a shared room on the nineteenth floor of the Tower. She had been allowed to gather a few clothes and shoes and personal articles. At the last minute, she'd reached out for the cross Sister Catarina had given her the day before, when they had prayed together.

During The Cleanse, an underground had developed. When all but one of the priests had been cleansed out, their last act was to hide whatever was left in the church. At that time there was such chaos that it wasn't hard to get around the electronic scanners, which hadn't yet been installed everywhere. Now it would have been impossible, but then, no. So the Sisters of Mercy had a rich cache of hidden valuables.

"Remember," Sister Catarina had whispered to El, although they were the only two left, "besides the pit, there are secrets hidden beneath the flooring stones. Everything you will need. Don't let them have it. One day, when you need it, come back. Ten stones to the north and twelve to the west. Remember that. Take this cross in your hand and swear by Almighty God that you will be good and not fall prey to them. Swear it and then I can go to Heaven in peace, dear El."

El took the cross and held it to her lips as the nuns had taught her. "I swear," she whispered, and kissed the cross before holding it for Sister Catarina to kiss. She struggled to hold tears back from overflowing. She wished she could save the sister. She wished she could stay there forever.

On the day of The Race, as El rounded a landing, Niko popped out of a cavernous space off the stairwell. His head was pattern-shaved in concentric circles for the event. Bands of bristle crossed the top of his cranium, and sparse sideburns pointed down to his jawline, where the bone jutted under darkly tanned skin. He wore black leather pants and a sleeveless tee with the image of a snarling tiger splashed tightly across his muscled chest. His sinewy arms were covered in so many tats it was impossible to tell where one ended and the others next to it began. Niko was taking a heavy risk on these stairs.

"I heard they tapped you to help Old Merrie," Niko whispered at her. "I know you can't be late but just stop for a minute or two."

"I can't," she told him, and started to trudge on, carrying two heavy canvas totes that said *Emilio's Friendly Market* in faded red letters.

He took the steps two at a time to catch up as she reached the next landing where he tried to take the bags from her.

"Let me carry them for you," he offered.

She shook her head and disappeared above him.

He followed, stopping a few steps just below her, and looked up at her firm calves. He reached out and placed his fingers around her ankle in a caress.

"Don't go." He said it softly, gently. He'd watched her climb these steps before to deliver food to the more affluent squatters on the top floors. They paid her enough to survive and she did other chores for them. He sometimes thought about the rewards he'd receive if . . . but he couldn't let his mind wander far. Not before he knew if he'd be the one. So he lingered there, his hand on her ankle.

Now she lowered the heavy bags to the concrete landing and turned slightly to look at him as his hand moved up her calf and he moved to the next step closer to her. He watched her intently for any signal at all, but she didn't move. He took one more step up, now only a step away from where she stood. Still his hand moved up, sliding around to the inside of her thigh. And he stepped up next to her.

That was when she put her hands on his shoulders and pushed him away.

"You just told me you know I can't be late. They're always watching everywhere. Do you want to get us both arrested and sent to a camp for interfering with The Race?" She backed away from him, but he moved toward her.

"There are no cameras here," he said, and looked around to verify the claim. "No one to see us. El, this may be the last time we'll ever be together. After tonight . . ." His voice had dropped to almost no sound, and a choke caught in his throat. He reached out and took her hand.

Off to one side of the landing was a small space that had probably been designed to house electrical equipment. But since none had ever been installed, it was just an empty room with a small doorway. Niko pulled her inside. The door was long gone. There were no windows and no cameras or InCom screens.

"I know," she said. "After tonight . . . Oh, Niko, it's too horrible."

"But we have now," he told her, and softly twirled a lock of her hair between his fingers. "We have each other for a few moments. It may be all we have."

"You're much braver than I am," she said. "And I promised the sisters. They made me swear before God."

"Do you think God would want me to die never knowing someone loved me?"

He moved closer, almost touching her with his body.

"Please, Niko. Please, don't say such things. It can't happen. Not you. Not now."

He leaned in and pressed himself lightly against her, and his hand once again moved to her thigh. He whispered her name, and his hand wandered up and up until she gave in and slid her arms around his shoulders.

"El, my lovely El," he said, and moved them as one against the back wall, where it was darkest.

And then they heard a clang. And another. Someone was coming up the steps. *Clang, clang, clang.*

"The bags," she whispered, suddenly petrified. "My bags are on the landing. I must continue up the steps. You hide here. I'll go."

And with a hurried rearranging of her skirt, she was gone.

Niko slumped against the wall.

El lifted the bags and began climbing again. Then there was another voice and El talked about how hard the climb had been, and how she'd had to rest before making the final push to the top.

He had to concentrate and hurried away from the stairwell down a long wall on the inside with nothing but a loose steel railing on the outside to guard against falling into the chasm of street far below. From up there, everything on the ground was a miniature: stunted as if squashed down from the top, or slanted at a crazy angle. He didn't look down but kept his gaze straight ahead until the wall ended at what had once been a doorway. By then, it was just a gaping hole, neither rectangular nor round but an amorphous shape, as if chewed by some great animal, huge chunks taken out at a time, and then left, abandoned like the rest of the building, to rot in the sun and wind.

He could see through the hole to the cavernous roof, one cracked cement wall, rusted girders holding up the building's frame, and down at the other end, thirteen motorcycles in perfect condition were lined up like soldiers between pillars: shiny, black, each front wheel tilted in the same direction as if at a showroom from long ago. He scanned the pitted wall with dangling rebar, looked behind the girders for signs of others, then walked slowly to the bikes, sauntered around each one, touched a seat here, caressed a handle bar there. Each had a key hanging from the ignition.

He swung a leg over the seat of the first one and leaned into the handlebars as if riding. He repeated this with each one. He dared not touch any of the keys, dared not start any of them. The sound would reverberate and bring others. Starting the machines would be later. Now only the electronic eye saw from the walls, but Niko had an in with the Watchers today. He'd brought them bruyaha leaves for a tea that made them temporarily forget their duties. He'd spent many dark nights collecting the leaves, but the bribe was worth it. He had to see these bikes for himself before they were hauled to the roof and placed in the final lineup.

Talk to me, he thought. *Tell me which one of you will get me through this night.*

On the twentieth floor, Old Merrie waited for the girl to bring the supplies. She sharpened a long, slender knife by methodically sliding the blade against a whetstone as she sang softly to herself. A squat woman of indeterminate age (but certainly old), her white hair was wrapped with a brightly colored scarf tucked into itself behind her ears, wisps of curls like a halo escaping all around the edges. Her dark eyes were never still and darted here and there, watching the floor for rats, the walls for roaches, the high ceiling overhead for spiders; her head tilted, she listened for any sound she couldn't immediately identify as normal.

Her bare feet told the story of her life. Wide, with the fat pads of soles spilling out, gnarled toes and calloused nails unclipped and yellow, thick and cracked lengthwise. Next to her were open-toed sandals made from an old tire with heavy treads, held together by rope wedged between horizontal slits in the front and back that she pulled and tied around her ankles to keep them on. Her ankles scarred where the rope had chafed over years of wear. Her dress, or whatever was covering her, hung loosely around her ample, bulging middle, like a sheet she'd wrapped sari-like. It was a heavy, bright-green material. On closer inspection, it might have once been an awning, judging by the faint flower pattern and the words, almost disappeared, that said *Bouquets, Baskets, Gifts*. Old Merrie had survived all this time by making food for the Tower units—and especially for the hot solstice. She was the most requested food purveyor, and rival units had tried unsuccessfully to steal her away.

She wielded the knife, deftly cutting up fresh vegetables. There were onions, leeks, potatoes, yams, ocas, cassavas, fat green beans, all piled into a huge battered steel bowl rescued from a burnt-out factory where once it could hold dough for fifteen loaves of bread at a time. Next to her, on a pitted slab of dark stone about eight feet long, were lettuces, fruits, and nuts, all in oversized wooden bowls. A cat lay under the slab, curled into a round ball of orange fur, its nose hidden between its front paws. It seemed peaceful, except one ear was missing a wedge, and one front paw was mangled so its pads splayed like leaves from a branch.

Merrie sang and hummed now and then, breaking into choruses of poetic rhymes about days gone by. She swayed slightly as if a breeze was rushing by her as she sliced and sang. Outside, the sun was bright, halfway to its zenith. She stood back and peered under the table.

"Tonight it will happen," she said to the cat. "First night. Full moon. No clouds. The summer solstice. Little cat, you best stay where you are. The food will be plenty, drink will be flowing. Dancing and cheering. Have I seen it before? Many first nights. Many dances with death. Many losers. One victor. Being a woman is hard. Being a man is harder. Being a cat is best."

She poked at the cat with her toe, but he did not budge. She finished cutting the vegetables, slid her wide feet into the sandals, tied them around her ankles until they were tight, and waddled off to another space where she found a dilapidated industrial-sized grocery cart with one wheel permanently off the ground and turned at a right angle to the post that held it. She pushed it to the table on its three good wheels, lowered the bowls into the basket, and wiped the table, using a ragged towel with the "H" insignia of a once-famous hotel chain. She swiped the knife clean against her dress and left it on the table beside the whetstone she used for sharpening.

She glanced one last time at the cat before she and the cart disappeared around the corner of an outside corridor, the one broken wheel of the cart wobbling crazily, its squeak echoing off the pitted walls. On this floor, most of the outside walls still stood, but all the glass windows had long since crashed to the street below. What was left were gaping squares that allowed air and weather to whoosh through the building. She no longer sang. Later, on the roof, she would serve the food. Later still, she would dance with the others.

There were clusters of ten- to twelve-story, nondescript building hulks left, but only the taller ones in The Ring were now inhabited. The rest were prey to the Leftovers, who scavenged mostly in the dark for food and water. The landscape was sparse, flat, interrupted only by the hulks of these crumbling, abandoned high-rises like planetary mountain formations that had been eaten away by galactic forces. They rose in clusters toward the sky, numbered according to their order of designated demise, which put them off-limits for habitation. When they had first been condemned, shifts of workers in pale orange suits circulated through the city, boarding up and painting "No Trespassing" signs on the doors and windows. These faded and rotted over the years. Scavengers tore them down to burn for heat on cold nights and, when there was any food to prepare, for cooking.

Yet far off, almost beyond the naked eye's ability to see, something in the distance glimmered. Not a mirage, for it had colors that were faintly iridescent green and a blue so deep it seemed to have no end. At times it appeared to lift off the ground and float as if pure light; at these times, it was bright white silver. Yet at other times it appeared wavy, like the far horizon of a great sea. That is when it seemed as blue as the deepest ocean. Only the Watchers could see this phenomenon from their perch in The Globe. But there was one particular spot at one far corner of the flat roof of the Tower of David. There, on certain bright, sun-filled days, at the very apex of the sun's path, by leaning so far over that a person felt in peril of falling and being lost forever to the ground below, a tantalizing glimmer appeared. It was mesmerizing, frightening, beckoning, enthralling.

Niko had seen it. He could not put it out of his mind. It reminded him of something in the ghost of general memory left after The Cleanse, something the elders whispered about when they were sure the Watchers couldn't hear.

"There is a better place," some of them said, nodding knowingly. "We still remember." Niko had heard them whisper, "A place called Zamora."

Some of The Cleansing had gone awry and had failed to fully wipe out all memory. It was said that, in The Globe, there were small machines that contained all the memories of past times. These were hooked up to the cleansing machines used to delete memory. Facts, dates, numbers, events, places, even the history from far beyond Infinius were stored. Hidden cameras acted as eyes. Sometimes, if a camera went blank, a robot was dispatched to repair the break.

Robots also repositioned listening and visual recording devices that were so small they were almost undetectable. With the buildings in constant disrepair, devices were easy to hide in the debris. That was an accepted part of life. If anyone happened to pick up one while sifting through trash for something to trade for food or drugs or drink, an alarm told the Protectors to shut that one down and send out a bot to replace it. Interfering with a bot was punishable by death. The people feared the bots almost as much as they feared the Protectors.

A small army of bots worked constantly underground to build new devices for the Protectors to dispatch. Bots had no loyalty, no conscience, no fear. And no love. They also had no greed and no cunning. They operated on whatever program had been installed.

From The Globe, a loudspeaker blasted orders for work and reports of infractions and punishments meted out to transgressors. These were called "Messages and Humiliations for a Better Day." On this day, the loudspeakers also announced The Race.

Floodlights will illuminate the city from dusk until dawn.

Bleachers have been installed on all roofs. Banks of seating face the Tower where The Race will be held. All viewers are required to be in their preassigned seats by first bell.

A hologram projection allowed people a close-up look. The messages repeated throughout the day, with new information added at random. This year's innovations were heralded broadly.

During this past year our trusted Overseers have assembled a list of prizes to be bestowed upon the populace of Infinius by aid of a random drawing. At the conclusion of The Race, a list of recipients will be read for all to hear. Cameras will pick out winners from the audience to broadcast over InCom to begin the

celebration at the culmination of our glorious yearly Race, where the victor will receive his rewards. Good fortune to all contestants this night.

Once Niko had seen the bikes and touched them all, he took the stairs quickly. Now he knew what he had to do. Someone would survive. No matter what it cost later, it had to be him.

With the image of El's delicate, oval face in mind, down, down, down he fairly glided, almost exultant, flight after flight. He would either be the one who lived or he would be dead when the solstice sun disappeared. There was nothing more he could do about it.

Except this one last thing. In a perverse way, this freed him.

Moving fast, heading to Building Twelve, as he reached the cracked and pitted sidewalk, a woman with a toddler balanced in one arm, a baby strapped to her chest, and tattered bags full of fresh foods hanging from each arm had just reached what was once a doorway and was now a gaping hole with sharp, twisted, and rusty rebar sticking out of the cement frame. He made the sharp turn at the end of the stairwell, colliding into her. They all fell in a heap. The toddler began to howl, and the fruits and vegetables splayed out around them. The woman didn't know what to save first.

As he regained his footing, Niko saw fear in the woman's eyes. At that moment what came to him was the little picture he'd traded with El. The picture of Jesus. And all the thoughts he'd had about the idea of being a servant to others. At another time he might have brushed himself off and hurried away. At another time he might have left the woman to cope on her own with her burdens. But in this moment, the little boy he couldn't help came back to him.

"You're okay," he told the toddler, and picked him up. He held the child so they could look into each other's eyes. A few seconds before he'd been thinking of The Race and of his own survival, but in that moment he smiled at the child and gave him a hug. "See, let's help your mama."

They gathered the produce, and the toddler came to his side and handed him an apple and a banana. He giggled and Niko poked him playfully.

As Niko helped, the woman picked up her sacks and looked again at Niko. She smiled. "You are a kind boy," she said. "I hope my boy will be kind like you." She reached up and cupped his cheek in her palm. "Bless you," she said.

Niko hurried on, the sensation of the woman's caress staying on his cheek until he reached Building Twelve.

At the third-floor landing, a corridor led to an interior maze of marred walls and battered doors. Farthest away from cracked windows and tenuous stairways inside the maze was a solid metal door with a heavy bolt and a round device halfway down. It looked much like a vault. There was a buzzer and a small window where visitors were approved or turned away.

On his sixteenth birthday, the Protector named Huston had summoned Niko to this door and told him to use the code word "dragonfly." Even though he was suspicious of all Protectors, having no alternative, he'd done what he was told. The door swung open to a world most of the populace would never see. Thinking back to that day, along with an anxious hope that his fate would not be death, Niko's anticipation of The Race grew. Gone was the cavalier attitude of just a little while earlier.

At the door now, he remembered that day and the world he had been allowed to glimpse exactly two years earlier, for The Race always fell on the birthday he had been given. No one, not even the Center where he'd been deposited, knew for sure when or where he'd actually been born. He was sure that world still existed behind this door and that if he knocked, he would be allowed entry.

The little window clicked open, and a pair of eyes took him in. It was a recognition device that had stored his face, and even though he had grown and changed since then, his eyes were the same. The door swung wide, and Niko stepped across the threshold.

Unlike the rest of Infinius—where one was always aware either of the baking sun, or heat rising from the streets at night, or the acrid scent when black clouds let loose with sheets of toxic rain—the entry hall was cool. Inside these walls there was the faint perfume of . . . what? Lilac or jasmine, delightful scents to lull the visitor. In the semi-darkness, Niko noted leather couches along one wall, expensive-looking rugs from another time, and a vaulted ceiling with recessed lighting that created a soft, pleasant glow. It was soothing, almost.

A young woman emerged clad in a silk robe that outlined her voluptuous body. She wore golden sandals with high spiked heels. Her nails were long, painted a deep red that matched the color of her lips.

"Welcome," she breathed, and took Niko's arm in hers as if they were old friends at a reunion. She was as tall as Niko. Or perhaps it was only the sandals that made her appear so. "Are you here to see someone special? Or can I be of service?"

She led him into a vast room with a wide bar at one end. On a large screen above the bar a movie was playing. There were men in uniform, guns, machines, a battle, the noise of war. Men sat at the bar watching the movie, drinking. Women surrounded them. Touched them. Fawned over them. Niko looked away.

"A drink?" the tall woman with red nails asked him. "Or a drug? I think you need something to relax you, no?" She smiled benevolently at him and squeezed his arm.

"You've been here before," she said. "I think I remember you. But it has been a long time." She maneuvered him toward the bar. "I've missed you."

"I'm looking for someone." Niko said it quietly so no one else could hear.

"What's her name? I can look her up in the log book," she offered.

Of course they would keep a record. I have to be careful, Niko reminded himself.

"No," he said softly. "A man. A Protector."

She stiffened, dropped his arm, and backed away.

"I can't help with that," she said. Her voice had lost its tempting lilt. She sounded cold, almost hostile.

"Who can?" Niko asked.

"I cannot."

She walked away and disappeared down a dark hall. Niko was left alone. He decided to have a drink and find out what he wanted from the bartender, a stoop-shouldered, bald man wearing a rumpled shirt and a loose bow tie.

Niko chose a barstool at the end by himself. The bartender sidled over, wiping his hands with a small, stained bar towel. He stopped in front of Niko and raised his eyebrows for the order.

"Beer?" Niko asked.

The bartender grunted. "Big spender."

Niko felt a flush of panic. He had no money. Nothing for bartering either.

The bartender pulled out a frosted mug (Niko marveled at this), filled it from a tap, and slid it over to Niko. A little foam sloshed over the edge of the mug.

"Um," Niko started, motioning the bartender over with a tilt of his head. "I, um, I'm supposed to . . ." Niko stopped, and the bartender waited.

"Supposed to what, kid?" He leaned over the bar to look up closely at Niko with red, watery eyes. "You one of them? If you're meeting anyone but a lady"—he voiced the word "lady" with disdain—"you shoulda said something at the door, cause you're in the wrong room for that." He held out his hand. "It's two big ones for the beer, kid. Anything else is outta my hands." He stared at Niko, who cleared his throat.

"No, no," Niko said, and took a sip of the frosty beer. He couldn't resist. It slid easily down his throat. Its sweet, musky flavor rested lightly on his tongue, and he thought for a fleeting second that he should have questioned it. But then, to have a Protector on your side . . .

"No, come closer, please," Niko told him.

The bartender leaned in, his hand still out for the money.

"I'm looking for a certain Protector. I'm supposed to meet him here."

"A Protector?" The bartender was obviously impressed. He stood up straight. "Which one? Because there happen to be three of them in the cardroom right now." Everyone knew who the Protectors were. It was rumored they had more power behind the scenes than even the Overseers. He took a swipe at the bar with his cloth while eyeing Niko. "He gonna pay for your beer?"

Niko laughed nervously. Even though it *had been* two years ago, he'd taken a big gamble that the Protector would want to support the minor investment he'd made. Hadn't he gotten word to Niko just today? If the Regime wanted to find you, they could. After all, he thought, at this point, the chances were fifty-fifty that he'd pay for a measly beer.

"Yeah." Niko drank again, then carefully positioned the mug on the bar and slid his index finger along the top edge of the glass. "Yeah, he'll pay."

This was a world where things were never what they seemed. One day the loudspeakers told of a food surplus at the northeast corner of Central Row at quadrant ninety-eight, but when everyone rushed to get there, the food had run out—if it had ever been there at all. Heat baked the crumbling cement, and good shoes were as scarce as rain. People's feet blistered and children wailed to be carried. The loudspeakers told of an air-conditioned theater giving out free seats, or a hydrant spurting fresh water. A few were allowed to take advantage, but most were turned away as having too many strikes on their ID cards. No one knew how to get the strikes removed. Periodically new cards were issued. Most were filled with strikes when handed out.

To be without your ID card was dangerous. You could be cleansed out if your card wasn't produced when Watchers demanded it. People got cleansed all the time. And agreements, pledges, assurances, and promises could never be trusted.

So Niko knew not to rely on what this Protector may have intimated with a free entry to a whore on his sixteenth birthday and a frosty beer or a text on his tracker.

Inside the cardroom, dealers at round tables that were covered in what once must have been thick green felt (but was now a mottled mix of brown stains and dark splotches) whipped out cards to men seated ten to a table. A spotlight loomed over each table, but the room's perimeter was so dark it took Niko a few minutes to pick out more than the tables. He stood at the door with an escort. He was a short, bald man who favored his left leg, which seemed a bit shorter than his right when he walked. He'd appeared from somewhere at the bar on some hidden signal, presumably from the bartender, but it could have been from an electronic detector somewhere in the recesses of the barroom. You could never tell who or what was watching at any time, from any place.

His escort nodded to the farthest table, and Niko made his way around the room, leaving the bald man to limp out the door.

The men at the tables played a game called "badger." It went fast. Cards fairly flew by. In the center of each table a stack of hexagonal chips grew and shrank as hands were won and lost. At times there were shouts of glee; at others, moans of disappointment. The room smelled of something sweet, slightly intoxicating. Not bruyaha, but something stronger, Niko suspected. He fought the urge to succumb to it and headed for the table where his Protector sat with a stack of chips in front of him and a long, lit meskitta hanging from the corner of his mouth.

As Niko approached, the Protector looked up and squinted at him through a curl of smoke.

"Ah," he cried, and raised a hand. "My rider arrives. Come, come." He motioned to Niko and then threw down his cards as he won a round and yelled, "Badger!"

The dealer shoved the pile of chips to him, and he pushed back his chair.

"Cash me out. I have to speak with my young friend." The Protector turned halfway around so he could reach up to squeeze Niko's shoulder.

The dealer counted the winning chips, then stacked them up while the others at the table grumbled that he should give them another chance at the cards. The Protector waved a hand at them and smiled coyly.

"Place your bets on The Race, my friends. You'll have your chance at big winnings there. You can sit in my box. All of you." He waved at them again and, with an arm across Niko's shoulder, led him away. He stopped briefly at the dealer's chair and took his winning slip.

"So, you came to discuss The Race?" the Protector whispered to Niko as they made their way back to the bar.

Niko wasn't sure what to call him. When he hesitated, the Protector said, "Call me Huston, now that we're in business together."

"Yessir," breathed Niko.

They walked past the bartender, who waved Niko's tab at them.

"Sir, uhhh, Huston," Niko muttered, "this is embarrassing, but I ordered a beer before and I have no way to pay for it." He motioned to the tab in the bartender's stubby fingers.

"Here." Huston pulled out the winning slip. "Cash this in." He handed it to the bartender, who reached down behind the bar and pulled open a large drawer. He gave Huston a wad of bills. Huston peeled off the top one and slapped it on the bar.

"Thank *you*, sir." The bartender's eyebrows shot up in surprise.

Huston turned to Niko and handed him the wad. "The rest is for you."

Niko was too stunned to say anything.

"Thank me later," muttered Huston under his breath. "There's a lot riding on your head. I suppose you're ready," Huston mused as they walked out the door.

"Yessir." Niko was not sure what was expected of him. "As ready as I can be."

"You know what a privilege it is to have been chosen. There were many others from your unit in contention." Huston's gait sped up a little, as if he realized he was late for an appointment. "The voting was close. But I rallied support for you."

"Thank you, sir." He wondered why Huston had supported him but was hesitant to ask.

Huston stopped to light a meskitta. He offered one to Niko, who accepted it and let Huston light it. They puffed hungrily, although Niko wasn't used to smoking. The pungent aroma surrounded them as Huston exhaled a cloud that hung in the still air. "Do you want something stronger for tonight?" he asked Niko with narrowed eyes, sizing up the boy who was about to become a man.

Niko shook his head. The meskitta scent was heady enough for him. At least for now. And he was already feeling its effect.

"Why did you support me, sir? I mean then and now. And take me to the bar?"

"Hah." Huston clapped Niko on the shoulder. "I gave you the very best that night, didn't I? She was a beauty then. Osana was her name, wasn't it? She didn't last long. Drugs. Killers for a girl that fresh. Too bad, really. But I was watching you long before then."

Huston puffed on his meskitta.

"I saw something in you. Who can say what? Early on, I saw you break up a Scrounger fight not far from here. You handled yourself well. Stood your ground and made a good deal that satisfied everyone involved. And took a good chunk for yourself. You put me in mind of myself as a boy. Life can be tough. Infinius . . ." He paused and looked around, then motioned with a slant of his head for Niko to follow his lead. They disappeared into a narrow alley lined, along a wall, by battered trash cans and a large half dumpster, its side missing. Huston leaned against the wall of the building and seemed to relax.

"Infinius . . ." he continued, "can be a hard place if you don't have friends."

If Huston was one of those men who liked other men, or if he liked both, Niko would have a problem. It wouldn't be good to anger or reject him right before The Race.

Huston laughed again and nodded with approval. "Caution. That's a good trait. I knew you were the one to win it all for me. Now let's get down to it." He motioned with his finger for Niko to come in closer. "You *will* win tonight. Take my word for it. And the world will open up for you like you can't believe."

"How can you be so sure I'll win?" Niko asked. "I mean, I know fixes are made, but others make them too. How can you be sure yours will stick?"

"It's not unlike that street fight. When we first met."

"Sir," he began, then hesitated and finally decided to go on. "Are you saying you set up that fight?"

"Call me Huston, please. We're in business together now. That is, unless you want your life to end tonight. And yes, I set it up. To see how you'd act, what the others would do. Would they turn on you? Or follow you? These things are important to know before . . ." Huston dropped the stub of meskitta and squashed it under his toe, swiveling his foot back and forth more than was necessary to put out the ember.

"Well, then, Huston, you mean before The Race?" Niko asked with a slight tone of authority now. "Why me? I know you couldn't go to The Hovels, but why pick me? There are hundreds of boys my age from The Ring. You could have chosen any one of them."

"True, I could have. But you managed the trials I put in your path better than the rest. And remember, there are other Protectors who chose riders. Each of us had a limited field. Anyway, it's done now." Huston looked up and down the street.

As they left the alley, the wad of bills crushed tightly against Niko's belt, were securely hidden from street hustlers and muggers. Even walking beside Huston he didn't feel safe. So when they parted, Niko cautiously made his way back to The Ring, where he lived on the ground floor of Building Three in a tiny room he'd created between two hollow concrete pillars. The only light came from a single bulb hanging from an exposed sewage pipe on the ceiling. Beside one pillar, a hot plate sat on a wooden crate next to a toilet with no seat. Across the cramped space was a mattress covered by crumpled sheets. An ancient laptop computer lay open on the floor. Niko had managed to tap into the jury-rigged electrical system by splicing his own line into the main one stolen from the street. The putrid odors of garbage and raw sewage mingled, especially in strong westerly winds.

It wasn't until he entered his own living quarters that he

looked at the wad and counted it with a staggering sense of luck, followed by foreboding. He had never seen so much money, never held it in his hands, never imagined he would come upon such wealth. He wondered briefly what would be expected of him after The Race in exchange for this windfall. Would it cost him much more than the money in his hand?

Such thoughts led nowhere.

At an industrial-sized dumbwaiter that could move large items to the roof, Old Merrie waited beside her wobbly-wheeled grocery cart. With her calloused fingers, she had pulled the ropes of this dumbwaiter in years past. Big, heavy ropes with bristly sides. She leaned against a pillar, listening for footsteps, and sang softly to herself, an old song from deep in memory that hadn't been completely cleansed.

On a night so beautiful
You came to my window, singing your song
About the dawn, about the dawn.
You were my love, so strong and true
And in your eyes I saw the blue
A summer sky.
Oh! Don't be far from me, my love
Out there so dark I cannot see your smile
Nor hear your voice as a whispering wind.
I had a dream the other night, when everything was still;
I thought I saw you come to me, singing your sweet song
About the dawn, about the dawn.

Old Merrie wondered how she could remember all the words after so many years since The Cleanse. She hummed the song again and then heard footsteps clang on those unsteady stairs. She was still humming and swaying a little as a few dance steps came back to her in a foggy film. El appeared around the corner, with the sacks of bottles and food she'd carried up twenty-three flights. She lowered the bags down to the cement floor and leaned against a girder. The bottles clinked against each other.

"How many bottles you carried in them sacks?" she asked El.

"I don't know, but this is my fourth trip so far." She pointed to a far-off corner where she had dropped off more bags earlier. "I hope it's enough. I don't want to make that climb again until tonight. What do you have?"

Old Merrie didn't answer right away. You never knew, really, who you might be talking to these days. Years ago, before The Collapse, when Merrie was still a young woman, she'd liked to meet new people, talk and laugh and sing and dance. In fact, she vaguely remembered a club she used to frequent with many friends. How they'd had fun and danced all night. Now all of them were gone, and she was left with memories like mists that passed across her mind and sprinkled droplets of images that dried up before she could catch them, hold them, examine them. She thought the girl looked harmless.

"What's your name, girl?"

"El."

"I heard of you from somewhere. Was you one of them foundlings the nuns took in, then?"

"Yes." El looked around for others, for hidden cameras, but saw nowhere they could be hooked up. "We alone up here?"

"Hmmm," said Old Merrie. "Appears to be. And this big dumbwaiter here for us to haul our goods up to the roof. I guess we might's well get started."

They moved the bags and sacks and produce onto the cavernous dumbwaiter. Old Merrie pushed her wobbly-wheeled cart in and began to pull on the ropes. The thing creaked and rolled up and up. El moved next to Old Merrie, and together they raised the thing to the final landing.

On the vast open space, useless corroded metal vent cones dotted the surface like sprouts of some alien vegetation gone to seed. In one corner was a huge refrigeration machine that had been installed by a work force of Scavengers pulled for this once-a-year event from their otherwise rambling efforts at collecting street garbage and detritus. Inside it, ice and drinks and food were jammed together for the throngs that would gather later, after The Race. On the other roofs of The Ring, the vents had long ago been scrounged off to break down and repurpose the metal. People from those buildings would view from their own roofs and celebrate after the event ended.

The area designated for party prep was distinct from where The Race would be held, but it was a grim reminder to El about what would happen soon enough.

El stacked the bottles on a high shelf inside the huge refrigerator while Old Merrie hummed, moving the prepared foods onto a lower shelf. They worked together but apart. El's stomach growled loudly, and Old Merrie glanced at her sideways.

"You hungry, girl?"

El nodded but didn't speak. Even on this roof, surely the Watchers would have a camera or listening devices.

Old Merrie took out a hunk of freshly baked bread that had a sweet scent. El lifted her head at the unfamiliar smell as it wafted past her.

"Take this," said Old Merrie. "They can't see you with this big door open."

El reached for the bread with one hand, cautiously like a wary cat. She devoured it and licked her fingers. She looked up at Old Merrie, wondering what this could mean. No one gave anyone anything in this city without expecting something in return. She waited, but Old Merrie only broke off another hunk and handed it to El. This time El took it without caution. It was too delicious to question the source a second time. Old Merrie broke off a smaller chunk for herself.

"My grandmamma and mama after her made coconut bread from the palm trees outside our house. When them nuts fell on the ground . . . *whump*, they went . . . us kids'd grab 'em up and pound 'em on the concrete walk until they got broke up enough so we could pull the husks off and get to the nut inside. Mmmm, mmmm, but those nuts was sweet when you got 'em open." She gazed skyward, her eyes wide as if some crevasse of memory had suddenly split open in her mind and she was seeing what used to be in that deep blue above.

El listened. She'd never heard anyone except the sisters speak of the past before; she had no knowledge of palm trees or coconuts. The taste of that sweet bread lingered on her tongue.

"What's a coconut?" she asked.

Old Merrie turned toward the girl, her head cocked like a robin listening for a worm underfoot. She smiled, a crooked little smile.

"What do you know about, girl? What did those nuns teach you over there?"

El's gaze wandered everywhere on the roof. From the stark vent stacks to the huge refrigerator, to the seating rows stacked in piles to the long tables that would later be filled with food and drinks, she looked everywhere but to Old Merrie's eyes, which regarded her steadily. Finally she allowed herself the luxury of looking into those eyes. She hadn't met a gaze head-on since leaving Sister Catarina, the last of the Sisters of Mercy.

"They taught me to trust only myself and my love of God," she said. "They taught me to guard myself from the world outside. They taught me to be careful and good."

Old Merrie nodded as if she, too, had been taught these lessons.

"And what did they teach you to do to survive?" she asked.

"I know how to plant edibles and sew my own clothes. I can cook and clean. I can do figures and write. They schooled me the same as anyone. They taught me how to build things too. I can take apart an engine or build a new one from old parts. They told me I was clever that way. And they taught me how to survive off the land."

"I tell you this: Young girl like you, beautiful as you are and just coming into your womanhood, this life is dangerous. Dangerous for everyone young I observed all these years. But for a girl like you . . ." Old Merrie shook her head.

They were facing west on that vast roof. The sun was bright gold, slowly descending. Old Merrie turned and motioned for El to follow her. When they reached the very edge of the roof at the corner, she squinted, looking out over the flat landscape to the horizon where, far off, a mountain from the earth rose like some glacial erratic.

"You look out there, girl. Look to see what's beyond. This ain't the whole world. You ain't seen nothing of it in your short life. Coconut trees and mangoes and papayas and all manner of trees you ain't never seen nor tasted nor smelled."

Old Merrie stood very still. After a few moments, as the sun moved further down beyond the mountains, the glimmer began. Faint at first. Pale green with a hint of blue.

El moved closer to the edge, but instead of looking out to the horizon, she peered over to the street below.

"Tonight they'll face this," she said. Inadvertently she weaved slightly toward the abyss.

"Nothing you can do about that," said Old Merrie. "You got to look out, not down. You got to think about what's better than what you got."

Then El raised her chin and fixed her eyes on the faraway place that now shimmered a hot green against the lowering sun.

"What is it?" she asked, her voice filled with wonder.

"The Glimmer," Old Merrie said simply. "And beyond that, somewhere, Zamora."

"Why are you showing me?" El asked without glancing at Old Merrie. She couldn't take her eyes off this sight.

Old Merrie pushed at a small chunk of concrete with the toe of her crude sandal. It tumbled off the edge of the roof and disappeared down and down where they could not see whether it landed on anyone or anything of consequence.

"They took away everything I could have had," she said without malice. "I never could have babies. They took that from me. It was all I ever wanted. They pushed me to a life of hard scrabbling for my supper. They wiped away my memory. But now it comes back to me. Now that I'm old. Because whatever they try to take away, it's stubborn and wants to stick. Now they don't pay no mind to me. They only care about the young. They'll take you away, too. They'll give you to some Protector or Overseer or worse because you're pretty. And then you'll never get away.

"I tell you this. There's a better place out there where the light shines. And if it was me, I'd take any risk to find it.

"What you see here tonight . . . well, it ain't the way it's supposed to be for a young man or for someone like you. If he wins, they'll take away his soul. He won't want *for* anything. But he won't *want* anything, neither. He'll stop wanting and he'll stop hoping. Because to win is to let them corrupt him. And if he loses, well, you know what happens then.

"And what about the girl? The winner, he can take any girl he wants. The girl he chooses, well how long will he keep her? And then where do she go? If I had a baby girl, and she was the one I raised and loved and fed and worried over . . . if you was that baby girl, I'd say find that light, girl. Find it or lose yourself forever."

El couldn't run back to the nuns. Not anymore. She'd heard about other girls, about what happened to them. She thought about Niko. About the way he looked at her. About the way she felt when he touched her.

They both stared out past The Hovels. Past The Protections. As far as they could see to where it seemed that, in the late-afternoon sunlight, the flat earth had begun to change to . . . what? A hill, a slope where the light now shone silver, bright as a mirror for a few more brief moments before it disappeared.

But now El knew it was there. Somewhere.

The boys weren't the only ones with high stakes riding on The Race. It was well known that the Overseers needed an ongoing fresh supply of girls to staff the brothels and gambling houses. Most of the men who paid to belong to these "clubs" preferred young girls, although even in the brothels, there was a strict hierarchy. Most of the women didn't live past thirty, if anyone even bothered to keep count.

It was forbidden to buy their way out unless under some extraordinary circumstance—if an Overseer wanted one of the girls to live under his roof, for instance. With the permission from (and a substantial payment to) Villinkash, this sometimes happened. Of course, what the girl became after that was of no concern to anyone. So that, even if everything else within Infinius was tracked and catalogued, girls were so disposable that they were no more than pieces of furniture to be passed around or discarded for the Leftovers to collect.

All the Overseers were men, with the exception of the wife of Villinkash, who had married him under duress when he was at the beginning of his rise to power. At the time, even she hadn't realized just how far he intended to climb using her money to get started. It was never clear to the public why she had married him. But one thing was certain: her status as an Overseer was a sham for publicity purposes.

The night before The Race, each building had held an auction of sorts, choosing by secret ballot which girls would represent their rider. Then each girl was given a ribbon in the color of her building. In this way, the whole city knew who was riding for what building and which girls could be chosen at the end as a prize for the winning rider. Girls whose riders did not win would be paraded through the city until they reached a central location where they would be trained for their new life in the brothels.

A huge hologram hovered over The Ring. It would broadcast The Race in excruciating detail. All the monitors in the city broadcast The Race. Everyone could see the cycles lined up on the Tower of David roof.

In The Hovels, Leftovers were encouraged to bet (bartering with whatever they had) on the outcome of The Race. To not support The Race was punishable by "deportation," where masked guards would bring the offender to the edge of a series of electrified fences called The Protections, then strap the offender to the fences to fry alive. Sometimes, this didn't take long. Sometimes, it took most of a day while the offender slowly lost consciousness before succumbing completely. All of it was documented and broadcast on InCom for the people to see and hear.

The gleaming bikes had been pampered far more than any newborn baby. It was one of many ironies that, after The Collapse, the Overseers retained certain parts of the old society they deemed valuable to their aims. Certain technologies would be essential. Controlling the population would be paramount. Efficient farming methods would be useful as well as strictly regulating methods of distribution. It wouldn't do to have a surplus of anything. Scarcity, after all, would cause competition for essential goods. This could maintain high values not many could afford. And when the Overseers deemed it useful to make goods available, the people would further conclude how they were good managers and concerned for the welfare of the populace. The problem of policing the society was solved through advanced technology. Since travel would be outlawed, except by the higher castes of Overseers and Protectors, vehicles wouldn't be needed. Of course, there would still be factories of sorts to make necessary machines, especially the motorcycles for The Race.

One of the plum jobs was employment at The Works, where old bikes were refurbished and new ones constructed by hand, like fine watches used to be. This would take craftsmanship, for sure, but it also would take dedication and trust. Experts in all the intricate parts of motorcycles would be handpicked by the Overseers at a young age and trained like little ballerinas for a lifetime of endless service until their hands and feet would give out. But until that day came, they would be cared for and protected. Older mechanics and restorers who survived the rigors of the factory became master trainers for the next generation in an endless cycle of servitude.

Just after El turned thirteen, two years before Miriam and Niko met, Miriam's editor had gotten approval for a story about how religious groups were what the Regime wanted portrayed as "thriving." Although no one admitted to outright censorship, there was, instead, a process for publishing stories that covered anything even remotely political. Religion fell into that catchall. So instead of censoring stories after they'd been written, a committee screened all story ideas before (and then again after) they were written.

The Regime felt stories about religion showed how deeply held beliefs were not only tolerated but encouraged. It allowed faith-based groups that held extreme views about biblical end times and backed groups that made financial donations or that delivered others for so-called subversive activities, which could be anything. Basically they supported an us-versus-them theology.

The old nuns operating out of a garage were left to themselves, not because the Regime particularly cared about their cause but because the Watchers, although brutal, were also a superstitious bunch. Some of them were known to make the sign of the cross whenever they passed the garage. Others left small items for the sisters. Old clothing, a baby blanket, cans of formula in paper sacks, even, at times, a baby whose mother had been dispatched to the camps. The sisters never acknowledged any of these acts. It was as if there was an unwritten peace treaty between the nuns and the Watchers. And so, the sisters managed their work in quiet, if not secret.

Miriam had interviewed the leaders of these churches and was able to speak with many of their followers. She noted how eerily they all said exactly the same thing in the same words and phrases. Whereas The Cleanse had wiped out memory, this religious fervor had been instilled piece by piece until it had become an automatic regurgitation upon any number of signals.

While researching this story she had come upon the nuns at the convent where El had lived. It was generally assumed all the priests had been cleansed out, and by the time Miriam arrived at the door of the garage where the Sisters of Mercy did their work, she saw that the drive-in door had been permanently bolted closed and painted a dull gray.

El answered a side door that had once led to an office. Two elderly nuns stood behind her and cautiously motioned Miriam in. After El closed and bolted the door, one of the nuns led her to a heavy, old wooden table.

"Welcome," she said. "Won't you take a seat at our table? I'm

Sister Mary Angelica, and this is Sister Catarina. She's our baby. Only . . . what are you now, Sister?" She looked over at Sister Catarina, who smiled back at her.

"She's teasing me. I'm one year younger than she is, but she's been holding it over me for six decades now. I'm eighty-one." Sister Catarina pulled out a chair across from Miriam and placed her hands flat on the table in front of her.

The sleeves of her habit were frayed at the wrists. Miriam put that in her notes in shorthand. El came over and sat down next to her. Sister Angelica followed, sitting next to El on the other side so Miriam was facing all three of them.

Miriam started right off because she never knew when an interview might end abruptly.

"What has been the hardest change for you since The Collapse?"

The sisters looked at each other.

"Ours is a service order," explained Sister Catarina. "Now it is so hard to serve the community. When a poor soul comes to us for help, all we can offer is prayer and a bit of bread that we make with our own hands. We still wear the habits so that anyone can tell who we are and what we offer. Still, we don't feel safe on the street. Even if we felt it was safe to get out to the neediest, we're old now, and frail. We depend on El for so much. But we worry about what will happen to her when we've gone to our Father."

Miriam turned to El and asked, "What do you do for the sisters?"

In her shorthand, Miriam noted that El was a beautiful girl with big gray-green eyes set in a delicately oval face framed by dark curls, which she had pulled back loosely with a black ribbon. She was otherwise unadorned and her skin seemed to glow, even in that semi-dark space. Miriam wrote she was beautiful and innocent, yet there was beneath that a will that came through. When she spoke, it was with calm and confidence that was "astounding given the circumstances," Miriam wrote.

"I do whatever is needed to help them survive, as they did for me," she said.

"And what of the dangers out in the city?" Miriam asked, for it was certainly no place for a beautiful young girl.

"I am protected by my faith," she said simply.

"Faith in what?" Miriam asked.

Before El could answer, Sister Angelica spoke in a quiet voice, as if thinking aloud to herself.

"Sometimes one must have faith in the future. Even when the present seems hopeless, we must remember that God is all around us. He manifests in the kindnesses we do for others and in the faith we keep."

"But Sister, not everyone shares your strong faith. What would you say to those people?"

"Sister Catarina and I have been here a long time, and we know that societies are fluid. None of them last forever in a pure form," she said. "Their structures are sometimes difficult to see clearly in the present moment. But they are always shifting like sands in a desert. Every wind moves them around. It makes new patterns, creates steep hills and ravines where there was once a flat plane. The moment we are in now will not last. It will harm many, as it has already done.

"Our own priests were victims of its irrational destructive force. But haven't we seen this all before in history? Nazis in Germany; Bolsheviks and then Stalinists in Russia; fascists in Spain and Italy; Spanish conquistadores; Americans with their concept of Manifest Destiny, which provided an excuse to annihilate native populations in order to absorb their great lands; Africans selling rival tribes into slavery to Europeans, who traded with Americans in people as if they were cattle; Japanese warmongers;

unspeakable Cambodian Khmer Rouge brutality; and, of course, North Korea starving its own people for the sake of nuclear weaponry. All examples of what history failed to teach us before the wars and famines and pandemics, before our planet revolted with heat and storms and frigid cold waves. And here we are hundreds of years later separated into disparate colonies, with micro climates that can't be predicted, our city tormented by brutal heat and people manipulated by the few at the expense of the many.

"Yes, we have seen it often through the ages. Now we are the ones in a state of torment. As El here says, we have our faith. In what, you ask? In the cosmos, if you like. In all the specks of dust we are and will be. Shall I speak of God? Of Jesus? You think because we are nuns of an order that we are blind to the world? No." She shook her head. "We are neither blind to it nor removed from it. This is the world we have. But not forever. Sister Catarina and I, we will not see the light shine through this darkness. But we have faith that it will break through the clouds. Time is merely a construct of people. And people know not the winding of the eternal clock."

This wasn't what Miriam had expected from the interview. She was looking for concrete answers to those reporters' who, what, when, where, how, but this time she wouldn't get that far, for Sister Angelica stood and motioned to El.

"Shall we have tea now?" It was less a question than a period on the sentence of the visit.

All Miriam could do was write of her impressions, of the physical space they occupied, of their daily life, and of El, who, now with quiet calm, went about the chore of making tea and slicing bread. They shared with her the honey they had gathered from their own hive, which they tended daily in the scrub yard behind the refurbished garage convent. The sisters had planted flowers from seeds El had gathered for them out near The Protections. The bees hummed merrily around the hive.

"They gather from as far away as a mile," Sister Catarina told Miriam. "Although Lord knows where they find more flowers, but they seem to. I do know that many people who took up residence in the Tower of David placed potted plants on their terraces. They grow vegetables all up and down the building, and some grow flowers. They sell the flowers in bunches for weddings and anniversary parties. You see how resourceful we are. Humans, animals, insects, all find ways to survive, no matter how dire the circumstances."

Why, Miriam wondered, did the people not rise up and destroy this horrible abomination of a system? Were they under some spell? In a way, they were. Oh, they grumbled and complained, but they also held back. Some of them thought things would right themselves into the normal order. But it didn't happen, and those who had studied history knew that such governments could last for hundreds of years. In time they got used to the way it was. And accepted it, as people do under extreme conditions. Better to live to fight another day, they must have thought, until the fight had nearly gone out of them.

By the time El was twelve she knew the city well. Knew where it was safe to forage and scrounge and who had goods to trade, who protected certain neighborhoods and who had street authority. Since she'd been collecting for the sisters for years, she knew how to find what they needed to keep their convent operating for themselves and for the needy who came to their door. Sometimes, out on the street, she'd run into Niko. He'd watched out for her even when she was a young girl. She didn't question why. She was cautious but grateful, and sometimes brought him a freshly baked loaf of bread or some other item to trade. At the convent, in a vast back room that was half underground, there were still stores of canned goods, boxed foods to prepare, sacks of flour and rice, bottles of red wine, and juices like guava, mango, and pineapple.

For years before and even during The Collapse, the priests had stockpiled goods. Not that this was a stated part of their mission or that their order demanded it. But Father Ignatius, who was the head priest of their parish, had grown up in the slums. He knew privation and vowed never to be without the means to help those who could not help themselves. Also he was a natural hoarder. Nothing was too small or too big for his basement reserve. He was also a tinkerer. When he wasn't holding Mass or tending to parishioners, he was fixing, mending, or modifying something he had found or been given.

There were other things about Father Ignatius that didn't quite fit the standard priestly mold. He swore like a street thug. Sometimes he'd forgo his clerical garb and wander the streets in jeans, sandals, and a tattered T-shirt. He had never specifically taken a vow of poverty, but he may as well have. And then there was his physical appearance. He was big. Tall, muscular, with biceps that looked more like thighs than arms, and a tough face marred by scars on the chin and right cheek below the eye.

Yes, Father Ignatius looked more like a retired boxer than an active priest. Yet he was gentle and kind, soft spoken, and had a hearty laugh that erupted unreservedly and without warning. He'd shadowbox boys he met on his rounds and always told them to come by the church for reading lessons or a hot meal. And they did show up. Sometimes in pairs, sometimes groups. He taught them how to read and write because after the Collapse, the schools were nothing more than recruiting grounds for boys to work for the Protectors, and for girls to work in the factories and assembly lines—or worse.

One steamy morning, as El was out scavenging just past dawn, she spotted a beat-up chair someone had abandoned near the sidewalk. She was about twelve at the time, and just beginning to look like a young woman. As she turned the chair over to assess its condition and whether it would make a good addition to the convent, a group of teenage boys wandered aimlessly down the street. They banged at dented garbage cans and streetlights with heavy sticks. One of them hurled a rock at a cracked store window that had been taped to hold it up. It shattered and crashed to the sidewalk, and the boys kept moving forward. Then they noticed El, who turned as she heard their racket.

They stopped. Standing still as a pack of hunting dogs pointing at a quail in the brush, they eyed her. And then, with no discernable signal, they began to move, spreading out to encircle her. But before they could close the circle, Father Ignatius rounded a nearby corner and strode up to the biggest of the boys and clasped his arm around the boy's shoulder.

"Well, you boys are out early today," he said good-naturedly as he spun the boy around to face him, bursting the circle as if it were a bubble.

The boys stopped as one and turned to Father Ignatius.

"I remember you," he said to one of the other boys. "Sam, isn't it? Sam, who learned to read with me. You still playing the drums?"

The boy named Sam smiled at Father Ignatius. "Sure. When I can," he said.

"Come by the parish house. We jam every Tuesday. Got some real good players. A sax, a trumpet, we even rounded up an old keyboard that works. We could use a drummer."

The boy smiled and nodded. One of his front teeth was missing. The other boys started grumbling about nothing to do, and Father Ignatius teased them lightly and told them all to come by and they could play in the band.

They wandered off then, banging their sticks against whatever they encountered, and Father Ignatius turned to El.

"Let me help you with that chair," he offered. "Where are you taking it?"

"Thank you," El said softly, almost under her breath. "Why were those boys angry?" she asked as she watched Father Ignatius lift the chair with one hand.

"Boys who have nothing to do and nothing to look forward to are often angry. What do they call you?" he asked.

"El."

"Where were you taking the chair, El?" He could be so gentle it was hard to reconcile that with the image of this big man.

"I live at the convent over by The Ring. With the Sisters of Mercy," she told him as they began to walk in that direction. "Why did you tell them to come to the parish house?"

"Because that's where I work, usually. I'm Father Ignatius. Didn't you know?"

"Will you teach me how to defend myself?" she asked him.

He looked sideways at this slip of a girl who was just beginning to grow up. And so began El's new education.

The day of The Race had arrived.

There they were: thirteen motorcycles lined up on that vast roof of the building that was supposed to symbolize the very best the city could produce. It was the ultimate in style and opulence. A feat of glorious engineering.

Like everyone else in the city, Miriam watched with horror. She admitted to herself that there was a prurient fascination with any gruesome scene. So she sat in front of the InCom in her tiny apartment, transfixed and, at the same time, repelled, in a way she'd never been in previous years. Because this year was different. This year she knew Niko would be up there for all to see on the jumbo screens. So, when the bell sounded and the riders' names were called and each number matched to a motorcycle, Miriam held her breath and, yes, said a prayer.

Calling the names and numbers was done with great fanfare, clapping, cheers, and yells. People shook their beer bottles and allowed the suds to erupt. Then they drank the rest and hurled the empty bottles out to the streets below so the sound of crashing glass added to the cheering. People threw fruits and vegetables into the air and from other roofs. These were not commodities ordinarily taken for granted. Huge balls of rolled-up newspapers were lit on fire and sent off the other twelve roofs, roiling through the air as they slowly burned, casting off sheets of flaming paper while descending to the pavement below. This continued as the sun sank lower toward the horizon on that solstice night. It was the last Race Miriam would attend, but she didn't know it yet.

A stranger just arriving on this scene might wonder why these young men subjected themselves to what amounted to almost certain death. The law said that when a boy from The Ring turned eighteen, he must register for The Race. He could be taken at any time thereafter until he was too old for the contest, although the cutoff age was never announced officially. If he refused to enter his name or refused if his name came up, he was arrested and never heard from again. People assumed such young men had been sent off to the camps, but no one knew for sure. There were cases of mothers going mad from the uncertainty, of fathers who pitched themselves over the roof in grief.

People whispered about one man who'd returned from the camps. He'd gone mad, they said, and was of no use anymore. But really, they'd sent him back because his wife had paid a ransom. She was pretty and young. They'd just been married. They loved each other very much. She had traveled on foot to the site where the camps were located. She had money and jewelry from her family. She had the name of the camp commandant, but he refused to see her. So she saw his assistant, who took her into a dark room with a window. On the other side was her husband. He'd been bound and gagged and hung upside-down. Many guards took turns beating his feet. By the time she'd arrived, the poor man's feet were dripping blood and his eyes had receded back into his skull. They removed the gag so she could hear his throat gurgling. Then the commandant told her that if she still wanted this wreck of a man, all she had to do was pay the fine and he would be freed to her charge.

She agreed and gave him the money and jewels. It was then they took her to the room to cut him down. But before they let her do that, they took turns raping her in front of her husband. When they were finished, she lay on the concrete floor, numb and bloodied, and then they cut him down and dragged him to her side and said, "Happy wedding day." And they laughed as they strapped their belts back on and holstered their pistols.

So going to the camps wasn't an option. And a one-in-thirteen chance seemed better than nothing to most of the young men. That one in thirteen was lavished with everything it was possible to have. And the losers' families were also rewarded: the Regime gave them money, prestige, and a plaque in a place of honor in the center square. The insidiousness of this was that families were convinced they had sacrificed for the good of Infinius and were awarded a new stature as if they had sacrificed in some military campaign to save their people from invaders. It was grotesque, and in any normal society, parents would never have accepted a reward for this cruelest of games. But this wasn't a normal society, and there were many cases of parents dying from grief. The Regime didn't care, though, and The Race continued.

And if a rider balked at the last minute, swerved away from the edge, leapt off his bike onto the roof, such a rider would be shot right there by a phalanx of uniformed guards whose sole purpose was to keep The Race going. And such a rider's family would disappear forever.

So there they were. Lined up and ready for the starting gun. The cheering throngs, the screens panning both the crowds and the roof where each boy stood next to his assigned bike. A horn blasted and the boys mounted their bikes.

Niko tried to clear his mind. *Concentrate. No doubting now. No holding back. Face your fate*, he told himself. *Do I look as scared as Thomaso? What about Gregory on number three; is he convinced he'll win? Do any of us really have a chance?*

On the jumbo screen you could see each face, jaws set; fingers encased in leather half gloves holding tight to throttle grips; booted feet, one barely on the footrest, ready to lurch into action. There was no going back now. No hesitating. It was full throttle down, go. And the people screamed with excitement.

Last-minute betting in the Overseers' stand wrapped up. As the camera panned past the reviewing stand, Miriam caught a glimpse of Huston. Was she the only one who noticed he looked like a man with a winning hand at the card table?

A second horn sounded, and the engines roared to life like an orchestra striking its first notes.

As his fingers gripped the handles and he felt the engine's sudden pulse, Niko stole a glance at the stands and also spotted Huston. At that moment Niko felt a wave of calm wash through him like an ocean breeze. There was no more time to speculate on Huston's motives or reliability. As he looked straight out beyond the roof, past the viewing stand and the people, past the other bikes lined up like thoroughbreds at the starting gate of a great race, past the course that had been set up for the riders, he marveled at his own calm. Now it was all or nothing. He would live or he would die. With choice eliminated, his mind had gone quiet.

The riders hunched forward. The crowds hushed. Then there was the crack of the starting gun like sudden lightning close at hand. A roar went up from the city streets and rooftops as the bikes shot forward.

Screeching tires and screaming crowds. Thirteen motorcycles careened around the track set up as an oblique eight leading to the far edge of the roof and a straightaway to the east side with the setting sun behind them and the street far below. When the shot broke through the city's momentary silence of anticipation, Niko full-throttled to lead the pack of riders at the start.

Then the city went wild. By the time the first riders reached the west edge and spun to the east, gunning their engines, some pulled their front wheel high in the air before gunning to the final straightaway. Then they leapt forward, gaining incredible speed on the last thrust to the end.

So fast did they approach the edge that it all seemed like a blur until the first ones hammered down on brakes that failed and the crowds witnessed the first bike plummet over the edge, flying out from the roof a few yards and then taking an arc to begin its epic fall, followed by the next and then two more and then three, and there was a horrendous shriek of brakes as the others went over and one miraculously stopped just short of the edge in a cloud of burned-off rubber. Its rear wheel spun sideways and the rider's left foot stomped onto the roof as the remaining bikes flew off in unison, the riders released from their seats like great birds with broken wings in a gruesome flight to death.

Niko alone had survived.

That's when the crowd really erupted. The sight of those poor boys hurtling off into the air, seemingly suspended for a fraction of a second as their momentum propelled them forward and they looked, if you blinked an eye, as if they were weightless and timeless. For that instant there was a gasp from the crowds as if a great wind had created a vacuum that sucked the city of its oxygen. And then that air collapsed as the ground under the riders was left behind. One by one they rolled and dove down and down until they hit the ground, where their bodies lay lifeless among the scattered and mashed metal and wheels splattered with blood now pooling in the gutters.

One final indignity came with the Collectors and the wide, flat shovels they used to scoop the broken bodies away. But that wouldn't happen until early morning before dawn, after the sky had turned dark on this longest of days and the people had finished their revelries, collected their winnings, or tossed their chits into the streets.

Miriam rushed to her toilet, where everything she had ingested that day erupted out of her in a gush of revulsion.

Part Two

The
Aftermath

After The Collapse, it was as though all the ugliest parts of people were like roadkill on public display. It was easier to become desensitized than to resist, at least for the older ones. The Regime ignored them. What revolution had ever been fought by old people? And the very young, well, they were ripe for indoctrination.

The Race was a turning point for Niko. Before The Race, Niko represented a small glint of hope for Miriam. It was Niko who'd begun to restore Miriam's sense that some people could be trusted or at least engaged in an honest way. She found out later that El was the reason for that.

After that first night when they'd met by chance at Miriam's office, Niko would show up occasionally when she least expected to see him. It was an odd sort of relationship, one separated by two generations and a cultural divide as deep as the Marianas Trench. Perhaps Miriam thought he viewed her as an adoptive grandmother, as someone so far removed from him that he could trust her. Trust in anyone was a rarity in those years. Miriam had long ago accepted that anyone could be compromised to turn on anyone else. Yet Niko persisted from time to time and so they seemed to strike an unspoken interlude in the normal wariness of others.

One day they met in a park at what had once been a boardwalk along the bay that bordered the city to the east. It was pleasantly warm yet not that blistering heat they'd come to expect. The sky was a clear blue, the kind Miriam remembered from her child-hood—a clean, crisp blue that seemed to have no end. The grayish brown haze that normally hung at the horizon was absent, and she remembered thinking that this was how it should be and won-dering how they could all forget normal so quickly. People are like any animal, adaptable to new situations because their lives depend on it. They go about their days the best they can because it's too hard to fight the system all the time, especially when it's an impossible uphill battle.

Miriam was one of the lucky ones whose memory had never been cleansed out. The journalists assumed they were spared because Villinkash realized he could use legitimate writers who had the tools to promote his message and tell his version of the news. Instead of distributors of the news, they became the cre-ators of opinion that passed for news. They realized he viewed writers as a low-level threat. The only thing that really frightened him was the prospect of mass uprisings. Writers were not particu-larly bold and only wrote about actions. Anyone who claimed the pen to be mightier than the sword had never faced a sword.

On that clear, bright day, Niko appeared from the darkened doorway of a shuttered building nearby. Miriam remembered a bank and some accounting offices used to be there. The gov-ernment had long since taken over all the banks and doled out post-tax salaries to individuals. Since businesses had all been absorbed by or made partners with the government, there was no longer any need for accountants or any banks that were not government run.

As she left her office for lunch, Niko fell in beside her for a moment and whispered, "Don't say anything. I'll meet you on the third bench by the old shelter."

Miriam had brought a small knapsack with some things to eat. No one ever knew when the street carts would run out of food or have only one thing to sell. Sometimes all they had were drinks, and other times condiments or only bread. There were still benches in the park facing the water, though no beachgoers went there anymore. In the heat the water was stagnant with algae blooms; the lapping tide looked like an undulating carpet of green goo, a vision straight out of some bad drug trip. But Miriam still liked to sit and imagine what it had looked like before the seasons had fused into each other. She sometimes wondered if it was like this everywhere or if only their city suffered under such impenetrable doldrums but after the Collapse they'd been completely cut off from the outside. Anyone operating a ham radio or anything that picked up news from other places disappeared and their equipment was confiscated. So her musings would go unanswered, for she would never leave Infinius.

Still, on that particular day, she was planning to sit and daydream about traveling somewhere west to cool mountain air with that bluest sky as encouragement for such reverie. The Regime couldn't take away their dreams. No one could take away their nightmares.

Niko was seventeen by then and facing what life would be like for him after he turned eighteen. When they'd met other times, Niko almost always asked about what life was like before. Before The Collapse. Before The Cleanse. Before Villinkash. He always whispered that name. Before the Overseers and Protectors. For him it was like listening to old fables.

He would ask over and over: "Did that really happen?" or, "Could you do that?" and, "There were such things then?" He asked about books and Miriam gave freely from her own library, which she had hidden in a series of battered trash cans in the basement of her building. Only rats used that space, so these books and other remnants of the past remained untouched as if entombed in amber. Niko was a quick study. He absorbed everything she gave him and brought back questions about what he'd read.

But on this particular day, when Miriam sat down near him on the bench and opened her knapsack, he shook his head when she offered to share her lunch with him. He stared out at the algae bloom of rust and green as if looking for some ship on the horizon. Miriam ate in silence, and he just sat and stared. Finally, as she finished lunch and started packing up the trash, he leaned forward, his arms resting on his knees, his head tilted up to the blue sky, and very quietly, as if he'd been thinking about it for a long time, he said, "Tell me about love."

Miriam had always tried not to show any emotion when he asked naive questions. She didn't want to discourage their discussions or his awakening awareness. But this question literally took her breath away. She tried to compose herself before blurting out some nonsensical remark. Niko, always alert to every nuance of his surroundings, followed this with a second question.

"You're probably wondering why I ask that," he said softly. "I read that play you gave me. *Romeo and Juliet*. Why did you suggest that one?"

"Well," she began cautiously, "it's probably the most read of any of Shakespeare's plays. And since the two main characters are about your age, I thought it might resonate with you. Did it?"

"What is 'resonate'?" he asked, so she explained the word to him.

He nodded and sat up straight. "So tell me," he said. "About love. Does it always end badly?"

At this time, Miriam didn't yet know about his involvement with Huston or his experience at Huston's club. If she had, she might have answered in a different way.

"Everything is dangerous nowadays."

"That's not an answer."

"Why don't you tell me what you really want to know then? Is this just because you read a play?"

He shook his head. Miriam looked at him and thought she saw the sparkle of tears in his eyes.

"I know this girl," he began, and she thought he sounded like a normal teenage boy from before The Collapse, with a crush on a high school girl. She imagined what it would be like if he were living in a different time and place where boys his age went on dates and to proms and played on teams and enjoyed their youth. Not this hard time, facing disaster at every street corner.

"Is she pretty?" Miriam asked.

"She's beautiful. She's strong and smart. I could watch her all day long."

And so he told her everything he knew about El. About how he knew her and what he wanted to say to her. Miriam didn't let on then that she had already met El during her interview with the Sisters of Mercy and understood how he could have fallen in love with her.

Finally, he asked, "Is it bad for me to feel this way?"

"No, it's not bad. Only . . . you know what the system is like. You could be putting yourself and her in very big trouble."

They both knew that even choosing a girl was, in a way, prearranged by The Regime.

"If I win, I'll have it all. If I don't, then it won't matter."

Such was the way young men were forced to approach the future.

"Only, if I don't win, what will happen to her?"

They both knew the answer.

After that talk with Niko, Miriam had a vague idea to try to steer El in as safe a direction as she could, so she made an excuse to see the girl again. Certainly, it was none of her business to do this, but her maternal yearnings had been stirred, and never having had children of her own, she felt a certain sense of satisfaction, even pleasure, at allowing them free rein. Since she had interviewed the two remaining nuns, she felt visiting the convent again to follow up would seem logical. The nuns didn't question it when she showed up at their door trailing three young Scavengers who'd arrived with a sack of items to trade.

People looked upon these roving bands of not-quite-children as no more than ubiquitous, innocuous streetlamps. That was how they managed to escape the Protectors, by blending in like old furniture. What they collected was of little value. Yet the old nuns always welcomed them. And in exchange for their paltry items, the nuns gave them food and sometimes fresh herbs or vegetables from the gardens they cultivated behind their converted garage in what had once been no more than a dumping site. Somehow, word of this never spread beyond the Scavenger community.

Over the years, such bands of children expanded to a loosely governed underground, where Niko had developed an increasing influence.

El offered Miriam a cup of herbal tea.

"This is delicious." Miriam sipped the aromatic mixture.

"It comes from our garden. It's a special blend of herbs. We grow them along the fence."

Miriam wanted to ask what El planned to do after the elderly sisters passed away, but the question was answered before it was posed.

"One day the old nuns will pass on," she said, speaking quietly in deference to them, although they had been left alone at the table. "Sister Angelica is not well. I can see her fading almost every day."

She was right, of course. Sister Angelica died not two months after that.

"What will you do then?"

"I won't be able to stay here. It will no longer be a protected space. What will you do with these interviews?" she asked again. This time Miriam had to answer her.

If Miriam was to help her at all, she must trust that El wouldn't betray her or anyone else. So she moved closer to El and, in almost a whisper, said, "I'm preparing a history. Do you understand?"

She shook her head, but her eyes widened.

"It's about what life has really been like since Villinkash took over. Since The Cleanse. And how it happened. Do you know about that?"

She looked down at her hands, and when she looked up, Miriam saw fear in her eyes.

"There are books and other things here. Things the sisters kept hidden from everyone. Even me. They taught me how to read and write and do figures. One day I saw Sister Angelica go to a secret room down below." She pointed to the floor. "I saw her take out the books she used for my lessons. I didn't like to do it, but one day, I went down there and found many things from long before The Collapse. And after. Magazines and newspapers. And other things I could watch on a little machine. It was terrifying."

"But you looked at them?" Miriam asked.

El nodded. And then she reached out and took Miriam by the hands.

"It wasn't always like this," she whispered. "And there's more."

"Yes," Miriam told her. "Much more."

By that time, El's lessons with Father Ignatius were well underway. Behind an old warehouse, Father Ignatius had cobbled together a gym of sorts. There he taught the street kids how to defend themselves. Along with physical lessons, he also taught moral ones, with varying degrees of success. To teach such concepts at that time was like ascending Everest in the dead of winter, such were the headwinds against him. Yet he persisted.

With El, he began with basic self-defense techniques. She was a quick study, and he found her an eager student. Rather than relying on the brute strength of fistfights or weaponry, he taught her in the disciplines that relied on using her own body's energy and the resistance of her attacker. She became a model for all his other students, and soon she was also teaching the techniques to others.

They met in secret, usually in the evening after the patrols had gone past. The Protectors never bothered to look behind the warehouse. It had been empty for so long that it caused no suspicion. After darkness came, Father Ignatius burned old oil lamps for light, using cooking oils he had collected around the city from restaurants that operated at the behest of the Overseers. These ranged from dives selling cheap, greasy fast foods to swanky (mostly private) eating clubs that served just about anything the elites could imagine. Such fare was smuggled in from exotic locales around the world, places ordinary people no longer knew existed. One of the more popular dishes at these clubs was songbird wrapped in rare orchid petals, drizzled with a sauce of blood siphoned from wolves.

The Overseers employed a select cadre to travel outside Infinius to hunt down valued prey for these establishments. Songbirds, prized as a delicacy simply because their ranks had been so depleted, were captured by vast nets strung along their migration routes. This type of seine fishing had been used in water forever, but catching songbirds this way was a relatively new development. As songbirds were brought in by the thousands and their numbers decreased, the price on their tiny heads increased exponentially.

The Birders, as the cadre of food smugglers were known, grew in numbers and value to the Overseers, and their hunting fields expanded farther and farther from The Perimeter. They were one link to the world outside Infinius, where the forbidden fruits craved by the Overseers tantalized with their difficulty to reach. And even though the greenhouses and vertical farms of

Infinius worked miracles to supply food for the city, some types of food resisted cultivation and could exist successfully only in the wild.

Realizing what El would have to face outside the convent once they were gone, Sister Angelica and Sister Catarina never asked about where she went on those evenings. She would quietly let herself out the hidden back door and climb over the fencing behind the garage. This way she wouldn't need a key to let herself back in the front door. The small door was hidden. It was half the height of a standard door and designed to be indistinguishable from the wall itself. It had been installed long ago. No one knew who built it or why, although Sister Catarina once posited that it had been meant only as an entry for after-hours deliveries of small machine parts. Nonetheless, especially during The Cleanse, when they had to come and go in secret at night to evade the street cameras so they could tend to the women who were due to give birth, it served the sisters well. In fact, before she had become Sister Angelica, she had been trained in midwifery and had since delivered thousands of newborns. This might have accounted for the babies left at the doorstep of the convent after The Collapse.

One night, not two blocks from the warehouse where she was headed for her lesson, a group of Scavengers rounded the corner like wolves on the prowl for an easy meal and stopped when they spotted her. The only one who stood out was the thug TMan. His hulking body and shifting gaze, with his head weaving from side to side as if from some nervous affliction, caught El's attention. She figured TMan was the one she would have to take on in order to dispel the group's energy. She stopped and assumed the stance she'd learned, of "watch and wait."

They also stopped, eyeing the street and then El. Scavengers were more dangerous than Scroungers. They had almost nothing to lose and were therefore willing to take anything that happened to cross their path. Scavengers usually lived in The Shanty Alleys, and they were routinely raided for contraband by the Protectors. Thus they were used to paying for protection. Every once in a while a small group of Scavengers, who never traveled in less than three, and usually more, would fall into a big score. The Protectors always heard from paid informants about these hauls and swooped down to collect their share.

A beautiful girl like El, just reaching her prime, would be a haul worth bargaining over, but only if she hadn't been *spoiled*, as they called it. Rape was always a threat to women—and almost as often to boys—but a girl like El was an unusual commodity. Especially out there on the street alone after curfew.

TMan, his head weaving, stopped to regard her carefully. He wasn't one to plan any elaborate strategy. He relied on brute force along with the backup of his troupe to overtake a situation. He moved forward, followed closely by the others, who were even less inclined to make a cohesive plan.

When they struck, with TMan out front, it was a grab-and-snatch kind of play. TMan reached for El. She let him get so close she could feel his breath on her neck.

Then, suddenly, she whirled sideways and gave him a bruising kick to the groin so targeted that he doubled over immediately and sank to the pavement.

The others, stunned at this, fell apart like matchsticks. Not knowing what to do next, they stood over TMan, waiting for instructions. One of them tried to get behind El, but she whirled again and flattened his nose with another kick and then chopped at his neck with her flattened hand. He dropped unconscious in front of her.

She took off running and disappeared around the corner, arriving by the alley into the yard where Father Ignatius had set up his oil lamps and the others were lined up for class.

"You're late, El," he said, and motioned for her to get in line. "You know it's important to stay focused. What we do here takes discipline. When one breaks that chain, it harms the others and we all fall behind."

He looked from one to the other down the line. They had all assumed the starting pose. El fell into line at the end, but her stance was off, so Father Ignatius approached her.

"Your legs are too far apart," he told her. "And you're not holding your neck taut enough."

"I'm sorry," she said, but he could hardly hear her, and then he noticed a slight tremor in her left hand.

"What's going on, El? You're always in perfect form."

"I'm sorry," she repeated.

"Sorry is not a reason." This time he'd heard her. "Sorry is an excuse. Sorry is an evasion. We must face our fears when we're here and uphold our high standards."

El almost said "sorry" again but bit her lip instead. She adjusted her stance and bent her elbows up in the opening position, but she couldn't get her left hand to stop shaking.

Father Ignatius took her hand in both of his. "What's this?" he asked. "You seem to be unable to control your body tonight."

"There were Scavengers two blocks before I got here."

Father Ignatius dropped his hands and stepped back.

"And you took them on alone?"

El nodded. The others broke their line to move closer to her. Father Ignatius didn't stop them.

"Do you know who they were?" he asked.

"The big one was that TMan. He came up to me, so I kicked him hard and he fell. I knocked one of the others out with a chop to the neck. And then I ran. They didn't chase me."

"I see," said Father Ignatius. He turned to the others. "This is why we study the art of self-defense. This is a good lesson."

"Let's go get them," a big boy named Rollo said.

"Yes," said another boy with a wide, flat face and big hands. "Let's take them all down."

"I'll go," said a boyish girl with chopped-off hair. She was older than El but only by a year.

Then they all clamored and shouted to run after the Scavengers.

Father Ignatius held up his hand for quiet.

"You'll bring the Protectors down on us all with your yelling. We are not here to become a mob seeking retribution against a few Scavengers. Believe me, young people, the day will come when you'll need all your training. When that day comes, you must be strong, organized, focused, and, above all, controlled. The Scavengers you meet today may be the army you lead tomorrow. Now get back into formation and let's focus on tonight's lessons."

He turned back to El as the rest reformed their line.

"And El, your future and that of all young people depends on keeping your mind straight and your body prepared. Tonight was but one encounter with a tiny rabble. The next will surely be a more organized foe. Remember: There was a time long ago when the Pope led an army across the continent of Europe. I may be a man of God, but He commands us to be righteous. Each of us must decide what 'righteous' means and how we must fight for it."

Cleaning up after being sick, Miriam began to think. Of course, Miriam had hoped Niko would survive The Race. It was an odd feeling to be rooting for one boy over all the others, knowing what would happen to the ones who lost. But she didn't know the others. That's how the system corrupted even its more honorable members: dehumanizing the "other" and making cruelty seem normal.

She'd hoped, if he did win, he wouldn't be corrupted by it. But Miriam was also a realist. In that situation, in the circumstances of their everyday life, how could anyone, if offered the brass ring, turn it down? And anyway, to turn it down wasn't an option for the winner. He was expected to continue to play the game by the established rules. Witnessing the winner take all his prizes was one of the ways the Overseers manipulated the population until next year's Race.

No matter what happened to Niko after The Race, Miriam hoped he would continue their conversations. Before The Race, although she'd never expected him to read all of them, she'd given Niko a number of books about authoritarian political systems. She chose both Orwell's *1984* and *Animal Farm* because she thought he would be more engaged by fiction. She also included, however, the complete set of Gibbon's *The Decline and Fall of the Roman Empire* and Shirer's *The Rise and Fall of the Third Reich*.

Along with the rest of Infinius, she saw the wild enthusiasm as Niko was led off his motorcycle at the edge of the roof to the viewing stand, where all the Overseers stood clapping and cheering as loudly as any lowly Hovel dweller down on the street or any Ring dwellers on the other twelve roofs.

He looked dazed, Miriam thought. And did she catch him glancing around for something or someone?

Miriam couldn't look away from the screens as Protectors in full uniform with swords at their belts draped him with the first spoils of his win. A huge gold medal was hung around his neck, from what looked like a purple velvet cord. Bags of gold coins were laid at his feet. Two Protectors opened the bags for the cameras to get a good shot of the loot. A large ceremonial key with a scroll announced his new mansion. It went on and on, with gifts and investiture into the Overseers Club. Each item was proclaimed by the announcer over all channels. He was deluged with promises of a perfect life of which others only dreamed. It was the lottery to end all lotteries. People screamed with excitement, and almost immediately, the revelries began. Loud music enveloped the city as people began drinking and dancing.

Clouds of meskitta wafted through the air as the sun descended below the horizon. Huge spotlights suddenly lit up The Ring. The final gift bestowed on him was the bike he had ridden to victory. It was rolled by two Protectors up to the viewing stand and lifted onto the platform in front of him. There was bugling and drumming as he was handed its key.

But still Niko stood on the platform, draped in his new riches, the key resting in his palm like a fragile egg and his mind racing.

What now? Do I belong to them? Have I completely given in? My future controlled and monitored like a robot? I'm better than that. There must be more for me—more than this life in a cell, more than scrounging and fighting and dying like bugs.

Then cymbals clashed and drums rolled as Villinkash himself arose, sitting atop an ersatz throne. It lifted up from below the viewing stand. For this, his one yearly public appearance, his beautiful wife sat stately and stiff by his side. He wore white silken robes and held a golden staff encrusted with jewels. As if from some cartoon version of an all-powerful ruler, a pair of German shepherds flanked him, standing at attention, their noses pointed up as if to sniff the air for prey. He raised his staff, and the whole city fell into an eerie silence.

His voice boomed over the loudspeakers.

"Niko, you are anointed, and the time for you to choose has arrived. Which of these young women will you take for your own? Let the city of Infinius celebrate your chosen one."

A parade of young girls, who were no more than seventeen, was ushered before the viewing stand. They were all dressed to maximize their beauty and youth. Their hair had been arranged by experts, makeup applied liberally, and their clothing revealed their most sensuous curves. As they walked past the Overseers and Villinkash, shouts erupted from the crowds.

"Choose number twelve."

"Get the redhead."

"Take number twenty."

The yelling went on as people tried to influence Niko. The drunker they got, the louder they yelled. The girls paraded around the roof, smiling for the cameras. All of them wore finer clothes than they had ever touched, trussed up for the auction of their lives.

And this was another horrifying part of The Race: Boys who lived in The Ring weren't the only ones at risk. Girls who were sixteen or seventeen living in The Ring were also called up as if for a stint in an army reserve. But this wasn't community service in the sense that it would offer any beneficial effect for the country as a whole, nor would it enhance the lives of either the girls or the people. No, this was pure depravity.

Miriam watched as the girls paraded around that roof. She searched for El's face, hoping it wasn't there. But knowing how Niko felt about her, she hoped at the same time to see her, and that Niko would pluck her out of obscurity and save her from the fate of those other girls. For the ones who were not chosen were destined for the brothels or the private bedrooms of the Overseers. Even worse, they could be cast into The Hovels to be groped and pawed and fought over by Scroungers, who would use and then sell them—or their services—to other Scroungers or to the Scavengers. Even worse than that was a lifetime of what was called "comfort service" for the Protectors. This was rumored to be more horrific than any other servitude. Most of those girls would never live to see adulthood.

Holding her breath, she hardly hoped to find El somewhere

up there in that throng of pulchritude, Miriam searched the screens as the yelling continued, fueled by the cameras panning the line of girls.

Finally, Villinkash raised his staff to silence the clamor. Without actually looking at Niko, he nodded his head and said, "Which one do you choose?"

Niko stared straight ahead. But when the girls stopped and turned to face him, Niko looked to the left and a bit behind the viewing stand. The crowds gasped. It turned into a murmur and then, as Niko did not single out a girl from the parade, there were shouts of "Niko, Niko, Niko," until it became a chant. People waved their arms back and forth and then began to sway from side to side. The cameras panned from the crowds to Niko and back. As the chanting grew in volume, Niko stared straight ahead. He seemed oblivious to it all.

At some point, as the chanting and calls of his name reached feverish levels, without any warning sign, he tossed off all the rewards draped over him and leaped off the stand.

Seen on the jumbo screens, it was like watching an escape movie come to life. The chants turned to cheers. People tossed empty beer bottles into the air and set trash on fire. The whole city seemed to come alive in a new way as Niko pushed through the crowd on the Tower's roof. With the camera following, he made his way to where El stood beside Old Merrie at the banquet table piled with food and drink.

He took El's hand in his. She was dressed for work, wearing an apron over her shirt and skirt, her hair tied back with the same simple piece of cloth Miriam had seen at the convent. On the screen, her skin glowed and her eyes sparkled as she gazed at Niko in wonder at what he was doing. Amid all the screaming and clamor, was it only Miriam who noticed Old Merrie's face up there on the jumbo screen? As the cameras panned, for less than the intake of a breath, she saw Old Merrie grimace as if someone had stabbed her. And Miriam suspected then what lay ahead for El.

He pulled her away from the table and held her hand high before he spoke.

"I choose El," he said simply. "I choose El as the one I want."

The city went wild. "Niko, Niko, Niko" drowned out the announcer, the drums, the music—even the rumble of the Collectors' huge trash trucks that had been summoned to prevent rioting. The cameras had followed Niko closely and now they locked on the beautiful young couple, and because the cameras and the people couldn't get enough of this image, no one witnessed what effect this was having on the Overseers and Villinkash back at the viewing stand.

Even in those years, news organizations had sources behind the scenes. As powerful as Villinkash was, even he couldn't plug every leak. So it became known that Villinkash was livid. He was not the type of man, however, to explode in the moment. He was too smart a political operator to show his hand or his outrage in public. There would be no sign of weakness or displeasure for the people to witness. And there was a simple reason for that. Villinkash did not fear obstruction or implosion from within his ranks, or even from a few disgruntled or overly ambitious lieutenants. He could always get rid of any number of Overseers or Protectors. To Villinkash, they were replaceable pieces of furniture.

He feared a massive uprising of common people. And the reason for that was simple. Without control over the hordes, he had no one to control. Once he lost control of them, there was no longer any need for him. A dictator who kills off all those he dictates to has no one left to prop up his power. Whatever system he had created would inevitably crumble under its own weight. But this lesson never seems to take hold for long. So Villinkash forgot it, and even as a new reality was beginning to creep over his own threshold, at that moment he was only reacting to the one event he could see.

Miriam heard, through the leaky grapevine up in The Compound, that Villinkash was in a fury like no one had ever seen.

"Who let that little snake win?" Villinkash sneered.

"We don't know, sir."

The same answer came back over and over. And no one seemed able to find out who had fixed The Race. Oh, it was common knowledge among the Overseers and Protectors that The Race was always fixed. The difficulty lay not in the dishonesty that everyone had a fix in but that everyone lied about who they'd backed. There were too many fingerprints scattered everywhere to trust any of them.

"Who let him pick that milkmaid? She's not one of our hand-picked girls. Where did she come from? How did he get off the viewing stand without being stopped? Why didn't anyone stop the cameras from covering all of it?"

"We don't know, sir," came the answer time and again to every question he fired off.

He continued fuming until one aide called in Huston to manage the "Supreme Leader's" rage. They also called for his personal doctor to administer a calming agent, but he brushed that off and turned to Huston with a sneer.

"Who is that little vermin? I want you to get to the bottom of this. We can't let The Race get out of hand like that. Where's the control? Who let go of the reins?"

Huston was, as always, impeccably dressed. And in control. Whereas the atmosphere was electric, he was neither rattled nor intimidated by the ravings and questions randomly flung about at no one in particular and everyone in the meeting room.

As Villinkash strode around waving his arms and periodically pounding his fist on the heavy oak table, Huston watched with a bemused expression, as if a small child were having a temper tantrum on the way to school.

He walked calmly to one of the large windows overlooking a shimmering lake where swans glided in absolute calm. On his way, he patted a couple of the aides on the shoulder as if to say, "Not to worry. Nothing bad here."

Gazing out the window, he said to Villinkash, "Look, sir, I think your swans have paired off into mated couples. Soon you'll have little baby cygnets out here."

"What?" Villinkash almost yelled out at the top of his voice.

"I said . . ."

"I heard what you said. Baby swans." He was silent for a few seconds. "Baby swans, you say? Well, now, that is something to blast to Infinius. Good news for everyone. Happy news. Happy times. Yes. I like that."

He pointed to an aide. "Get that out over the InCom right away. Tell them we'll have eggs to watch soon. And then a hatching."

"Yes, sir. I'll take care of it right now, sir," he said, and scurried off, relieved to be out of the room and off to do something else.

"Now then." Villinkash turned to Huston. "What about this other business? I'm not happy about it. No, not at all. We have to spin this some way."

"I was just thinking the same thing, sir."

"The question is how. If we let this squirt get away with not following protocol, we invite eventual insurrection."

"Of course." Huston quietly motioned the others out of the room. They backed away like the obsequious servants they were. "And I agree with you, as I always have. We'll manage him just like we have all the others from past years. He's no different."

"Yes, yes, I know. You've handled all of them." Villinkash waved as if to a crowd standing in the room. "You've been there through everything we've accomplished. I want you to take on the dual title of Overseer. No reason for you to remain a Protector. You deserve the promotion. Take care of that. Which reminds me: What about the Tower and all those squatters? They're stealing electricity from the street poles. We should charge them."

"All in good time," Huston said. He pulled a chair away from the conference table and moved it to the window where he'd been standing to watch the swans.

"Come, sit down. You'll be able to think better once you feel more detached from the problem."

Villinkash followed his suggestion. Now he was as docile as a bovine coming back to the barn for milking.

"Ahhh," he sighed as he sat to take in the scene below.

It was a lovely scene. From above one had an especially captivating view of the entire manicured landscape. It was like entering a painting. The lake, fed by springs, was an amorphous, undulating shape with an arched intricately carved footbridge at one narrow point. This was exquisitely reflected in the water below it. At parts of the lake's perimeter, weeping cherry trees waved softly. In the hot wind they skimmed the edge of the water, creating a ripple pattern that spread outward. Besides the swans, peacocks wandered the lawns, and under the tree canopy, llamas and small deer rested for the night. During the day, birds sang; although they could not be heard behind the glass, one could see them flitting here and there. Butterflies plied the many flowering shrubs, and hummingbirds darted from flower to flower. Scattered throughout the landscape were patches of roses planted in full sunlight. Some were bright yellow, others dusky pink, and some with orange fringe at the far edges of the petals of their white-throated interior. From this viewpoint, the armed guards, barbed wire, watchtowers, and security barriers surrounding the building and the lake were invisible. Of course, the glass through which they gazed was bulletproof as it was everywhere in The Compound.

Miriam sat on a bench next to a collapsing park shelter near the water's edge. A scrawny tree gave partial shade from the searing sun. She'd bought a cold cucumber sandwich from Old Merrie, who'd said she'd gotten a fresh load of cucumbers early that morning from a farm somewhere outside The Perimeter. A real farm. Not one of the Regime's greenhouses. Everything *they* grew had the faint reminiscence of cardboard. How anyone got hold of fresh vegetables Old Merrie couldn't or wouldn't say when Miriam asked. But just imagine, Miriam thought: a black market even for vegetables.

"The less you know, the better," Old Merrie said with a wink as she plopped three of them into Miriam's canvas bag along with the sandwich. "And here," she added, shoving into the bag a loaf of freshly baked bread wrapped in a crumbly sheet of paper. The bread was still warm, and its aroma spoke of whole grains and molasses. Then she turned her face sideways and whispered, so low Miriam could barely hear her, "Cucumbers from Zamora."

Miriam paid her and squeezed her fat forearm as a thank-you.

"We got to watch out for one another," she whispered, which surprised Miriam. On the other hand, though, she'd had the feeling lately that something was brewing. It was only a vague sense. Like watching a fog hanging over a misty lake that might grow denser still or simply evaporate, leaving behind the distinct outline of a far shore.

Old Merrie slowly wheeled her beat-up cart down the street, where someone else stopped her and bought a bottle of soda. The cart itself was something of an enigma, holding as it did, in different compartments, both cold and hot foods and, on the top, fresh fruits and vegetables under a wide umbrella she'd cobbled together from an old awning and the ribs and posts of two scavenged beach umbrellas. It looked too large for the old woman to maneuver, yet she managed to push and pull it up and down the pitted streets while hawking her wares through songs she made up as she went.

Miriam crunched into that cold cucumber, and with the first bite, a flood of memory came to her. Of summer salads and all the family crowding around their picnic table under the giant old oak tree in the backyard, the grass just cut, its sweet scent speaking of hayfields and munching cows.

As she ate, Niko appeared seemingly from nowhere.

"You probably thought you'd never see me again," he said in a low voice.

She must have jumped a little with surprise, because he grunted softly. And it also vaguely registered that she'd heard the soft roar of a motorcycle while she'd been eating, but she had taken no particular notice of it because the Detainers sometimes made rounds on bikes. And there was usually some noise in the background whenever you were outside.

She looked over at him then and noticed a cut on his face, running from his cheekbone to his jaw. It was a clean line, and she thought it was too bad because he would be left with a scar on that handsome, young face. He was dressed as he always had been, and this surprised her as well. She thought he would be enjoying living in luxury by this time, wearing expensive clothes and riding around in a big car. He looked raggedy, like he hadn't slept or showered.

She wanted to ask about the cut but instead answered him. "No. I never expected to see you again. Not after The Race."

He shrugged and said, "I had nowhere else to go. I mean after what happened." He stopped talking and stared out at the undulating sea.

She wanted to ask for details but held back, figuring he'd sat down next to her because he had something on his mind.

Instead of talking she offered him a piece of her sandwich, but it wasn't easy to separate just a piece, so she gave him half and watched as he bit into the crisp cucumber. When he opened his mouth, he winced in pain from the fresh gash on his cheek.

As he munched on it, Miriam finished the other half and waited. When he stuck the last corner into his mouth and wiped the juice away with the back of his hand, he said, "I'm not supposed to be here."

"Where are you supposed to be?"

Instead of answering, he said, "I did a terrible thing."

Miriam opened her mouth and was about to try to relieve him of this burden by saying she was sure whatever it was hadn't been his fault. That the system made us all do awful things and that he was a good person and shouldn't take on the sins of the city. But before she could even utter a word, he pointed to his cheek.

"This happened because I was weak and selfish. I should have asked her first. I should have told her. But I really didn't know until it was over, until I was standing there and the crowds were yelling and I was draped with all those prizes. I mean, how could I have known that he really had fixed it for me? I couldn't. I didn't know. I thought, *maybe* he could do it. But why would I have trusted him? Why trust anyone in the Regime? What was in it for him? All those others—the ones that went over the edge. All that blood and the bodies. All those others . . ." His voice faded.

Miriam watched the muscles of his face contort as he tried to regain his composure. He looked intently at the water in front of them. It looked thick near the shore with a recent algae bloom, rolling like a sheet of green rubber.

"But he told me I would come to him one day. And I did. I did and he fixed everything. For me. Why for me? What had I ever done that he would want me to win? Nothing. Not a damn thing. Yet he did it. And then all those prizes. Do you know where the winner gets to live?"

He didn't wait for an answer.

"There's a compound way up in the north end. Surrounded by high walls and small guard towers. Guards sit there all day long just watching. Inside the walls there are actual houses. Not high-rises but low buildings. And swimming pools. They put huge ice blocks in them every morning to keep the water cool. All the food is fresh. Fish just off a boat. There are sports fields and coconut trees. I never saw a coconut tree before. And servants who take care of you. They clean your house and water your lawn. Yes, there's grass everywhere. There's a zoo with animals you've never seen except in books and birds nesting in the trees and singing. They even gave me my winning bike. Every day a mechanic would tune and clean it for me, they said. They said I can ride it anywhere I like in The Compound. They even built a track for the winners. I've never seen the others, though. They must be there somewhere. There's a team of what they call handlers assigned to me. I don't like them. They told me I could have anything I wanted any time I wanted it."

He stopped to take a breath, so she asked him, "What *do* you want?"

That seemed like a simple question, but Miriam felt that most people had no idea what they wanted. They know what they think they need. It's usually related to money or things. Even the people who have money usually want more of it. And then they're afraid someone will take away what they have, so they start looking at other people with suspicion. And trying to arrange society to protect themselves and their money. They wall themselves off. Like being inside The Compound.

He looked over at her with a blank stare as if she'd interrupted his thoughts and he'd lost where he was. The cut on his face looked deeper from this angle. For a moment, she wondered if he'd fought his new keepers and she wanted to ask him about it.

"Before The Race I thought that I just wanted to stay alive. I had a one-in-thirteen chance. Not very good odds. But better than refusing, I figured. And I had some idea . . ."

He paused and looked down at the ground. She waited, not wanting to interrupt him again.

"I mean, I thought I had a shot. You know, like Romeo thought. What the hell, he thought. He was in love, and it mattered more to him than anything. So he took his shot. It didn't end so well, but while he was at it, he was happy for a little while. Wasn't he?"

He looked up at her like a wounded deer. It was almost as if he was asking her to put him down. She was afraid to ask but did anyway, softly as if he were a small child and she was his mother.

"What happened, Niko? You chose El. Isn't that what you wanted?"

He jumped up from the bench. His arm muscles tensed so hard they looked like boulders. His jaw set even harder, and he balled up his fists into tight knobs.

"You don't know what it's like," he hissed, and whirled around to face her like a cornered snake.

For an instant Miriam was afraid. She didn't take her eyes off him, but the thought crossed her mind that he'd been followed and they were both about to be in trouble. Then his expression changed again, softened, and his head drooped. His muscles relaxed for a time, and he looked up at the sky in a pose of supplication. Then he whirled again back to face her, his jaw set again, his eyes narrowed, a scowl between his eyebrows.

"Do you?" he challenged. "Do you know? Do you have any idea?"

She shook her head, not sure what he was referring to. She thought it best to go along without asking more questions.

"They tell you everything's going to be laid at your feet. Anything you want. They want you to choose a woman. Choose someone you don't even know. They don't care who or what she is. To them, she's just a body. Someone to screw. Or do whatever you want with. Like the ones at those clubs they go to. You know about the clubs?" he asked sincerely, as if Miriam was so far removed from life she had no idea what really went on.

"I know," she told him.

"Yeah, like them. But I didn't want any of those girls. I only wanted El. And I thought she wanted me, too. That she wanted us to be together and have it all. That she would be glad."

At this his head drooped, and all the anger drained from his face. He sat down again, crossed his arms on his knees, and lowered his head to rest on his folded arms.

"What happened?" Miriam asked. Looking back on it later, she realized how little she'd understood of the whole situation, how deeply perverse was the structure they lived under and how it twisted everything, even love.

It began when Niko stepped off the reviewing stage and inadvertently created an uproar. It didn't take long for drunken revelers, partying until the sun emerged, to graffiti the city with one word scrawled over and over on every available surface and so the name—NIKO—instantly morphed into a rallying cry and a major problem for Villinkash and the Overseers. And inside the well-cloaked rooms of The Compound, Villinkash ranted with a series of Vesuvius-like eruptions. The news of this got out to certain circles, journalists among them, and took on its own anti-humor scree cascading freely and picking up heft as it traveled through the city. People would suddenly erupt in wild yelling or machinations, ranting "Niko" over and over. Others would pick it up, sometimes in groups, sometimes just one-on-one, almost inaudibly mouthing "Niko" and repeating it as a kind of secret society's signal.

But Niko hadn't begun to react to what had happened. While the city transitioned from pre-Race suspense to post-Race debauchery, the handlers led Niko and El away from the cameras.

Niko was in a daze, the kind you hear about after someone's been in an accident. Husky, heavily armed handlers, the kind Niko wouldn't want to tangle with on the street, led him off the roof with El by his side, shaking like a kitten. He wanted to tell her everything would be okay but couldn't find the words, thinking as he allowed the handlers to shove him forward that they were going to be treated like royalty, wherever they were being taken.

From the corner of his vision, he saw some men lift the bike he'd ridden onto a platform and wheel it out of sight. Later, when it was presented to him, he would thank them and say, "It's a fine bike. And good brakes." He'd laugh at that: a short, nervous laugh. It was ironic because when he was driving the course, he couldn't even remember how to apply the brakes, as if his mind was stuck in some gear. And then, when he saw the first bike go over, his brain came back alive and he started calculating how his odds had turned. It all went by so fast, he couldn't tell how long it lasted or who went over next or how many were left. By then he just drove that thing as fast as he could, figuring if he was going over, he wanted to fly really high into the air, wanted to feel free for that second before the fall. So he just gunned it and went all out. And when it was over it was like he was in a trance. Like there was a bubble around him and all he could see was El and all he wanted was her in that bubble with him.

The handlers led them off the roof onto the big elevator that had brought all the bikes and food and chairs and everything up to the roof. They had to work the cables by hand as they went down and down, slowly to the ground floor. It seemed to Niko longer than The Race itself. When they finally reached the ground the screaming surrounded him, and it was then he noticed another sound. The sound of an engine. And scraping, like some sound Niko remembered from long ago. The sound of metal against concrete.

Around the corner, three big black cars were waiting. He couldn't see inside of them. They were idling, but that wasn't the engine he'd heard. He looked past the black cars to the street and saw the blood. And the bikes, all busted up, tires split, wheels at right angles. Some of them had fallen on top of others. Handlebars all jerked to hell. Lights hanging by a wire. Fenders crushed. Chips of mirror all over the place and molten metal bent out of shape.

There were body parts mixed in with bike parts, all twisted together, with blood all over everything and running in a river down the street. Niko broke away from the handlers somehow and ran to the biggest pile, and whoever it was had a skull so crushed there was no face left. So he ran to the next pile and then the next, where there was one bike and one rider alone. It was Thomaso from Building Five. Niko remembered he was a good guy. He played the trumpet with Father Ignatius. Both his arms were gone, but his face stared right at Niko. He was smiling. Just a small smile like he was happy.

Then two of the handlers grabbed Niko and dragged him back to the waiting cars and shoved him inside next to where El was sitting way over against the other door. They smacked the car hood hard, and it took off. And there was someone else in the front seat, but Niko didn't care who. All he could see was Thomaso's smile. The whole ride to wherever they were going, that smile went with him like a ghost. As they sped away, he caught sight of a mother with tears streaming down her face, a face of agony, scratching at the man holding her back and, behind her, the Collectors riding in on their huge scooping machine to scrape what was left off the concrete.

The sun was searing now, and Miriam shifted on the bench to try to get maximum shade from the flimsy tree. Niko didn't seem to notice the heat or anything else around them. She felt sorry for him in an abstract kind of way. Sorry for what all these boys had to endure. Sorry for the ones who hadn't made it and, again, in an abstract way, for the parents who were grieving. She didn't yet understand the depth of Niko's pain.

"I'd never driven in anything like that before," he said. "That car was plush and cool. They had drinks for us in the back. And velvet cushions. And soft music. At first all I could see, all I could think about, was those bodies on the street, all mangled and bloody. So much blood. I wanted to scream or hit something. Finally, I shook off enough of the shock to sneak a look at El. I wanted to take her hand. I guess, in some way, I wanted to feel less alone back there in that quiet car. But she was hugging herself and crammed against the door, so I didn't see any way to approach her. And she wouldn't look at me either. She just stared out as we passed all the street people. Drunks. Scavengers. People dancing and yelling. One of the other black cars was in front of us, and the other behind us. I think they were shielding us from all the people in the streets. I'd never seen so many people out all at the same time."

Miriam nodded a little to encourage him to keep talking. Looking at him in profile as he sat there, she could see his face was set in a grim stare. And the cut on his cheek had turned a deep purple that she found compelling and repellent at the same time. He seemed to be aware she was staring at it and raised his hand to cover it lightly with his fingertips. It seemed like a loving gesture to her, which was odd and out of context.

And then he said, "I'll tell you about this." He let his hand drop, and she noticed once again the tattoos on his arm. She wondered what they meant and when he'd gotten them.

"I guess I lost track of where we were in the city, and I think I nodded off for a few minutes with the motion of the car and the cushy seat. I suddenly felt so tired. I do remember that.

"And then we stopped and the car doors opened and those handlers were there again. They took El by the hands away from the car and one of them opened my door, so I stepped out. I had no idea what would happen next. We were inside The Compound I told you about. Everything was scrubbed looking, even the plants; they were clipped and neat. There was no moon, and the lights were all low and dimmed but placed in a way that lit up what you needed to see to get around. I climbed out of the car, and now I was waking up again. Alert, I guess. In case I got jumped or something.

"I saw them lead El into a low building nearby. And as I turned to follow her, someone took my arm and turned me around. The handlers faded back away from me, and there he was, Huston, facing me. He'd been in the front seat all along. He was smiling and he said, 'You did real well tonight. And now you get to see how a winner lives. Just be careful. Choosing her'—he nodded toward where El had gone—'was a really risky move. Villinkash won't like it at all. You're on his list now. I'll do what I can. Just remember this: You're always being watched. And you know what's expected of you tonight. With her'—he nodded toward the building a second time—'make sure she's . . .' and he seemed not to know what to say for a few seconds. Then he sort of pushed at my arm and said, 'You know what I mean. They'll examine her tomorrow, so you better be sure you get the job done tonight.' And then I knew what he meant."

Miriam did, too. They were the Purity Squad. A bunch of pseudo-doctors who people suspected had never actually studied medicine. They rounded up the girls before The Race to make sure they were—what did they call it?—*intact*. Sure, she knew.

Niko had started talking again.

"But I thought it wouldn't be a problem. I thought El and I had an understanding. So I just nodded. 'Don't worry,' I told him. 'I've got this under control.' And he smiled and let go of my arm and motioned to the handlers to take me away. He got back in the car and it rolled away, and I smelled meskitta smoke in the air. It must have been Huston lighting up in the car."

Miriam began to see where this story was going and was also sure she didn't want to hear about their quasi-wedding night. So finally, she spoke.

"Niko, you don't have to tell me the details," she said. "I'm sure you did what was natural, and there's nothing terrible about it."

Immediately she was sorry she'd opened her mouth. She almost apologized, but he snapped at her before she could speak again.

"You don't get it, do you?" His voice was harsh for the first time, and he turned to look at her, his hands raised. For a moment she thought he was going to grab her throat and choke her. It was the only time she had ever been afraid of Niko, and she saw, in that instant, how ruthless he could be, if needed.

"I'm not telling you this for all the . . . What's that word you taught me once? *Salacious* details? Are you that stupid? Don't you realize what I'm telling you?"

"Niko," she began.

But he raised his hands as if to tell her to stop.

"Please," he begged. "Let me tell it all. I have to tell someone. I have to tell what happened. What I did. I can't tell anyone else. You're the only one. I did something else bad once. But I never regretted that. At least I don't think I did because I had to survive. But this . . ." His voice trailed off.

Miriam nodded and said, "Okay, Niko. I understand. Go ahead. Tell me everything."

"I know you come from another time. You think things can go back to the way they were. But they can't. Not ever. They're getting worse all the time. I know that now."

Miriam gazed out at the water. He was right. She used to hope for change. But now . . .

"They led me to a room with low lighting. There was music playing softly somewhere, and I could smell something, some flower blooming at night somewhere outside the building. And there was a girly guy in white pants and this sort of tunic thing. He told me what the flower was, said it was jasmine. He led me to a huge bathroom where another girly guy had towels and oils and soaps and stuff, and they told me to undress. They didn't say 'strip,' but 'undress.' They called me 'sir.' They had filled a big tub with bubble bath, and I thought, *If they try to fuck with me, I'll kill them both*. But they just told me to soak and wash and pull the bell cord when I was done. Then they laid out new clothes for me and left me alone. I looked everywhere for the camera, but I couldn't find one. I really was all alone. And I have to say that bath was the greatest thing I've ever experienced.

"I don't know how they knew what size clothes to give me, but they fit. They were loose pants and a sort of jacket thing that buttoned up the side. Very comfortable. Black, I think, or navy blue, with my name embroidered across the chest in white. I don't know how they got that done so fast. And these sandal things that were very soft. After I finished and pulled the bell cord they came back in with a tray of champagne. Yes, champagne. I know because they told me that too. And they said there was a dinner ready in the dining room. I drank a glass. It was great. Kind of like what I imagined drinking sunlight under a splashing waterfall might be like. And they led me to where the food had been laid out. There was a big dark wood table and two comfortable chairs. This big chandelier over the table and candles, lots of candles burning everywhere.

"I sat down and started in on the food. Stuff I've never seen before. Everything fresh and so delicious I could have eaten every single thing on that table. And I realized I was famished. But after a few bites, a door across the room opened, and El stood in the doorway under a pale spotlight. And I can tell you I will never see anything more beautiful in my life. I stopped breathing, she was such a sight. They had done her hair long, with curls, and put on a dress that was more like something you would use for sleeping. But fancy. It was the color of the champagne and had lace and feathers and tassel things down her arms and a belt that wound around her waist and up the middle of her chest and over her shoulders. She wore some kind of slippers with high heels and more feathers. And they glittered like the necklace she had around her throat. It all looked as soft as one of those clouds."

He pointed to the sky, and Miriam thought a hint of a smile crossed his face. And then the cloud above them joined with another one and turned dark at the edges. She wondered if they were in for one of those freak storms, where clouds suddenly formed and rumbled and tumbled until the pressure of all that water had to find some release. But so far there were only a few clouds and they helped dispel the heat some, although the air felt heavy with the threat of something ahead.

"Someone or something pushed her from behind, and she entered the room. The door closed and I thought I heard a bolt. It was then I noticed—I think because another set of lights came up at the end of the room—that there was more than this dining room. In fact, it seemed to be a whole apartment. I got up, thinking I would offer her some food and a glass of the champagne. Which is what I did, walking over to her with my hand extended. Many times El had given me food and drinks and honey from the convent. This seemed perfectly natural and a way to repay her the kindness she'd shown me in the past. But she looked past me to the table, so I said to her, 'Are you hungry? Come and sit down. They gave me all this food. And have a glass of this.'

"I reached out my hand with the glass in it, and before I knew what was happening, she raised her arm and smashed my hand, and the glass fell on the floor and shattered. The champagne went all over the place, and all I could do was stand there, stunned.

"'Why did you do that?' I asked, but she brushed past me to stand by the table. She grabbed food with her fingers and stuffed anything she picked up into her mouth. There was a pitcher with water, and she lifted it and drank after every few bites.

"I was too stunned to say or do anything for a few minutes. I just watched her. When she had crammed a lot of food into her mouth and swallowed it, she turned to face me, and I saw hatred in her beautiful green eyes. And she seemed to be searching for an escape route. She whirled around and tried the door that those girly guys had used, but it was locked. Then she skirted the table and tried the door she'd come through, but it was also locked. She stood there, looking confused and angry and scared. And then she walked carefully down to the other end of the room and disappeared. I thought she'd found a way out, and I sat down to think things through, to try to figure out what was going on.

"My mind began to wander back to earlier that evening. And then I couldn't stop the flood of images. It was like a movie playing fast forward in my brain. I thought I should lie down for a while, but I didn't know where. And then I wondered where El had gone and thought she must be tired, too. So I headed to where she had disappeared. And I wanted to find out why she was acting so strange. I guess I wasn't thinking too straight. I guess I should have understood what she'd gone through. But, honestly . . ."

His voice cracked a little, and he made a kind of choking sound, then took a deep breath. Miriam waited. She didn't want to upset him again. The air felt heavy, and the sun was blocked out now. The tree above them had taken on a dark gray-green tint like mint leaves boiled for tea. Looking out at the sea, she saw patches of gray-blue water where once she could only see a green algae bloom. She guessed it had died off some. Or was it wind blowing the water? She had a fleeting thought that it was an omen, but then she mentally chided herself for such superstitious thinking.

But Niko went on.

"Then I went down that hallway and through a door to a dimly lit room. It took a little time for me to understand that this was a large bedroom. The bed was up on a platform and looked very plush. Lots of pillows and stuff. Beside it was a table and what looked like another champagne bottle in a bucket. I saw a lot of what looked like feathers on the floor. I think I was confused by that, and before I could get everything straight in my mind, someone kicked me from behind and I doubled over. Then I saw a foot coming at me again, so I jumped out of the way and spun around and it was El. The dress she'd been wearing was all torn up, and the feathers were gone from it.

"'Hey, what are you doing?' I yelled at her. But she just launched another kick at me and spun around like a top and kicked me from the side. Well, I guess I just went on autopilot because I grabbed her foot and pulled her, and she lost her balance and fell at my feet. I bent over and reached out to get her by the hands and pull her up. I didn't mean to hurt her. I was confused. I swear I didn't mean her any harm. I chose her because I loved her. I thought she felt the same. Or would once The Race was over and we were together.

"And that's when she pulled out the knife. She'd been holding it in her dress somewhere. I never saw it. Everything happened so fast. It must have been when I bent down because her hand flashed in front of my eyes, and then I felt this stinging pain."

He touched the cut again with an expression on his face of anger and sadness, like a bewildered child who doesn't understand why his pet puppy got hit by a car.

He was quiet for a while, so they just sat in silence.

Finally, Miriam said, "Sometimes people react without thinking. El must have been confused and terrified. No one had prepared her for what had happened to her. Her whole life had suddenly been stolen."

He stared out at the water and then up at the darkening clouds, but Miriam had the feeling he was really looking inside himself as if searching for some answer to a question not yet asked aloud.

"That's not all," he said softly. "Not nearly." He turned to her with a puzzled look, his brows knit as he touched the edge of the gash on his face again with his index finger. "I thought she would be happy," he said. "You know. To be chosen. To be with me. To be taken care of. Not to have to live on the streets anymore."

He took a deep breath and exhaled. His shoulders slumped. And then he stood up, agitated again.

"The next thing I remember is seeing the blood. My blood. But it was like—I don't know how to tell you—like all the blood, you know, on the street. After . . . after The Race. All those bodies. The others. The ones who didn't win. A river of their blood. It was like something broke in me. It was the blood that made me crazy, I think.

"I grabbed her hand and twisted that knife and threw it across the room, and then she tried to bite me, and that's when I tore her dress. Right down the front. Underwear and all. I didn't mean to.

It just happened so fast. And there was her skin and her breasts. Right in front of my eyes. She tried to shield herself I think. It's not very clear now exactly what happened next. What I did or what she did. All I remember was blood dripping down on me. My face was burning by then and that's when I grabbed her by the arms and pulled her over to the bed. I must have pushed her down. It's a blur now, how it happened, I mean in what sequence. Maybe I saw the blood dripping after I pushed her.

"She tried to kick me, but she couldn't do anything anymore, and I ripped the rest of her underthings off. Blood was still dripping. Right onto her stomach. All I could see was red. Like my eyes were filled with it. I was going to do it, you know. I really was. And then I heard something like from far away, as if I was in a tunnel and someone at the other end was calling my name. "Niko." It was El. She was crying and saying my name. 'Niko. Niko. Stop.'

"It was like some storm had gotten inside of me and I wanted to let it out inside her. But when I heard her voice something snapped and I pushed back off her and all I could think was what the blood looked like on that street as we drove past and this one thought kept repeating inside my head: *I did that. I created that. I should be there on that street all bloodied and broken.*

"She could have killed me at that moment. She could have gotten up and grabbed for the knife. It was like I was caught in an invisible trap. Unable to move or scream or anything. But when she didn't get up, I left her there and got my own clothes. These." He pointed to what he had worn to The Race. "I didn't even look at her again. It was like someone else was operating me. Like I was a bot or something. Next thing I knew I was outside and there was my bike. I guess they'd delivered it to me after they said it was part of what I'd won. They must have serviced it. I got on it and rode and rode all over the city and finally got so tired. But I had no place to go, so I slept for a while under a bridge, and when it got light, I scavenged a drink. And then I came over here."

As he told Miriam what had happened, he began running his hand absently over his pattern-shaved head. He ran it over and over from his forehead back and then to the front again. Like someone with senility, endlessly repeating the same gesture. When he stopped talking he kept doing it, as if trying to dislodge some foreign object stuck inside his mind.

When he finally spoke, he said, "I almost became like them. Like all the high-ups. I never had anyone love me or take care of me. El was the only person in this world who cared for me. And look what I did. I don't want to be like them. Not for any wealth or power or anything." He looked at Miriam in a way that begged for forgiveness, understanding, relief from his burden.

"I never should have chosen her, never should have put her in that position. But why did she turn on me like that? I only wanted us to be together."

Miriam didn't know what to say. She couldn't give him absolution for what he'd done. She understood how guilty he must have felt. Understood the turmoil that must have driven him. And then there was the knife slice down his face. And the tears running down along the cut and dripping onto his knees because his head was bowed now. He was a bird who had smacked into a window, dazed and disoriented.

Miriam thought he might need stitches for that cut, but she only asked, "Where is El now?"

He didn't have a chance to answer. The moment after she asked the question, a splinter of lightning broke through the dark gray clouds that had lowered over them, and almost immediately came the crack of thunder. They saw the bolt strike the edge of the beach not far off. Miriam gathered her few things, and Niko ran to his bike.

"Come back to my apartment!" she yelled to him, and ran off in that direction.

Miriam let Niko sleep on the floor of her rabbit-hole apartment that night. After she cleaned his wound and bandaged it the best she could, he washed in the shared shower down the hall and ate the cucumbers and bread she'd bought. He slept for the rest of that day and most of the night. The rumble of his bike as he rode away awakened her before dawn, and she listened until the sound faded.

That morning, when Miriam went to work, the whole office was in turmoil. It had been ransacked. Everything was strewn around and mixed up. It seemed random, but while trying to restore order, they began to notice a pattern to the apparent chaos. It wasn't that unusual for the Regime to invade offices in a general search for so-called subversive material, but this seemed different. After they'd put everything back where it belonged, there was nothing missing. That, in itself, was odd.

Strangely, Miriam's desk was almost untouched, which made her even more suspicious. Had they been watching her meetings with Niko? She would never know for sure, but this interruption, like all the others, reminded them that at any time they could all be hauled away, and that nothing really belonged to them.

Just before dawn, El managed to escape from The Compound by hiding herself under a pile of linens on a laundry truck. The Compound was serviced by outside vendors. Laundry was too menial an occupation for anyone actually living within its walls. She saw an opportunity when the truck backed up to the building, so she took it and climbed aboard the back.

Once outside the walls, she ripped a sheet in half and wrapped it around her body sarong-like. Then she took off the heels they'd put on her feet and tore them apart to make them flat. She waited until the truck stopped to unload, then jumped out before the driver came around to the back, and hid behind the laundry's wall.

The laundry happened to be midway between the now-boarded-up convent and where she'd been meeting with Father Ignatius and the others. She had no idea where he lived, so she skirted the alley and slid under a tear in the fencing, where the weeds and vines that covered it were so dense they afforded her cover. She found a dark spot in a corner against the back of the building and crouched there to wait for someone to appear. She fell asleep half sitting with her legs folded under her, her head resting on her shoulder against the old brick building. That's how Father Ignatius found her.

Upon hearing his footsteps, she stirred and saw him spin around, as if to confront a foraging rat. She was wide awake now and tried to shrink back even farther in the semi-darkness.

When he realized who it was, he approached her slowly, extended his hand and leaned down to her. "El," he said. "Are you all right?"

She looked up at him with vacant eyes, like someone lost in a foreign land, almost as if she couldn't understand the language he spoke.

"El, come," he tried again, softly, "let me help you."

When he tried to take her by the hand, she shrank back against the wall. She began to shake despite the heat.

"You're afraid," he said. "I understand. But you can't stay here. The others will be here for class. Let me help you. I'll take you to my place, and you can rest there. It's just around the corner."

She looked up at him as if assessing his motives. Her eyes narrowed. She looked around at the vacant lot where she'd trained with him, and she seemed to get acclimated in some way as if remembering it. Slowly she stood, and when she did, Father

Ignatius could see that she had tied a sheet around herself. Fragments of a torn dress hung loosely under it. Her arms were bruised, and he saw dark circles under her eyes that hadn't been there before. There was now a haunted look about her.

"Follow me," he said simply, and did not reach out to touch her again.

He lived in a sparse room on the ground floor of an undistinguished, three-story gray building that, long before The Collapse, had been erected of heavy granite from a now-defunct quarry outside the city limits. The room was rather longer than it was wide, with one window at the far end. This window looked out at the other side of the yard where Father Ignatius taught his outdoor classes. There was a pallet on the floor with a blanket and pillow. Also in one corner was a battered dresser. On the opposite wall, a wooden bench and one old chair were back to back. Above these, on the wall, were a shelf, two candles, a cross. Next to the shelf, hanging from a plain hook, was a purple stole of the kind priests donned to receive confessions.

Father Ignatius closed the door with a soft thud and said in a low but steady voice, "You may take the chair."

He pointed to it and El followed his finger obediently, taking her seat while he lifted the purple stole from its hook. It was the last remnant of his life as a practicing priest. He kissed it and slipped it around his neck over his T-shirt, making the sign of the cross. He lit the two candles and blew out the match. It left a faint acrid scent in the air followed by the odor of melting wax. He turned to the bench and sat with his back to El.

"I will hear your confession now," he said simply, as if this was any normal act of penitence.

El began with the usual ritual recitation, and Father Ignatius answered as required.

"Father," she began, "I know we are all sinners. I know I have sinned. I have stolen, I have used bad language. I have had evil thoughts and have wished evil upon others. I am not worthy of God's forgiveness for those things. But why did this happen to me? Why was I singled out for such . . ." Here, she stopped abruptly as she fought to control a strangled sob. "Father, tell me why."

"I am supposed to give you penance for the things you just told me. But El, to receive absolution you must be honest in your confession. Honest with God and with yourself. I myself have sinned and continue to sin against God. Yes, we are all sinners. But there are degrees of sins, I believe. And these degrees must be recognized and brought into the light where God can grant ultimate absolution. Sometimes, we are burdened with more than we think we can bear, and many of those burdens are not caused by us. They are not our direct sins. There is no way I can explain to you what has apparently happened to you, and I won't try. All I can say is you, too, El, must bring your burden to the light. Do you understand?"

"Yes, Father."

She was quiet. Her head drooped down, her chin resting on her chest bone. She closed her eyes and sighed.

"I don't know why he chose me," she began. "He never told me it was his plan. I would have said no, but when it happened, I had no way to refuse. All those people. All that noise. And they led me away. And I thought . . . well, I did think about the feelings I had for him. I can't deny it, Father. I would have gone with him already, been with him if he had asked me to. If I thought he wanted that. But he never said anything. In all the times we'd met, he never a word about what would happen after The Race. Still, I thought he had feelings for me."

She stopped and took a deep breath. "Father, can I turn around? It's hard for me to tell all that happened not facing you."

Father Ignatius answered, "My child, I told you I have sinned.

I am as mortal as anyone. I left my priestly garments behind. I stopped going to confession. I went out on the streets, collected children, taught them how to defend themselves and, yes, how to fight. All this isn't within the responsibilities of the priesthood, although hundreds of years ago, the Pope himself led an army of men. I suppose I harken back to that time because I see the people of Infinius under such an evil spell that to fight it is the only way to restore it to its moral core. All that said, I am still a priest; therefore, when I hear a confession, even under these unusual circumstances with no true confessional available, I must not look upon you, nor you upon me. But be assured, I listen not only with my ears but with my heart without judgment and with a mind open to all the frailties we humans must endure."

He waited, sitting quietly on the hard bench, his hands folded in his lap, aware of the conflicted feelings inside this young girl who had come to him for solace.

"Why do people do violence to each other, Father?"

"I do not know the whole answer to that. What is tormenting you?"

"I did violence to someone."

"What did you do?"

"I took a knife from a table set for a big meal. I hid it in my sleeve, and when he approached me, I kicked him as you taught us. But when I tried to kick him a second time, he was too fast for me and I was caught. It was then that I pulled the knife from my sleeve, and struck him in the face. I meant to do him even more harm. Father, I will go to hell for this; I am sure of it."

She sobbed then. The tears flowed freely, her shoulders shaking, great heaving breaths between sobs. Father Ignatius waited, certain there was more to her story that would not be revealed in sequence. He had heard such stories before. They spilled out in seemingly disconnected pieces.

"They did things to me, Father. The men who were there when we arrived. I tried to resist, but it was no use. There were five of them, dressed in white coats. But they were not doctors. They told me they had to examine me. They held me down on a table, and then, Father, they took my clothes off and I was naked, and they held my arms down and spread my legs. I screamed. I called them horrible names. I spat at them. And then they put a needle in my arm, and I couldn't speak or move anymore. But I was awake. They put a light between my legs, and one of them did something to me. I couldn't see, but I felt him feeling me. You know . . . there. I felt I was going to pass out, and then it was over. And one of them said, 'Put in the report that she is pure.'

"They took me into another room and stood me in a shower and washed me everywhere. And then two women came in. They had new clothes for me, and they talked to me about what was expected. That's what they said. 'What is expected.' They said I would be treated well. That I had nothing to fear. That everything I would do would be natural. That I was there to serve the Regime, but it was fair. That I should be proud to serve this way after The Race. That it was an honor.

"I still felt numb, but I could move on my own by then. But they finished dressing me and put makeup on me and did my hair. They sprayed me with perfume that smelled like the lilacs I remembered from the convent garden. And then they led me down a hall to a door. A man was there. He unlocked the door and sort of pushed me forward just inside the door and then bolted it behind me.

"Father, if it is such an honor to serve the Regime, why do they have to lock you in?" For a moment she seemed genuinely perplexed, but it passed quickly and she began to speak rapidly, as if she feared someone would stop her before she got everything out.

"I thought the worst was over when I saw that room with the big table and all the food. I was hungry, I remember. Very hungry and thirsty, so I went to the table. They had me wearing shoes with high heels. I never wore shoes like that before. I thought I would fall down walking in them.

"And then he spoke to me. Niko." When she spoke his name she faltered, and her voice changed.

"I don't remember what he said but I know that's when I got so angry. And Father . . ." She stopped for a long rest.

"Yes, El," Father Ignatius said. "What do you want to tell me?"

"I wanted to kill him. He was the cause of my humiliation at their hands. It was all his fault. If he had just done what he was supposed to do, I wouldn't have been there. I wouldn't have been handled. And drugged. And dressed up like a . . ."

"But you didn't kill him."

"No, but isn't it just as evil to think such a thing? To want such a thing?"

"You must forgive yourself for reacting to such trauma, El. None of this was of your making."

"That's not the end of it, Father."

He had been steeling himself to what he knew must be coming. He had heard stories about the aftermath of The Race before. He knew what was expected of the young people. He knew more than El. Knew how perverted it was. Knew what they wanted of her. But he kept silent, at least for the time being. Because he knew she must go back to them, back to their examinations and control over her. That they would punish her severely. So he would alter his plan. He would help El in the only way he could, and he would be risking all their lives. For this he would have to face his own penance. Someday.

"When he approached me, as I was gorging myself on the food, all I could see in front of me were those white coats. And that's when I . . . I don't know exactly what happened, but there was glass on the floor, and later in the bedroom I used the knife. There was so much blood. It seemed to be all over me. I don't know exactly what happened then, but he attacked me. He got the knife away and dragged me to a bed. Then I went numb and thought he would attack me, you know, in the way men attack girls. There was blood dripping from his face and the look I saw frightened me. It was like he went vacant, like a dead person looks, like the way the sisters looked after they had left life and so I tried to call out to him, 'Niko,' I said, but I don't remember if the words made any sound at all. I think I said 'Stop,' but I can't be sure."

She broke off, sobbing again. "Why did he do that to me? Why did he choose me for such degradation? And even while I was using the knife against him, somewhere in me was watching and saying 'This is wrong. This is not Niko.'"

Father Ignatius spoke softly from the bench behind her. "You have gone through a terrible ordeal, El. It is normal to try to protect yourself. God does not expect you to be perfect and you must not punish yourself for these experiences. God has mercy. You must also, even if the mercy is directed to yourself."

El was quiet then, thinking about what had happened and what Father Ignatius said. She thought about Sister Catarina and Sister Angelica. What would they tell her to do, to feel, to want? She tried to calm herself but the gnawing anger welled up in her again followed by a trembling fear and a sense of loathing. Still too upset, she couldn't sort out what options she might have had or what she could have done differently. All she knew for certain was that she had been changed in some deep way and that survival must be an instinct that a person could not control and that instinct made her attack Niko and that instinct drove her to escape.

Father Ignatius spoke again.

"As for the young man, he also went through a terrible ordeal with no good options. He was allowed to live and he chose to fight for that life and not give in to the Regime. And you must also. I think, as time passes, you may find you have a friend and ally in this young man who right now must seem crueler to you than all the others. I do not forgive or condone what decisions he made. And although you suffered because of his choices, in the end he pulled back. He has humanity in him still. But I do understand that a system like ours fosters inhumanity in all of us and that's what we must fight against, rather than fighting each other."

El had one more confession.

"I hear what you're telling me, Father, but I don't think God will forgive me, because, you see, if he were to stand in front of me right now, I think I would try to kill him rather than give in."

"You are very young, my child. You may have difficult choices ahead of you. Maybe one of them will be what to do if you're ever confronted by Niko again. I will not say you must accept what happened to you with no anger or hatred. I will only say that such feelings, left without resolution, will lead to a bitter future. And a future without forgiveness is a future without hope. We have too much work to do, El, to move forward without hope. I will try to help you heal in any way I can."

He made the sign of the cross again, replaced the purple cloth on its hook, and left after telling El he had a class to teach. He said she could stay and rest, if she liked, but that she must know they would search for her to bring her back to The Compound.

"I'll go back to the convent, Father."

"Hasn't it been boarded up?"

"Yes, but I know a way in."

After Father Ignatius left, El sneaked back out onto the street and made her way furtively along the alleyways. She kept her head low and hoped no one would stop her or notice the ragged, bloodstained dress.

When she finally reached the boarded-up garage, she followed the graffiti-covered north wall until she came to the old wooden fence. It was only then that she noticed spray-painted *Niko* everywhere. She glanced around at the other buildings and saw his name emblazoned on every surface.

At the fence she knew exactly which board was loose and swung it to the side, letting herself into the yard that once had been a garden. Inside she sank to the ground and ran her fingers over it, dipped her face down to smell the earth there and even the pungent scent of weeds that had taken root. But there were also remnants of the flowers they had planted, and jasmine, a lemon tree, pole beans, and even some roses along the side.

After Niko's escape and El's disappearance, the rooms they'd been assigned had been searched by Regime Detectors. The team of four inspected the blood, the torn sheets, the pieces of El's clothing, and finally the bloody knife. At first, it was unclear which one had been the aggressor and which the victim. All they knew then was that Villinkash had ordered both of them to be caught and brought back to him personally.

Under ordinary circumstances this might have worked. Except that no one knew where El had gone. She had simply disappeared from The Compound, and no matter where or how they searched, they couldn't find any trace of her.

After they'd finished their physical examination and dressed her for the night ahead, they'd done an extensive photo shoot of El. Then they pushed her into the room where Niko waited. The photos were to be plastered all over the city as further proof of how The Race turned ordinary girls into princesses. But now they were to be used to find El and bring her back.

So the search began.

Pictures of her, all done up for her "wedding" night, circulated everywhere. A blimp hovered over the city, streaming her name and likeness in a floating banner. She looked so pure, so beautiful, so alluring. She was the perfect image of the perfect bride. But it was the foul lie they perpetuated that grabbed the people and held them in its thrall: that she had been spoiled by her lover and would be thrown to anyone who wanted seconds. That meant to anyone who turned her in.

This was their lure to drag the bottom-feeders out of hiding. And to top it off, there was a bounty richer than anything that had ever been offered to snitchers and weasels.

Although Villinkash set about to remake Niko and El into dangerous rebels who must be stopped, no matter the cost, this took time to organize. Three days after The Race, the Regime broadcast the first arrest order, with Niko's picture on every InCom in the city. On the fifth day, they posted El's picture and offered the reward.

El found the key to the back door of the convent exactly where it had always been: in the broken flowerpot by the old hose bib. The hose was still attached, but water to the convent had been turned off when the electricity had been shut down.

After she'd let herself in through the half door, for the first few hours of hiding inside, she crouched in a corner, shivering, alert to the minutest sound—a creaking floorboard, a mouse skittering inside a wall, a person walking on the sidewalk, Scroungers rattling trash cans. She was afraid to light a candle, and since the place hadn't been touched, there were many candles the nuns had left.

Finally she fell into a deep sleep, slumped against a wall, hugging her knees to her chest. At some point she awoke with a heart-pounding jolt. She was afraid of nothing and everything. Slowly it passed and she stretched out on the floor, consciously trying to remember Sister Catarina, Sister Angelica, and safer times.

She had no idea what day or time it was, but she was stiff and sore. And she felt an overwhelming need for soap and water. Long before the building was a garage and then a convent there had been a small house where now there was only a scruffy backyard. And in one corner was an old well with a hand pump. El knew it still worked because the sisters sometimes used it in times of drought, when the Regime cut back the water supply.

Since the Regime had designated this a low-priority section, there were no inhabited buildings nearby. So even though the pump handle creaked and water came out with a gushing sound, El felt safe leaving the building with a bucket and filling it at the well. She had no way to heat the water, but the night was warm.

She made a few trips. Each time she dumped the water into a large washtub the sisters had used for laundry. She took a small cloth and towel, soap and shampoo, and slowly cleansed the indecencies that had been perpetrated on her body. She was careful and worked with patience from her head to her toes, taking special care to soothe herself, and at one point, she began humming a hymn the sisters used to sing.

She found some of the clothes she'd left behind and dressed herself. Finally she felt clean. And so began her recovery. She was not the same sweet El. She had become a warrior.

Niko knew the city better than any of the Regime's Detainers. This was his turf, and he navigated it with expertise and cunning. Although it would take a day after his disappearance was discovered for the roar of Detainers' motorcycles to permeate the city, the night was his friend and gave him the edge he needed before dawn to locate Gruen, who was out scoring bruyaha. And besides, his wasn't the only motorcycle out at night. There were the regular Detainers and others who paid them off to be free to score and rob.

No one took notice when he parked in a dark back alley near

where he figured he'd find Gruen doing business. He waited until he heard Gruen's scuffling walk out on the street.

"Hey," he whispered.

Gruen spun around, ready to strike.

"It's me."

"Hell, don't come up on me like that. I could have knocked you out."

"I need help."

"Hell's yes, you do, man. What are you thinking? Leaving The Compound. People die to get in there and you run off? And what's up with that cut? What'd you run into, a knife fight?"

"It's a long story. No time to tell it now. I need to hide and then . . ." Niko broke off. He didn't really know what he needed.

"Your name's all over this city. People shouting it. Graffiti on all the streets and buildings. Someone even painted your face on that tall fence over by Quadrant Two. You're the most famed man in town. What you need now is an escape plan, man. Unless you wanna lead the revolution, man, you need to get your ass out of this city. Because they catch you, they string you up and blast it on every InCom they got. You got no chance, man."

"Where can I hide for a day or two? Just long enough to make a plan."

"You can't come to my place. And The Hovels are out. They'll turn those shacks inside out lookin' for you." He looked down at the ground and then out to the street.

"So what's in this for me?" he asked. "I'm taking a big risk to take you on this joyride."

Niko thought about the rules of the street. Tit for tat in everything you did. He and Gruen were not real friends. He wouldn't have protected Gruen for nothing. Why should he expect anything but the same?

Gruen walked farther into the alley and saw the bike. "Wheee . . ." he whistled. "That's the one?"

"Yeah. My big win."

"Some bike. I could sell it for a fortune if it wasn't so hot. They'd know it right off and arrest me." He shook his head. "What a pity."

"Tell you what." Niko lowered his voice. "You help me escape and you can have it. You can repaint it and grind off the engine number so they couldn't identify it."

Gruen thought for a minute.

"But that still leaves me with a bike that I can't explain where I got it. It ain't like bikes are easy to . . ." He broke off, thinking. "I know. It's perfect. You know Father Ignatius? Trains the kids in self-defense? He's got a small army of 'em. I know, 'cause I traded him some weapons a while back. He'd help you. That is, if we can get you to him."

"An army of street kids against the Regime?"

"You'd be surprised. A lot of them kids is clever. And they're streetwise. The Detainers are soft. Yeah, they got big guns, but they don't know shit about getting around in this city. I hear these kids even have tunnels and back ways through buildings. They can disappear a hundred ways and never get caught. And I hear they got explosives from somewhere. I ain't sayin' how I heard that or where they mighta got 'em."

"The less I know, the better, I guess. What about the bike?"

"How can I turn that down?" Gruen said. "Even if I keep it for myself. What a bike."

"Where does this Father Ignatius live?"

"I don't know. I only know he trains out back in a lot down in Quadrant Five. It don't look like nothin' from the front, but out back it's a different story."

"Why wouldn't he turn me in?"

"He's been preachin' revolution for a while. He's a good guy, they say. I only had that one deal with him. He had a case of wine to trade. From his old days as a priest. He give that up when he went out to the streets to the kids."

Gruen looked around. The night was fading. Soon it would be light.

"We better get to it."

They walked up to the bike.

"Can I drive her?" Gruen gripped one handlebar. He whistled under his breath. "She's sure a beauty."

"Sure. It's yours." Niko waited a minute, then added, "As soon as we find this Father Ignatius. You drive."

El found food in what had once been a mechanic's pit, which was one of the convent's secret hiding places. It stayed cool and dry down there all year, especially in the cold storage room they had dug farther back and underground from one wall. The entrance was under a heavy wooden plank that covered the pit and stairs that led down to it. The plank looked like part of the floor, but El knew just where to grab hold of it and pull to lift it at one end and prop it open. She used an old oil lamp for light, and in the pit she found the single-burner emergency kerosene stove the sisters used when the power went out. With all the babies and children they'd cared for, they'd made provisions never to be without food, water, and a way to cook.

She ate until she was full, then went up to the big table with a mug of tea. She had to think about what to do. She couldn't stay at the convent too long. Yes, she was safe for the moment. But that couldn't last. Instinct told her to gather supplies for a trek. She didn't know where or how she would go or if she would get anywhere. But she had to do something. Not sit around and wait.

As she searched for what she might need for a long journey,

she found plenty of materials that could be useful: a fully stocked medical kit; a knapsack perfect for stuffing; extra clothes, tampons, soap, shampoo, a couple of small towels; socks and even a pair of hiking boots. She laid everything out on the table in small piles. She found a waterproof poncho folded into a tight pouch. And food. She had to take along food. She even located a camping set of plates and forks and knives, canteens and cups. What were the sisters thinking? They might once have camped out with children, before The Collapse. Before there was nowhere to go. She found a small flashlight and a sharp hunting knife and lighters. She would have to make a fire somewhere.

With everything laid out on the table, she began to speculate on where she might go. And then it came to her . . .

Zamora. Yes, *Zamora*.

Old Merrie made the daily climb down twenty flights from what was more a giant kitchen than a living space. She had moved in after the lower floors were occupied, one of five thousand squatters who had migrated into the unfinished Tower of David. They were more desperate than superstitious about its past. Rather than live in The Hovels (or worse, The Shanty Alleys), they occupied the Tower knowing a day would come when they'd be evicted. Until that day, they made a life.

Weddings were celebrated, babies were born, children were taught to read and write, feuds were settled, policing was done, and people came to accept that this was their mini village inside the bigger city.

At one wedding, after the groom's family had carried all the food and drink up sixteen flights of stairs to a cavernous space where no apartments had survived, the bride's family set up tables and chairs. Musicians arrived from other floors and tuned their instruments. An officiator arrived, because no priest was left to perform the ceremony, and friends and families made the laborious climb and took their seats.

Finally, the bride had arrived. She was out of breath from the climb from her apartment on the fourth floor, her train held off the cement by four little girls. And the event began. They exchanged vows and rings. There was music and laughter. Dancing and eating and drinking. Finally, the bride and groom had waved farewell and climbed the stairs higher and higher until they reached the twenty-second floor, where a large apartment had been draped in sheets for privacy, as there were no walls. Flowers had been strewn in a path to a mattress on the floor. This is where the couple spent the night. A honeymoon in a hulking, half-finished high-rise where the only beauty was a full moon that cast its silver light through the gaps in the sheets.

So people carried what they needed up and down every day, took their dogs out walking, carried their rusted motorcycles up to makeshift garages, and stole electricity from the street in elaborate lines that crisscrossed each other up and down the building. They had jobs and hobbies, beauty parlors and dress shops; there were seamstresses and tailors. Everything they needed was within the Tower.

Old Merrie had made it her business—and it *was* a business—to know every one of them: from the tiniest newborn to the oldest grandpa. She brought them food, for a price, but she brought much more. They could order just about anything from her, and she'd supply it. She was a scrounger's scrounger who specialized in delicacies no one else could find. Her cooking and baking were legendary. She supplied food for all occasions and was always in demand.

For those who'd been cleansed, her meals were a new and exciting experience. She was sly and could fool anyone into thinking she was on their side or that she wasn't quite right in the head. No one considered her a threat to the system.

She wandered where she pleased, pushing her cart, singing her songs. She was a fixture on the streets and in the Tower. Everyone trusted Old Merrie. And everyone needed a sympathetic ear. So they told her things.

Rosalie's baby had colic. That old man on floor five had been caught peeping again. The lab mix on two had a litter. Joe Beppo had lost his job and slashed his wrists. Angie and Eduardo's wedding had been postponed because they couldn't get enough money for the permit. The boys on floor nine had a fight over a girl, and one of them got stabbed. A gang had moved into the old pharmacy next door and started doing business in the front apartment on the ground floor right under the noses of the Protectors. So it was assumed they must be paying off someone high up. Mrs. Oberdorf on seventeen was screwing the boy who stayed in that closet by the stairs on floor twelve. He climbed up to seventeen every morning right after her husband, that bus driver named Gus, left for work. He keeps a regular schedule, you know.

Old Merrie knew it all. She just took it in and never repeated a word to anyone. Except that one time on the roof with El. Something about the girl's quiet way moved Old Merrie. What was it? She couldn't say. But she saw it in the girl's eyes, in the way she held her head and the sway of her hair in the breeze, in the way she gazed out to the Glimmer, in the hope Old Merrie saw in those clear, bright eyes.

Yes, there was something about that girl.

Father Ignatius had no illusions about what the Regime would do to him if he was ever caught. It was an inevitable result of his work. When he decided that his faith could not be contained inside the walls of a church and he would fight rather than be eliminated like the other priests, he'd asked God for guidance. He had wandered the streets for months as a beggar, witnessing the decay and hopelessness of the city he'd once loved. After much prayer, he realized he could no longer accept the evil around him.

Then one day he saw a woman give birth on a piece of cardboard in an alley. He had heard her cries for help and rushed in without thinking and used his own shirt to hold the child as it came out of her body. It was as if an angel had come down to deliver a message to him: it was the children who needed him.

He knew the Detainers would one day knock down his door and drag him away to be humiliated, tortured, strung up, or worse. He prayed that day wouldn't come before he had executed his plan. And so he taught children day and night. He divided them into squads. He taught them tactics and self defense. He taught them how to fight as guerillas. To use the city as a battlefield. Taught patience and discipline. The ones who caught on fast were elevated to decision-making posts. Some were skilled as shooters, and others as strategists. They played endless war games on paper and then on the streets.

Even when the Detainers would see the kids practicing maneuvers, they laughed at the kids playing soldier. This had been part of the Father's plan: make them seem like harmless kids—until the time came to act for real.

Father Ignatius had no idea when that day would come. Until The Race. Then all the gears meshed.

They rode on backstreets and through alleys where Gruen told Niko that no one was likely to be out. The bike was loud, but bikes were not uncommon and people paid no attention. Most people were still asleep or just getting up. Gruen rode as if he'd had the bike all his life. Finally, they got to the street where Father Ignatius held his classes. It was quiet as Gruen pulled up to the warehouse.

He stuck out his foot as he stopped the bike.

"This is it."

"What is? Nobody lives here."

"He trains the kids out back behind this building. It's an old warehouse. The Detainers don't bother with it."

"Yeah, but where is he?"

"He'll be here. He comes every day."

"I can't just sit on the curb and wait."

"Listen, man, I got you this far, but this is it for me. I got stuff to do. And a woman waitin' on me. I don't show up, she's likely to start asking around where I am. You don't want that, do you?"

Niko swung his leg over and got off the bike.

"Thanks for helping me," he said. He looked up and down the street. There was an alley on the far side of the warehouse. He could wait in there.

"Hey, good luck, man. You gonna need it. I'll keep an ear open for you. Thanks for this." He patted the bike.

"I may need to borrow it sometime."

"No prob, man. You know where to find me."

And then, with a roar, the bike disappeared around a corner.

When Gruen was gone, Niko walked quickly to the alley to a broken-down dumpster and some slabs of wood. He climbed up on these and looked inside. Empty. The Collectors either had just picked up or no one used it in this deserted section.

He lowered himself into the dumpster and waited. He wasn't sure for what. Waiting was always the hardest part. His stomach growled. His head ached. The cut on his face burned. He tried not to think, but he couldn't help it. Where was El? What had happened to her? Remorse overwhelmed him. It would have been better for everyone if his number hadn't been the winner. Damn that Huston.

Even Huston, who seemed to have a remote sensor on every beating pulse in the city, had no idea where El and Niko had gone, nor how they'd gotten away. Except the report that Niko's bike had disappeared came to him immediately.

"The Premier will want answers," the captain of Compound intelligence—named Wilder, who was a stout man with thick arms and a twisted mouth—told Huston. "He'll want answers right away."

It was Huston's habit to rise with the sun, so he'd been at his desk for two hours by then. It took less than ten minutes for the news to travel to him by phone, and in another minute, this brute was at his door, almost smirking. His racer had lost and he'd dropped quite a bundle on him. And he'd never liked Huston or understood why Premier Villinkash depended so heavily on him. As far as Wilder was concerned, Huston was an elite pansy.

"Ah, Wilder, you're so right. And I will supply them. In the meantime, suppose you give me a complete rundown on what your people know so far. I see you have a folder already. Has there been foul play?"

Huston was neither cowed by, nor concerned with, what Wilder may or may not think of him personally. He had a record on the man that could shut him down permanently.

"I think it's for the Premier to examine this file."

"Right again. However, as you are no doubt aware, the Premier sleeps late and doesn't like bad news before he's eaten and taken care of his personal needs. And I believe he was up rather late last night celebrating with, shall we say, some friends? So it's best if you and I handle this at the outset. On the other hand, if you think it wise to disturb him this early . . ." Huston made a sweeping motion with his hand toward the door and slightly bowed.

"I think we'd best find out more facts first."

So that was that.

"And the folder?" Huston held out his hand.

Wilder laid it on the desk and opened it carefully as if he expected a viper to pop out.

"Mmmhmm," Huston murmured. "So there was more blood than . . ." He hesitated.

"Yes. Much more than one would expect from a first encounter. And she had been examined by the team. She was unspoiled. There should not have been so much blood. The tests were inconclusive. The blood samples were mixed together."

Huston turned the first page over and read the second.

"And the food had been eaten but also disturbed. Like an animal had gotten to it? That makes no sense."

"There are photos." Wilder pushed the paper aside and spread out a batch of pictures.

"Well, we've never seen this before." Huston studied the pictures. There was the dining table, which looked as if a fight had taken place. Dishes on the floor, food spattered around. And the bedroom. So much blood. "There's a trail of blood. Look here." He pointed to one of the pictures and then arranged them in a pattern. "Leading from the dining room to the bedroom. Just drops and then . . . look at the bed. It's been used."

"More than used, I'd say." Wilder pointed to the bedclothes strewn on the floor and pillows askew.

"What the hell went on in there?"

"Whatever it was, it didn't end there."

"Leave these with me, and I'll inform the Premier as soon as it's reasonable. What other information do you have?

"His motorcycle is gone."

Huston looked up at Wilder, whose mouth was twisted to one side in a triumphant, crooked smile.

"He's your boy," Wilder said. "Your winner. And he got away with that stunt after The Race and now the city's waking up to this. His name's already all over the place. There's no telling where this could lead."

"Are there pictures of her? *Before* pictures?"

Wilder riffled through the folder and slid out photos that had been taken of El after they'd dressed her and done her hair and makeup after the purity examination—and just before they had pushed her into the room with Niko.

In a rare show of his true feelings, Huston whistled under his breath. "She *is* a beauty. She couldn't have gotten away unless they rode out together."

"We've put out an all-city alarm for them. They can't possibly get far."

On an order from Villinkash, Huston came up with a three-step plan to quash what the Regime most feared. A developing insurrection

First they would call out riot troops and Detainer squads to patrol the city, question individuals, make arrests, and generally promote more fear than usual. This included an even more stringent curfew, which made it more expensive and cumbersome for the Scroungers to do business. Not that they cared about any curfew one way or the other, but skirting it became more onerous.

Next came the constant barrage of InCom propaganda and lies about Niko. But as an added bonus, a large reward had been offered for anyone or any group giving information that led to his capture. Now this was a bit tricky for the Regime because it forced them to admit that Niko had escaped their grasp and chosen to throw their accolades right back at them. This wasn't good publicity, and it spread across the city with the vengeance of stampeding cattle. What individuals couldn't speak out loud, hordes of people whispered. That whisper reverberated.

Finally, there was the Regime's fruitless effort to quell any uprising. The minute the Collectors scraped one spray-painted "Niko" from a wall, three others popped up somewhere else. Niko banners appeared on toilet paper streamers and were stamped onto sidewalks. Young people in their teens and twenties held secret meetings, came up with resistance strategies, and mobilized themselves into platoons.

So while troops in riot gear stormed through the city, they couldn't be everywhere at all times. Whenever they left one sector, groups popped up like cockroaches coming out of hiding in the dark of night. Spontaneous fires erupted, seemingly from nowhere. Cauldrons of burning oil spewed from rooftops. No one knew the backstreets and alleyways like the Hovelers and Scroungers. Riot police were like bumbling rhinos chasing their own tails while the city dwellers scurried everywhere like mice and hid anywhere. They called in false tips that kept the Collectors busy. They erected roadblocks faster than Detainers could knock them down. And those who knew how reprogrammed their trackers, making Detainers scurry around to fake addresses in fake quadrants.

The more time passed, the more furious Villinkash became. And so, as a final step, the death threats began. Villinkash called for random captures of people he could post on the InCom pleading for their lives. Two were actually placed before a firing squad and shot on camera. This only disgusted and inflamed the city more. Anyway, people recognized these two as informants. Bands of young Scroungers tore down and smashed InComs, then ran away and disappeared into the general squalor like scattered ashes.

And throughout it all, Niko was nowhere to be found.

Father Ignatius heard the first shouts of "Niko" after The Race ended. Though he had no idea where they came from, he realized in an instant what it meant. While it was still dark, he'd rushed out of the old brick warehouse and stood on the sidewalk and listened in wonder and joy as if a cool rain had suddenly broken a long hot season. He spread his arms to the city that, despite everything, he loved with a deep faith in its goodness. That faith that underpinned everything he'd done since taking his mission out of the church and onto the streets to the young people.

Now, surely, was the time to act.

When the cries of "Niko" grew louder and erupted into a chorus with banging sounds made from metal trash can lids and iron pipes against light posts, Father Ignatius walked with a calm air to the fence hole where the kids entered, bent down carefully to squeeze through it, and meandered back to the very farthest corner of the brick building wall that butted up against the pitted one next door.

Before running his fingers down the line of bricks third from the end, he glanced up at the sky and around to the old buildings' walls that surrounded him. Since The Collapse, when all manufacturing had been taken over by the Regime and moved far north of The Compound, no one ever used these. What used to be made in these buildings—clothes, toys, shoes, bedding, flashlights, fans, refrigerator and washer parts—had all been closed down and moved offshore for cheaper labor or to the camps where slaves from their own city worked fifteen-hour days with no time off and no accounting to anyone. You could live or you could die in the camp system and no one would know.

His hand rested on one brick that stuck out a little from the others. He positioned his thumb and index finger over the end of it and wiggled it from side to side. Slowly it moved out toward him, and he pulled it out completely. Inside, he knew, was an oblong, sealed plastic box. This he removed, then slid the brick back into place.

For the rest of that night and very early the following morning, he wandered the city, seemingly at random. In reality, he knew exactly where he was going. He made twenty-two stops. At each he deposited a small, hand-drawn map with an X on it into an old coffee can whose faded and scratched trademark said "Maxwell House." Each can, with a rock on top of it, was set at the base of an innocuous wall and covered in dirt so as not to be noticed. It was just one more discarded piece of trash littering the city. He left each one camouflaged as he'd found it.

The leaders also knew what to do. The oldest was nineteen, the youngest fifteen. But he'd chosen each of the twenty-two captains for their stellar qualities. Intelligence, stamina, determination, dedication. He'd trained his troops well. He headed back to his small apartment to pray and prepare for what was to happen.

He was like any general on the eve of a battle for which he'd spent years preparing. Beset by a series of conflicting emotions and sensations, he felt excitement, certainty, and anticipation followed by worry, caution, and dread. These young boys and girls, who were not yet fully grown, trusted him with their lives.

That simple cross, hand carved from a tree branch and hanging from a nail on the wall with the rough-hewn figure of Christ forever in limbo, draped with a swath of cloth, seemingly in torment and at peace all at the same time—is this what the Father felt? He wasn't delusional. He knew what he was doing. He had no illusions that he was Christlike or that it was his burden to free these people from their yoke. And yet wasn't he doing just that? Hadn't he prepared this battle? Wasn't their cause righteous?

He knelt on the floor, stared up at the cross, and prayed that the children he was using as soldiers would be successful, would survive, would triumph and forge a new path for the city. He stayed on his knees for a long time that night. And as the night wore on toward morning and the cries of "Niko" hadn't abated, he knew that soon the coffee cans would be unearthed, and after destroying every paper scrap he'd left for them, his group leaders would follow their instructions.

From the bottom of the bashed-up dumpster, Niko also heard his name shouted throughout the day. At times he thought it would cease. In fact, it did stop from time to time. But then it began again with more fervor, more voices, a more elaborate chanting.

When the sun lowered enough that the alley was in shadow, he managed to nod off for a few minutes here and there. Finally, dusk gathered across the city, bringing a soft light. But the cries did not stop. And as dusk faded to semi-dark, the sounds of the city took on a more strident tone and Niko heard motorcycle-riding Detainers roar through streets not too far away. He knew he couldn't stay where he was forever, so it was time to find Father Ignatius.

He stood up and stretched before peeking over the dumpster rim. With no one around and no noises he could detect nearby, he hoisted himself up and jumped down to the dirt alley. It was narrower than a street, so he figured it used to be some sort of service way for the buildings on either side. These extended far back to where the alley dead-ended at the back of another building facing the next street over.

Niko had a strong urge, so he relieved himself behind the dumpster at one corner and quickly zipped up his pants. He noticed they were stained with dried blood. A flood of memory returned, and he shivered in the dank, breezeless night air. What if he couldn't find Father Ignatius? Or if it turned out he wouldn't help Niko? He shook off such thoughts. No sense making an alternate plan until he knew the first one was a dud. He inched toward the sidewalk and out of the alley, looked around, saw nothing of note, and walked quickly to the warehouse Gruen had pointed out.

Seeing boards across the front door and no windows, he skirted the building to the fence with the gaping hole. He peeked around to the back and then squeezed his way through the fence.

Once inside the lot, he spotted an old, scratched, and dented metal door with a padlock. He was sure he could bust it with a big rock, but that would make noise and could draw attention if anyone happened to be nearby. He knew the Detainers patrolled methodically, street by street, building by building. He also knew how easy they were to bribe because while Villinkash kept the people at the top happy with graft, it didn't always flow downward, so many of the foot soldiers stayed hungry. Anyway, he had no barter on him.

Just as he turned to look for something to pry the lock off, he heard the fence jangle slightly. Every hair on his body tensed. He spun, ready to kill if need be, and searched the ground for some sort of weapon to give him an edge.

Father Ignatius didn't see him right away. He walked calmly toward the door, but when he was about twenty feet away, he noticed someone standing in the dark not far from the door. He stopped, thinking it was one his leaders. His mind raced. Which one? Was there a problem? Had someone been caught? Had someone turned on them? No, that wasn't possible. He knew them all too well.

He approached the shadowy figure slowly, his hands at his sides. Certainly he could fight anyone. But he didn't want to, hadn't needed to since he'd stopped training, wouldn't hurt another person except in self-defense, if even then.

"Who are you?" he asked quietly, in a nonconfrontational way, and then added, "Do you need help?"

Niko stepped away from the wall into the dim, ambient light from the street. Father Ignatius recognized him right away but also noticed the cut on his face.

"Can you help me?" Niko came closer.

Father Ignatius reached into his pocket and pulled out a key chain.

"Follow me," he said, and unlocked the padlock. He put a finger to his lips and motioned for Niko to precede him as he swung the old door open for them to pass.

A few feet inside the door there was a second door, which the Father unlocked after closing the outside door. It was pitch dark inside the warehouse, which had no windows. And the double door assured that once the inside light was on, it wasn't visible outside the warehouse. He opened the second door and led Niko by the arm inside before closing off the second door with a tight thud. Then he switched on the light.

What appeared in front of them stunned Niko.

"Infinius," he whispered, and simply stared at the replica of the city. Every building and street, even all the dirt alleys that led nowhere. Lampposts and InCom stations, the park where he had met Miriam, even the bench they had sat on. And The Compound with its lake and wall and guard stations. Looking at it now, from above, Niko was astounded that he'd managed to get away at all.

Constructed on top of a large wooden base, he could see each detail from a standing position and walk around the entire city to study it from every angle. And this he did, inspecting it carefully, noting The Hovels and the dirt fields and then The Perimeters, barriers, bridges, and tramways that ran through the city on tracks. They all showed on this miniature Infinius.

"How did you do this?" he asked without looking around. It was so intricate, so exact. How could anyone make such a thing?

"Niko," the Father said, "we have to talk about what happens next."

"I know. But first, there're two things missing from your little city here."

While the thuggish Wilder ordered his Detainers to fan out through the city, Huston retired to his quarters to think.

Right now it was important to control the search efforts. But he was also concerned that Villinkash had to be managed properly. He had to get the Premier over the InCom, had to show that he was in control. But how? How could he make it seem as if Niko was one of them but, at the same time, someone to rally behind for the people?

He rang a bell under the desk he used when working from this apartment. He had a lovely view from the other side of the lake. He could watch peacocks strut the grounds and deer loll under the shade of tall trees.

A knock at the door roused him. He pushed a buzzer. The door opened, and a tall woman Huston had taken out of one of the brothels entered wearing a kimono and tall spike heels with little pom-poms over the toes. She shut the door noiselessly behind her and seemed to float over to the desk. There was about her an air of certainty and serenity incongruous in this environment. She rested the fingers of her right hand lightly on his shoulder, and he immediately relaxed.

"You rang, sir?"

"It's been a rough couple of days."

"Yes. I can feel your tension."

Huston sighed and leaned back in his chair. He closed his eyes. "Are you still as beautiful as the first time we met? I can picture it as if it happened yesterday."

"None of us are the same."

"You're always right. I think that's what drew me to you."

"What do you need now?"

Huston sighed again, a deeper sigh. He straightened up, then hunched over the desk, his head resting in his hands, his elbows on the desktop. "I wish I knew. A thorny puzzle. Everything happened too fast. Didn't plan on this."

"You think too much," she said. "Always planning and scheming. Ever since we met."

"How else would I have gotten where I am? Look where I started. A nobody. And now look at me: second to the most powerful man in the city. With connections far beyond here. If it wasn't for me, he'd be sitting in a jail cell trading for smokes. And he knows it, knows what I know. What records I have. And the connections I've made for him so he can expand his power after Infinius. And now this. Just when I thought it was all sewn up."

"You're too tense. You need to loosen up."

"I've got to figure this out. Where is that kid? Where could he possibly hide in this city? And the girl. She can't get far. We'll have her face plastered on every InCom. She'd be better off turning herself in to me personally than to let the Detainers get hold of her."

"Stop thinking about it, about her. I'm here, you know."

She had stopped massaging his back. She ran her fingernails up and down the back of his neck. He reached back and grabbed her left hand and pulled it to his mouth. She let him insert her finger between his lips.

"Now, are you ready?" she asked.

"Not here. Let's go to the library."

He rose from the chair and, still holding her fingers in his, led her to a short hallway and another door that opened to a sort of study room lined in bookshelves. All the books were histories or biographies of leaders from the past. Leaders as far back as the Chinese dynasties and the Egyptians. There were the Roman emperors and the Greeks. The Hebrews and Assyrians. Even the Inca and Mayan cultures were represented in numerous volumes.

There was a leather couch with plump cushions, a reading chair with a side table, a deep-pile rug, and a bar loaded with glasses and bottles of all kinds. He kicked the door closed and turned to her.

"Cassandra," he said, his hand around her neck, his fingertips and thumb feeling the pulse of blood flowing through her carotid arteries.

Her kimono slid to the floor as his fingers tightened and she gasped for air.

Part Three

—

The
Perimeter

Father Ignatius took in Niko's rumpled clothes and slashed cheek. What could this boy know? In his years of planning and preparation, was it possible the Father had overlooked something? Could he trust Niko, who had put his own life in the Father's hands? The reward alone would be worth handing him over. Surely that showed something. These thoughts racing through his mind led to a conclusion that trust was like risk. Sometimes you had to take the leap. Niko had done it. Now it was his turn.

"I'm listening," he said.

"It's very impressive, what you've built here. I don't know how you plan to use it, but it only shows what's on the ground."

"And what else is there?"

"What's underground. And what's wired in."

"I see." Father Ignatius approached the table with the model. "And do you know anything about those missing links?"

"I do. But before I tell you what I know . . ."

"You want me to tell you what I know?"

Niko nodded and came to the table. He pointed to The Perimeters. "Do you think it's possible to get beyond them? Without getting killed, I mean."

"I think it's possible if the Detainers and guards are otherwise occupied."

Niko whistled softly. "So that's what you're up to. How many are you planning on getting through?"

Father Ignatius looked up from the table and stared straight at Niko for a long moment. In a way, his hope was like a prayer. You never knew about people, about just what they'd do under pressure. Finally he said, "Just two."

"How will you choose them?"

"They're already chosen."

Niko looked at Father Ignatius with a mixture of hope and caution.

"That's right, Niko. You are one."

"Why me?"

"Because of what you did after The Race and what it meant to the people. You've heard them shouting. You've seen the graffiti. They've never been more ready. There's never been a more incendiary situation. Right now, the whole city's one big ammunition pile ready for a match."

"You said two."

"You know who the other is, Niko. You made that decision. Now it's too dangerous for either of you to stay."

Niko shook his head and leaned forward, his hands on the edge of the table. He bowed his head and shook it from side to side slowly.

"She'll never go with me. Never."

"I think she will."

"You don't know everything."

"Yes, Niko, I do. And I say she will go."

Niko turned his head sideways to study the Father.

"She told you?"

"Let's just say I know how troubled you both are. And that the only way forward for each of you is to get away. I don't know for how long. You can't be around for what's going to happen. But later . . . later, the city will need you again. To heal. To find a new way. If everything works out the way we hope it will, that is."

"And what if it doesn't? What's your plan then?"

"I think it's better for us to make our plans as solid as possible right now. It won't do any of us any good to look too far down the road. So show me what's missing on this model of Infinius. And where."

At that moment they heard a commotion out in the street. Father Ignatius put a finger to his lips and moved to the front of the warehouse to stand with his head pressed sideways against the wall to hear what was happening.

"What is it?" Niko kept his voice low, standing next to the Father.

"It's beginning. Staged street fights to draw off the Detainers. Come, I'll show you on the model what will happen."

In The Compound, Villinkash called an emergency meeting of the Overseers. Usually when he called such a meeting, it was more of a dressing-down than anything urgent. Ever since The Collapse and The Cleanse, Villinkash had made damn sure the Regime ran as smoothly as a high-performance machine.

Now that Niko had thrown a rock into the gears of this government, that machine was failing.

Villinkash couldn't fully grasp how one punk upstart could be a serious threat to his powerful Regime. So he fumed at his people gathered around the big conference table in the high-ceilinged glass room, while beyond the Compound walls, cracks in the system popped up like mushrooms after a heavy rain.

It was a further irony that the scuffles starting in the streets were not shown on the controlled broadcasts of the InCom screens. Instead they still broadcast the glories of the Regime. Every once in a while, Niko's face appeared with dire warnings of treason and the offer of a reward for capture. Soon an army of disenfranchised people who had nothing left to lose would look on these very screens as objects on which to vent their wrath.

Also there was a growing sense among the Overseers of something not quite right. They had begun to perceive a steady, if slow, deterioration of the Premier's mental state. It had happened so imperceptibly that to most it was nothing more than a series of quirks. And those who had witnessed his decline were unwilling to acknowledge it. If he failed, where would they all be? They who had benefitted the most from his rise to power. They who had grown rich, who were protected, whose families lived in untold luxury and who controlled all the wealth of the mechanisms within the city and access to the natural resources beyond it.

So they blindly followed along with whatever Villinkash commanded. If they had questioned his ability to lead, they might find themselves under suspicion. Cleansing could be applied to anyone, if ordered. Thus, year after year, they accommodated themselves to his whims, made excuses for his memory lapses, failed to acknowledge his absentminded lip smacking or the phrases he repeated (or his obsessive reminiscing about past triumphs or his seeming inability to speak truth even to them). It was as if his internal program had gone awry, saying one thing one day and claiming the opposite the next.

Such changes seemed to be advancing more rapidly. Huston noticed them all. He made sure to keep meticulous notes for later reference. Yet no one was more solicitous of Villinkash, more devoted, more vigorous in his defense, nor more ready to carry out any program he initiated, no matter how brutal. In fact, it was Huston who had first proposed The Race, while crediting Villinkash with the concept the second it had been adopted.

There were other instances when Huston had maneuvered Villinkash into a successful position that further cemented his power. The Premier had one quality that was useful to all his subordinates: he could sway people to his will. He was like every charismatic autocrat. He knew the art of manipulation. It was embedded in his bones, enmeshed in his speech, entwined in his gestures. He was a hypnotic speaker, and before the public knew what had happened to them, he had enslaved them. Except for a few. Except for the children.

Now, as he pounded his fist on the table and railed at them about controlling the people, Huston, who now had the double role of Protector and Overseer, sat quietly by his side.

"I want him found and brought directly to me!" yelled Villinkash. "I want the troops called out. Mobilize the city. Bring in the secret guard. Arm them to the teeth and round up people until someone squeals. Go to the brothels. Beat those whores until they talk."

He went on like that for a long time, pointing at first one Overseer and then another until they all cowered.

"And," he said, lowering his voice so they sat forward to hear, "I want that girl." He spat out the word "girl," as if something rotten had settled on his tongue. "I want to deal with her *personally*."

He whispered the last word, and they all took note. The Premier's appetites were well documented. Even Huston had lost count of the women who had been brought to him over the years.

One of those women Huston had brought had become Villinkash's wife. Wealthy and from a powerful old-guard family, his wife had accepted his proposal only to save her father when Villinkash took over Infinius. Villinkash had wanted her money under his control. And to get it legally, he wooed her at the same time he was building a case against her father that would have had him tried for treason and executed. The only limitation on accomplishing this goal was that the family wealth would go to his daughter when her father died. To save him, she said yes to Villinkash. That was the beginning of his takeover from the old guard and the installation of the Overseers as his cabinet.

It was clear from the start of their marriage that Villinkash kept women on the side and would not stop. His wife lived in obscurity, keeping her father nearby, rarely showing herself in public unless her husband demanded that she be at his side in a ceremonial role.

She was an intelligent, kind, and generous woman who devoted herself to the sick and the abandoned. Without her husband realizing it, she had supported the Sisters of Mercy and others. And over the years, she had made clandestine contact with Father Ignatius, even before he had left the church for the streets. Even Huston, with his far-flung spy network, was at first unaware of her efforts, which she directed through a maze of secret intermediaries.

Gruen hated Villinkash. After what had happened with his eye during one particularly brutal beating delivered by the Protectors on the specific orders of the Premier, Gruen, who had been a good-looking and powerful youth, was reduced to accepting sexual exchanges from the lowest caste of street women. Before the beating he'd been desired by the ladies and always successful with them, but afterwards, he was even barred from the brothels.

When Gruen dreamed at night, after a day of scrounging and bartering and making deals, it was always of retribution for what had been done to him. Always his dreams were filled with violence and bloody outcomes, with him running away in some dreams, toward an unknown in others.

The first skirmishes after The Race happened outside The Hovels and far from Gruen's rickety housing "unit," which wasn't much more than a shed. Nothing so thrown together could ever be considered a unit. Its mildly protective panels had been slapped together, and they turned to mush after a storm. He was constantly patching and replacing elements, and the whole assemblage relied on power stolen from wherever he could find it. But this was common in The Hovels.

His one prized possession, just acquired, he kept chained to a cement block with a large iron ring on top. He'd traded for the chain and had poured the concrete block himself. It was still setting but already strong enough to do what he needed.

Gruen let it be known that he would happily kill anyone who fucked with his bike.

In the middle of one of his chase-or-be-chased dreams, he had been awakened by the sound of a crash or a boom. His first instinct was to jump out of bed and check his bike. He pushed aside the tattered covers under which he slept and ran to the doorway. But something stopped him. Another crash, which lasted longer and ended with a loud thud. It was too far away to be right outside his door, so he stopped and listened.

He heard another, unusual noise, as if something heavy was being ripped apart. This was too tantalizing to ignore, so he pulled on wrinkled pants and went to peer out into the dark night.

Nothing. No sound at all. It was still hot, and the humidity felt as heavy as a blanket against his skin. He thought he must have imagined it. Thought his mind was playing tricks. That his dream had invaded his waking. He turned to go back to bed and then . . .

A crash nearby. And after the crash, a pounding sound. It came from the direction of one of the InComs. And then came repeated bashing noises. Now he had to find out what was going on out there.

He threw on a T-shirt and some shoes and headed out toward the noise, rubbing the sleep from his good eye and sliding his hunting knife into the sheath strapped to his leg. He crept along the walls of the other hovels and soon came upon a sight he could not believe.

An InCom was completely ripped from its stand. This was no small feat. These screens had been welded to their stands, and the stands were embedded deep into concrete. The screens themselves were protected by an outer layer of thick plastic, and the speakers were located high above. Whoever or whatever had done this had some mechanical help. Or perhaps some explosive had been used to weaken the base? He wondered how that could be.

Sirens, loud and insistent, told Gruen he must get away. But he lingered, thinking it might be useful to overhear what the Detainers would say. Or they would send troops for this. No, not a big enough problem to rouse troops. It was well known that all InCom machines were tied to a grid the Watchers monitored at all times in case of malfunction. So of course, they would already know about this one going down.

But then Gruen heard more sirens, these seeming to go in the other direction. And with the first group almost upon him, he hid behind a nearby pile of rubble. Crouching down, he heard the first vans pull up. Out came a number of Detainers.

"Another one, for shit's sake," the first Detector out of the van grumbled. "What's going on?" He wasn't trying to keep it quiet, either. "Why does this have to happen in the middle of the night anyway?"

"What're you grousing about, Stanyard? You haven't been called out in over a month. What, d'you have some in with the captain that he lets you sleep all the time?"

"I heard he's screwing the captain's wife, and she won't let him get called."

They all laughed and Stanyard said, "Have you seen that bitch? I wouldn't screw her if the captain paid me."

Gruen heard scuffling and then . . .

"Looks like there's been an explosion." It was Stanyard's voice. Gruen could tell them apart already.

"Yeah, electrical I bet," one of the others said. "But it also looks like something dragged it off its base. Look here. Tracks."

They shined powerful flashlights around the area, and Gruen crouched down lower. If they found him, he'd pretend to be sleeping off a drunk.

Then Stanyard was talking to The Globe. Telling the Watchers what they saw. And then . . . more sirens far off, coming their way, followed by loud shouts of "Niko, Niko, Niko" that faded as quickly as they'd begun.

Before they piled back into the van, Stanyard said to the Tower, "Really? That many? Well, they can't all be electrical." He stopped talking for a few minutes and then told the Tower, "Hey, there's no way a bot could fix this. Get a crew out here with a replacement. But the wiring's all mangled, so they'll have to fix that too. And we can't tell what it looks like underground. It's dark out here, you know." He listened again and then said, "Yeah, yeah. We're doing the best we can."

Talking to the Tower stopped, and Stanyard said to the others, "Something's going on. They don't know what. Nothing we can do here. Might as well go back to screwing the captain's wife."

They all laughed, and Gruen heard the van motor start.

Gruen had never thought of himself as particularly smart. Cagey and tough, but not all that bright. He knew he'd have to ask Niko about this. He'd go back to that warehouse to look for Niko early in the morning before anyone else was up. Niko would know what it was all about. Unless he'd already escaped. But no, Gruen thought, there was no way he'd have gotten out so fast.

He set his old wind-up clock to four and fell asleep quickly, wearing his pants with the knife still strapped to his leg.

"It's started on its own," Father Ignatius explained to Niko. "I hadn't expected that, but it's good because the Regime didn't expect it, either. It will take time for them to figure out what's happening and how."

As they spoke, they could hear faint shouts outside of "Niko, Niko, Niko."

"Let me show you what's been prepared."

They went to the model of Infinius, and as they skirted its perimeter, Father Ignatius pointed to tiny color-coded pins strategically placed here and there.

"The red ones are ammunition stores. Orange for fires to be set. Green for InCom screens to topple. Blue are hiding places with quick access. Plain silver denotes relatively safe gathering spots, and black where to put graffiti or signs."

Niko followed the Father's pointing finger. He nodded, taking it all in. "Even right outside The Compound?" he asked. "Isn't that too risky?"

"We have someone who knows how to take scraps of technology and repurpose them. He's made some remote-controlled devices to set off explosions once they've been hidden. The bigger challenge was recruiting someone with access to The Compound to place the explosives. They're small, so once placed, they're undetectable. And the Regime doesn't sweep The Compound for devices because they're arrogant enough to think no one could get inside. Once the signal goes out to set off the charges, The Compound wall will have gaping holes all around it."

"What about The Perimeters?" Niko asked.

"That's more difficult because of the Watchers in The Globe, the guards at stations all along The Perimeters, the fact that there are multiple layers, and that it's all out in the open." Father Ignatius shook his head. "Now that you're here, we have to come up with a plan to get you through there. And there's El. We have to get both of you as far beyond Infinius as possible so they can't track you."

"The smugglers get through all the time. They have tunnels, I've heard."

"That's true. But guards know all about the tunnels. They're all on the take. No one gets out or back in that way without paying a fee." Father Ignatius studied the model intently, seeming to look for an answer in its miniature streets and buildings. "We'll have to get you out fast."

"Maybe I should stay and help you fight. I know the street. Its people. The gangs. I've done business with everyone."

Father Ignatius shook his head. "As long as the Regime can't catch you, they can't parade you around to show the people how you capitulated, how you support them. No, you're more valuable as a rallying cry. As a symbol for people. No, you've got to get out. And the same for El. Her name will appear soon, too. And her picture will be copied from the InCom screens and plastered all over the walls and hovels and fences of the city. To make your names and images stronger, both of you have to disappear. In many ways a myth can be more potent than a man."

"Do you know where El is?"

Father Ignatius nodded. "She's safe for now."

"I gave her something, Father. Before all this happened. She promised to hide it for me. Something valuable that you could use."

Gruen awoke to his alarm buzzing and the loud hum of motorcycles outside as they circled the edge of The Hovels. The hum turned into roaring and shifting gears. Behind their roar, shouts of "Niko" broke the predawn.

He slid his feet into an old pair of sneakers with deep treads, the pair he always wore on marauding forays. He unchained his bike and stowed the chain and lock behind the seat and took off, blending with the other cycles. He'd never heard so many Detainers out on bikes at the same time. He figured they must have called up all the off-duties and reserves. All this to catch one kid. *Fuck them*, he breathed, and headed for the warehouse.

Gruen was no revolutionary. Nor was he some altruist out to save his buddy. No, he remembered something he heard once: In confusion, there is opportunity. He figured with all the turmoil, there was money to be made. *Maybe I can turn in Niko for the reward*, he thought, but then immediately disregarded it. He had his own set of principles. Turning on Niko would mean capitulating to the system he hated. He'd sooner die fighting than give in to that cheating, lying, scumbag crowd of thieves who'd disfigured him.

With all the motorcycles roaring through The Hovels, no one took any notice of him as he escaped into the backstreets toward The Ring. It was still dark, and he noticed that some streetlamps had already been toppled. This worked to his advantage also, and soon he pulled up in the alley where Niko had hidden. Gruen walked his bike behind the very same crumbling dumpster. Then, scouring the street with his one good eye, he crept toward the boarded-up warehouse. Seeing no entry point, he found the fence and the hole and figured this must be the way they came and went.

Gripping the handle of his hunting knife, Gruen squatted down and crawled through the hole, following the building wall to the padlocked half door. Seeing it was unlocked, he pushed it open and walked into the small vestibule between the two doors.

This one was solid . . . and locked. Should he knock? Wait? No use trying to break it down or pick the lock. He heard muffled voices. One sounded like Niko. But was he sure? He rapped quickly on the door, and the voices ceased. Standing as far to the side of the door as he could in the cramped space, he pulled out the knife and held it in striking mode.

The door opened inward but no one appeared. Gruen held his breath. He could feel his pulse thumping against his temples, feel the stagnant heat of the space, and then cooler air coming from the other side of the open door. One movement, one signal that he was in trouble, one sound. The knife was poised to strike.

Then Father Ignatius stepped forward and turned to see Gruen.
"Yes?" he said. "Who are you?"

"Where's Niko?" Gruen spoke in a harsh voice. "I gotta find Niko."

"Are you a friend?"

Niko appeared at the Father's side.

"Gruen. What're you doing here, man? It's dangerous. You can't be seen with me."

"Let me in."

They led him inside and locked the door.

"You know what's going on out there?" Gruen turned from one to the other. "The whole city's going crazy. They want you bad, man. And they'll find you, too."

"You planning on that reward?" Niko asked.

Gruen sheathed his knife and took in the model of Infinius. He poked his chin toward it.

"What the hell's that?"

But Niko was wary. "How about it? You takin' me in for the money?"

Gruen shook his head and walked over to the model. "That's some juiced thing right there," he said. "Naw, I ain't wanna take you in. I wanna help you. But also I got an idea."

Father Ignatius started to speak, but Niko held out his arm to stop him.

"What idea's that?"

Gruen wandered around the model. From the other side he looked up and turned his head to see better with his good eye.

"You remember that guy, Fuller? The one who got sick and told you about them papers?"

"Yeah."

"He sent his Scrounger over my place yesterday looking for a score. We traded a couple things, and then I got to thinking about how useful he might be. I'm thinking he could fuck up the InCom. And even the Watchers' machines? Wouldn't he be? I mean, suppose somebody other than Villinkash"—Gruen whispered the name—"could get a message out on the InCom? Huh?"

Again, Father Ignatius started to speak, and again, Niko cut him off.

"How would he get inside?" Niko asked. He was calm, very quiet, like he knew Gruen had something.

Gruen showed a sly smile as he came all the way around the model.

"See, this here tells me you got a plan. Plus there's them papers you showed me that one night. Remember?"

Niko nodded slowly, sizing up Gruen.

"Well, I got something could be used to help your plan along."

"What's that?" Niko asked.

"First, what's in it for me?"

"I can make it worth your while, depending on what you've got to offer."

"Someone who can get into the systems," said Gruen. "And once inside, Fuller can do his number."

Niko looked at Father Ignatius. "This is what I meant before," he said. "I have plans that show what your model here leaves out. And if Gruen can get Fuller inside the tech systems . . ."

Father Ignatius nodded, looking from Niko to Gruen. "Are you sure you can get someone inside? That part of the city is really well guarded. Even more than The Compound."

"I have this guy . . ."

Father Ignatius held up one hand. "No, don't tell me. If I'm captured, the less I know, the better. I'd rather lie than know. They'd stop at nothing to torture it out of me. That's why we've kept each operation walled off from the others. No one knows the whole plan."

"Except you," Niko said. "You came up with it, no?"

"Not entirely. Anyway, I'll die before I endanger anyone else. I decided that long ago."

"Then we have to get those plans of the underground and tech systems," Niko said. "We should go before it gets light, which is soon."

"I can ride you wherever they are," Gruen offered. "Where did you hide them anyways?"

"It's better if you get Fuller and whoever this infiltrator is. Tell them to be ready. When?" Niko looked at Father Ignatius.

He looked at his watch and counted with his fingers. "Tomorrow night, midnight it will begin. Is that enough time?"

Gruen shrugged. "It'll have to be. But they'll want payment."

Niko moved toward the door. "The Father and I will get the plans and the payment. Meet us back here at ten tonight when it's dark. I'll have plenty of money for you then."

The first big blast occurred at 11 p.m. It rocked The Hovels. In The Shanty Alleys, cardboard walls collapsed on top of people asleep on their mats. People pushed out of their shelters and ran in all directions. Nobody knew what had happened. Babies wailed, mothers gathered children, men hurriedly slipped on shoes and grabbed whatever was handy for defense. A fire broke out somewhere, sending a ball of smoke into the sky. It wasn't clear where the blast was located, so people shouted directions and theories. No one listened to anyone as the chaos gathered momentum. Not knowing where to go for safety, people gathered in knots together. These knots grew larger and then broke apart, scattering to new places.

At regular intervals across the city, and as far as The Ring, blasts sounded like massive fireworks celebrating nothing.

After Gruen left Niko and Father Ignatius, he rode to The Ring, where Fuller lived in a second-floor apartment in the Tower of David. One of the last squatters to claim a space in the building, he had paid a family of eight to move out of their three rooms and go to a higher floor because he was just too big (whenever he referred to himself, he used the word "big") to make it up more than one flight. Even that was so difficult he rarely left his rooms. He moved in right after the Regime had reorganized him out of the underground abyss known to the Regime as Information Services. Money was tight for Fuller. Free rent, no matter what the living conditions, was better than paying a monthly fee to some grubber of a landlord. After the Regime took over, all landlords' money ended up back with Villinkash and his cronies anyway. So Fuller thought of squatting in the Tower as a blow against the bastards who had used him and tossed him away like a rag.

Fuller was a guy with some peculiar abilities. For one thing, he had a photographic memory. Everything he had seen while working in the dingy computer rooms was stored in his brain. Things like passwords, strings of code, names of files, were all accessible to him at any time. He was about as antisocial a person as you could find, rarely speaking, uninterested in chatting or gossip, never interacting with groups, never uttering a pleasant "good morning." But there was no technology beyond his grasp. Which is why the Regime had cast him aside. Because he didn't operate the way everyone else did, they viewed him as a threat they might not be able to control.

In the end, they were right.

Day after day and night after night, Fuller spread his enormous bulk across a mattress atop the platform he'd built to accommodate not only his size but also his array of computers and devices. The Regime limited access to technology as a perk for their members. So when he moved to the Tower, Fuller instructed a twelve-year-old Scrounger, who was called Shag because of his unruly mop of hair, to install a tiny wireless device on the roof.

It was so small that no one ever noticed it. Using it, Fuller could connect to any part of any system with just a few codes and passwords.

Because of his peculiar abilities, which were known only within a small circle, sometimes a person looking for particular information would show up at his door to pay for Fuller's talents. He compensated Shag for his services *and* his silence. He was Fuller's fetcher, gofer, and informer, and that way, he had made a new life and amassed a significant nest egg.

For Fuller there was little distinction between day and night, so when Gruen showed up at barely five in the morning, Fuller's fingers were busily pecking at one of his many keyboards. He might have closed and locked the door to his unit, but there had never been a door. Most of the glass windows had been blown out long ago, except for the one in the room he used as a bedroom, the largest of his three rooms.

"Hey, Fuller," Gruen called out as he walked into the unit. "You up?" He peered into the dark room. You never knew who could be around any corner. Gruen heard something that sounded vaguely like a belch and followed the sound toward Fuller's preferred room.

"Who wants to know?" Fuller asked, his voice scratchy as if he'd been asleep.

"It's Gruen."

"Yeah, so you wake me up to tell me who you are? What do you want?"

Gruen walked farther into the room. It smelled like old sheets that hadn't been washed. Dirty dishes lay stacked on the floor, and there were empty glasses near the edge of the huge bed that took up most of the room. Besides pillows and rumpled sheets, an array of computers and screens surrounded Fuller.

"No. I came because I need some help."

Fuller maneuvered himself into a semi-sitting position against a wall of pillows. He closed all the open laptops and systematically darkened the other screens.

"What kind of help? And hand me that bottle, would you?"

Gruen took a water bottle from the floor and handed it to Fuller.

"Dangerous kind of help."

"Oh, yeah? Dangerous to who?"

"Both of us."

"Is it for you? This help you want. Or a second party?"

Gruen was uncharacteristically quiet. He walked over closer to the bed. "I'm going to tell you something. Something you could use to get a lot out of the Regime. Something Villinkash would pay more than you can imagine to get."

Fuller blinked. "And you think I would be interested in helping that piece of shit?"

When Gruen heard what Fuller said, he suddenly realized that there was no light coming from the apartment's InCom screen.

"Where's your InCom?" he asked.

"Ha. That's the first thing I reprogrammed. Now, what is it you want from me?"

"Before I tell you, what would you want to dismantle and reprogram the entire InCom network?"

Fuller opened the bottle and put it to his lips. After drinking from it, he held it by its neck as he said, "You don't have enough for that kind of a job. No one's ever done anything like that before."

"I know. But that's not all."

Fuller laughed and then had a coughing fit. He drank more from the bottle.

"What else?"

"The electric grid. Could you get into it and shut down power to The Compound and The Perimeters? And all the watch towers and The Globe?"

"You don't want much, do you?"

"And there's one more thing."

"Yeah?"

"It needs to be done by tomorrow night at eleven."

Fuller put the bottle down and stared at Gruen. "You must be crazy. What's all this for, anyway?"

"I've told you enough already. Any more and you'd have a tough time denying any of it."

"So, let's say, for argument's sake, I could pull this off by tomorrow night. What are you willing to pay and when do I get it?"

"How much do you want?"

"I want gold. No currency. And I want it delivered here."

He wrote down an address for Gruen and handed it to him.

"Who do I see? And how much do you want?"

"Give me the paper." Fuller wrote something else on it and handed it back. "Ask for Jake. He'll take care of it for you. Have it there by three today. I'll take it on faith at this point and start working. But I won't put anything into motion until I know the gold is there."

"How will you confirm it's done?"

"My boy, Shag, will let you know. You still live at the same place? In The Hovels?"

Gruen nodded, astonished that Fuller knew even that much about him. "How did you know that?"

Fuller patted one of the closed computers. "I make it my business to know things." He squinted at Gruen. Light was beginning to filter through the windows in the other room. The sun would be up soon.

"So, change is coming to Infinius," Fuller said. "Let's hope we survive it."

"We must go now. Not a good idea to wait until it's too late in the morning. Put on this hat and follow me out," Father Ignatius told Niko.

The hat was old and worn, a peaked cap with a faded logo of some team from long ago. Niko had to adjust the back to make it fit properly.

"Are you hungry?" Father Ignatius asked.

"Yes. Do you have anything we could eat before we leave?"

Father Ignatius went to a carton on the floor and pulled out two bananas and some biscuits. He also took two bottles of juice, then closed the carton.

They ate in silence. Niko didn't look at Father Ignatius; he was thinking about El.

When they finished, they dropped the peels and empty juice bottles into a bag, tied it, and locked the doors behind them. They slipped through the fence hole, and after a few blocks, Father Ignatius dropped the bag into a trash bin by a lamppost. They passed an InCom screen and saw Niko's picture with a warning flash across it. Then there was a picture of El all dressed up from The Race night.

No one was out on the street yet. Niko whispered, "See that? Anyone could recognize me . . . or El."

Father Ignatius kept walking. With every step he felt the fate of many young people in his heart. They were young people who would, in a few short hours, risk their lives at his urging, and now he also felt the pressure of getting Niko and El out of the city. Where should they go? For how long? Such questions spun in his mind like a pinwheel round and round, pushed by the winds of change. In the vastness of time, all things pass, yet in the moment, every detail seems filled with import. He weighed the challenge of reuniting these two young people against what would happen to them at the hands of Villinkash should they not escape.

No matter how he turned it over in his mind, the conclusion was the same. He had to find a way to make peace between them.

El slept on and off, waking each time she heard a blast outside the convent. Some were muffled, and she figured they were far away. Some were loud enough that she got up and listened at the door, ready to hide in the pit if she heard anyone trying to get in. At some point she fell asleep, falling into a deep rest with no dreams until something roused her and she sat up.

Part of her felt comforted by the familiar surroundings. She had left everything intact when the last sister died and she had to move out. She wondered why the Collectors hadn't ransacked the convent. She'd heard they were superstitious about some things. Maybe that was the reason. She looked up at the cross on the wall.

She was sore from fighting Niko. She couldn't get it out of her mind. Even if the sisters had been alive still, she couldn't have told them what had happened. Thinking about everything Father Ignatius had said, she felt clammy with shame. Tears pricked at her eyes. She lowered her face into her hands and wept.

After her personal storm had passed, she got up and washed herself again, using the cleansing soap and water as a ritual to feel whole again. Moving around helped relieve the soreness. She made an herbal tea and ate canned soup and crackers. She even found dried figs. With her stomach full, she looked around the convent and thought about all the years she'd spent there and how safe she'd felt although she knew about the dangers that were always waiting outside. Now she was vulnerable. She couldn't stay inside those walls forever. But what to do? Where to go? How to survive now that she was being hunted?

After cleaning the few dishes using water pumped from the old well out back, she sat at the big wooden table to think. Her situation was untenable. That was the only certainty. Outside was nothing but danger. She began to imagine what could happen to her when she had to venture outside of the convent. It was too frightening to contemplate, so she focused her mind on what few resources she had. A mental image of Old Merrie came to her, and she wished she could speak to the old woman to ask her what to do.

Then came the faint sound of a scratch at the secret door. At first she thought it must be a feral cat. The sisters used to leave food for them. But then she heard a creak that told her the door was opening. She ran to a small storage room off the kitchen and crouched down, her heart thumping wildly. She had not even thought to grab a kitchen knife.

Faintly, she heard someone call her name.

"El? Are you here? Don't be afraid. It's Father Ignatius."

Such relief flooded through her that she all but ran into his arms and collapsed against him, her fingers so tight to his jacket that she could feel the muscles tense to hold her up.

"Oh, Father," she breathed. "I've been so afraid. But now you're here."

"Yes, child, I'm here. Hush hush. It's still not safe out there. And I am not alone."

He gently disentangled her from his arms. That's when she saw Niko behind him.

In one instant her expression shifted, with the fluidity of water, from relief to disbelief, then fear, back to disbelief, and then to anger as she pushed at Father Ignatius and stumbled backwards slowly, as if the fact of Niko's presence would not come clear in her mind, as if she was having a recurring nightmare as she distanced herself from them by half the length of the room.

Father Ignatius held out his hands to calm her.

"It's all right, El. No one's going to hurt you. We've come to help you and to ask for your help."

"Help?" she asked in a hoarse whisper. "Help him?"

Father Ignatius took two steps forward, placing himself between Niko and El, but before he could say or do anything, Niko rushed to the kitchen and began pulling out drawers until he spotted a long slender carving knife with a sharp point. He grabbed it and moved swiftly around Father Ignatius until he was in front of El.

He threw the knife at her feet. It clattered and lay there, easy for her to grab.

"There," he said softly. "Use it. I won't blame you."

El bent down and picked it up by the handle. Holding it as if to stab, she approached him slowly, deliberately, her eyes narrowed, her mouth set in a hard line.

Niko did not move.

"You . . ." she began to speak. "You come here. You want my help. You think you can make everything between us like it was before?"

"No, El. No."

He spoke quietly, his lips set in a grim line. He stood in front of her like an animal that had been trapped and realized there was no escape. He tilted his head up towards the ceiling beams as if searching for some signal and it was then El saw his face contort in pain. Out of him came a sob of anguish like nothing she'd ever heard before.

El didn't know what to do. She fingered the knife, thinking that if she killed him now, that act would stay with her, forever layered over what he had done by choosing her and what she had done to him. There was no going back, she realized. And to add to that pain by creating another one would only hurt her further.

"Whatever you do to me, I deserve. Whatever you think of me, I deserve," Niko sobbed. "I've done too much. And to have hurt you is too much for me to bear."

Father Ignatius stepped forward and spoke.

"Please, both of you, I want you to understand that there is no going back in life. We all do terrible things. Sometimes to the ones we love the most. And terrible things are done to us. I wish I could explain to you why, but I cannot. In all my years and with all my experience, I still cannot fathom why people are so cruel and so filled with all the sins in the Bible. No one can avoid all those sins. No one can say he or she is absolutely pure.

"Niko has harmed El in a way that she feels cannot be forgiven. El has harmed Niko in a way that will show on his face for the rest of his life. The system you were born into has harmed us all. So we must change. First ourselves. Yet how? By forgiving, as the prayer says, those who trespassed against us. And then we must change the system. Because corruption breeds corruption. Greed breeds greed. Evil breeds evil. It isn't hard to breed these things. All it takes is turning people away from their innate need to love, to forgive, to build a better life. Because destruction is so easy. But creating is so hard."

El stood there, the knife still in her hand.

Niko looked up at her with tears streaming down his face. He held out his hands, palms up.

"Forgive me, El. Please, forgive me. I don't understand what happened. I never wanted to hurt you. I will never hurt you again. But if you must seek revenge, do it quickly. And then I hope you find a way out of Infinius. Because if I die here, at least I'll know I didn't completely kill the feelings we once had for each other."

El relaxed her hold on the knife. Could she believe what he said? Or was he saying these things only because of Father Ignatius and because he was in trouble? It was impossible to know for sure. He seemed sincere. But how could he know what she'd gone through and how she felt now? It was still about how *he* felt, about what *he'd* done. It was still not about her, not about her feelings. And now her feelings were more confused than ever. Because she *did* remember how she'd felt before. Before The Race and everything that came afterwards.

She turned to face Father Ignatius.

"I see you are confused, child," he said softly. "And that is normal, too. Even expected. But the wonderful thing about humans is their capacity to heal. It's something miraculous that we see all through the natural world. We are a part of that world. If you strike a tree, it will grow tissue back over the wound. After a forest fire, new life sprouts. So it is with us. Part of healing is rediscovering trust. In yourself and others. Not blind trust, but trust that is warranted. I cannot guarantee that you will never be hurt again, but if you carry this hurt forever, without forgiveness, you will never heal." He reached for the knife, but she held back.

"How can I forgive him, Father?" El asked.

"Perhaps you can't forgive him now. Perhaps in the future you'll find a way. For now, try to trust that he is remorseful and that he truly cares for you. Blame the system. And blame his desire to be close to you. He chose you because he wanted something real, not some tawdry, meaningless, empty liaison."

El stood there looking from Father Ignatius to Niko, still crumpled on the ground like a fallen leaf. Her hand shook as she released the knife to him.

Father Ignatius put them knife back in its drawer and carefully shut it then leaned down to help Niko to his feet.

"I wish we could stay here and speak about the future and how to unravel the emotions you both have experienced. I wish many things for you, Niko and El. But there is no time. You're in too much danger. The Regime will hunt you relentlessly. There will be a price on both your heads and many people will try to make money on you. So neither of you can stay in the city. And neither of you will get far away on your own" He turned to El. "We have made a plan for your escape, but that is only a part of the plan.

Many things will begin to happen tonight, and the city will be engulfed in turmoil. The Regime will be out in force but so confused that I think we can slip you past The Protections. From there you'll be on your own."

Niko now spoke. "But Father, where can we go? Escaping Infinius is one step. Where can we escape to?"

"We'll escape to Zamora," El said.

"If it exists," Niko murmured.

"I'm sure of it," El said.

Niko paused as if searching for other options, but then relented. "All right. I'll trust you. Maybe it does exist. And if it does, and you can trust me, we'll find Zamora somehow."

Gruen had never actually seen gold coins.

Where and how the priests had acquired and stockpiled the stacks of coins El and Niko handed to Father Ignatius from the depths of the converted mechanic pit would forever remain unknown. There were bags and bags of them. Sturdy canvas bags stored in a metal trunk with a heavily padlocked latch. Niko had to struggle to break that lock using a crowbar Father Ignatius found in a closet.

"Did you know about this?" He looked at El with wide eyes.

She shook her head. "Not that it was gold. The sisters told me there were valuables, but not down here. I only knew about the things about the past that I told you about and other things that were stored here, but I had no idea . . ."

She looked up to the top of the steep set of steps where Father Ignatius was waiting. "How much should we take now? You might need some later. After we're gone."

It sounded so permanent, suddenly, and El felt a wave of fear about the future. She faltered at the thought of depending on Niko, of being alone with him. She looked around to reassure herself, but he was counting the bags and had opened one.

"I don't know the value of even one of these coins," he said. "But they must be worth plenty, so I think if I give twenty of them to Gruen, he'll keep what he wants and pay off his guy with the rest."

"And leave the others here?" asked El.

"Yes," Father Ignatius called down to them. "Leave them."

"What about these?" El picked up the roll of papers she'd taken from Niko. "You asked me to keep them safe. Before . . ."

Niko stood up and took the papers from her. As she handed him the roll, he saw in her eyes fear and something else. A cold loathing.

"I promise you, El. You will never have to fear me in any way again. Never. I want you to know that."

Whether this reassured El or not, she was curious about the trunk's contents. Looking down in the faint light, she saw an old photo album and an oversized envelope. She stooped down and opened the album. Inside were pictures from a wedding. Old pictures, but not ancient. The bride was beautiful in a simple white dress and held a bouquet of white roses. The groom was . . . El couldn't believe it. She had seen him on the InComs before. Villinkash. Making frightening, angry, threatening speeches. She squinted at the picture and was about to lift the album out of the trunk to see it in a better light.

"Hurry up, you two." It was Father Ignatius standing at the top of the steps, peering down at them.

El closed the album and stood up. Niko closed the trunk with a thud. There was no time to say anything else or investigate further. They climbed the steps and closed off the pit once again. Father Ignatius pulled the rug over the trapdoor, and they moved the heavy table over it.

El said to Niko, "I'll pack for you," and walked away to begin gathering what they might need. She had no idea how long they'd be running or where they would hide, but her fear had vanished and been replaced by caution.

The image of the girl in white holding roses stayed in her mind. Later, much later, she would wonder about that picture and what other secrets were hidden in the old trunk.

The cart trundled along with Old Merrie singing her songs as if this was lunch hour on any other day. People ran from street to street, not knowing when the next explosion would rock the city or where it would happen. Siren wails filled the air. Dust clouds fell intermittently here and there, like isolated spring showers.

One man dressed in a business suit yelled out to her from the other side of the street as he hurried by, "Old Merrie! Get out of the street. Go home."

She just smiled and wobbled along, calling back to him, "Old Merrie need to make a living out here. I got fresh pineapples and some yams today. Make you a nice supper." She chuckled and bounced her cart over a flat stone that had landed on the street.

Finally, a woman stopped her. "You got potatoes, you say?"

"No, yams today. Special price. All this . . ."—she waved her hand around at the buildings—"not much business out here."

"Well, I still gotta make supper for my kids. Give me four yams and take this money."

"Now ain't that right?" Old Merrie leaned down and pulled opened the tin door of one compartment. She lifted out four fat yams and placed them in the woman's sack. "We still got to eat, no matter what they doing. How 'bout a fresh pineapple go with them yams? Mighty tasty."

The woman hesitated, looked around and up as if expecting a bomb to fall on them, then said, "Yes. Give me one of them too. My kiddies love pineapple." She handed Old Merrie some bills.

"Mmmhmmm, you gonna have some nice supper tonight."

She counted the money, nodded a thank you to the woman, and stuffed the bills into a pocket of her voluminous skirt.

The woman hurried off. Old Merrie knocked once on the side of the cart with the flat of her hand as the cart bounced on. She skirted The Hovels on a narrow street that seemed to lead nowhere. But Old Merrie had been plying these streets so long she knew exactly how each one connected to another, which were dead ends and which ones wound around until they reached where smugglers hid to make it through The Perimeters.

Along with the sirens, the sound of motorcycle engines could be heard. Every now and then the screeching of brakes added to an overall sense of a blanket of turmoil over the city. The bumping and clattering of Old Merrie's fruit and vegetable cart drew no unwanted attention no matter where she pushed it.

Old Merrie's cart rumbled along down a street near the convent. She pushed it forward with more caution than usual. Now she didn't sing or tout the fresh vegetables or fruits hidden in the large confines of her food cart. The tattered beach umbrella that shaded the cart and partly protected her from the scorching sun weaved from side to side like an intoxicated tightrope walker.

Old Merrie squinted at the buildings, their doorways, the vacant lots she passed. She kept her left hand hidden in a pocket that held, among other things, a half-used ball of twine, a dried-up rubber bottle stopper, a screwdriver, a hand towel, a pair of broken sunglasses, two plastic drinking cups permanently stuck together, three playing cards—an ace, a queen, and a three of clubs—five keys on a brass ring, a roll of toilet paper with few sheets left, and a small unopened bag of peanuts. With her hand thrust deep into this pocket, she fingered a solitary gold coin Father Ignatius had given her not one hour ago.

Stopping her to buy an orange, which she'd just offered to a passerby as one of the fresh fruits she had to sell that day, Father

Ignatius had leaned in close to her and whispered something that surprised her more than anything she'd ever heard. He bought the orange, and she mused on his request as she left him and headed in a circuitous route toward the convent, which was now coming into view. She saw its old familiar door, its backyard garden hosting a variety of weeds that, in previous days, never would have been allowed to compete for survival. She wanted to be sure no one had followed her, so she took her time, stopping now and then to rest or to sell something. She also had a few fresh pears, hard-boiled eggs, and freshly baked flatbreads that stacked neatly inside the cart's front compartment. She had tried to barter for lettuce but, finding none, had settled for parsley. If no one else bought it, she would make use of it in a soup.

Once the lunch hour had begun, she usually sold out of the fresh produce quickly by singing of her wares. Today it was even more important that she clear her cart's compartments. The large block of ice she had placed inside the insulated top every day maintained a cool enough environment below to keep her produce fresh. Other vendors cooked food for the office lunchers, but Old Merrie was a specialist in things most of them thought it too much trouble or too dangerous to obtain. She specialized in things that required dealing with Scroungers and smugglers, and often paying off guards at The Protections.

So Old Merrie was well known out at the western edges of the city. Well known and certainly no threat. Now she came closer to the convent. Would her cart fit through the fence, allowing her access to the back door the Father had told her about? Would she be able to complete her mission?

Arriving at the fence, she saw that her cart would never make it through. She even doubted if she alone could squeeze through that narrow opening. Her only other option was the front door. Well, she shrugged, it was worth trying. If they did not answer, she would have to get through that fence somehow, which, she determined, would arouse even more suspicion if anyone happened by.

She drew her cart across the sidewalk and tapped on the door softly. Since there were no offices in this neighborhood, no one was on the street looking for a place to eat. She glanced around, still fingering the gold coin deep inside her pocket. Again she rapped on the door, this time daring to sing out a tune she made up on the spot.

"Old Merrie's come to call," she sang. "Old Merrie with her fresh things to eat and her song to sing."

She knocked again, insistently, and then saw El peering through a crack from behind the boards.

Old Merrie leaned forward. She recognized El and held a finger to her lips.

"The Father sent me," she said. "You got to be quick and get in my cart. You in the front storage, the boy in the back one because it's bigger. Then we got a long way to go, and you two got to be real quiet the whole way."

El turned to Niko. "This is it," she told him. "It's time to leave."

They left from the small door the way they'd entered.

Old Merrie pulled the cart right up to the fence and opened both storage bins. She had already moved all the food to the smallest top one to make room for her passengers.

Niko climbed in headfirst. He folded his knees up as far as he could, held his knapsack against his chest, and crammed his feet against the sidewall. He knocked once on the door to let Old Merrie know he was in, and she shut and locked the front panel. El climbed into the small side bin the same way. She also held her knapsack against her chest and placed another small bag on top of it. On this she rested her head by turning sideways because the bin was too low for her to sit up straight. Old Merrie locked her in the same way, patted the top of the cart once, and, with a great effort, pushed it from the sidewalk onto the street.

With her mouth set uncharacteristically hard, she began the long push to The Protections toward the opening of a tunnel where Father Ignatius had told her they would make their escape that night. Where were they going, Old Merrie had asked him, for risking everything as she was, she felt she had a right to know. The gold coin was a bonus, but it meant less to her than being alive after all this was over.

"Zamora," he'd told her.

"Ah," she'd said. "Toward the Glimmer."

In his cushioned, vaulted office in The Compound, Villinkash hadn't stayed calm for long. He barked orders and paced like a convict waiting to be strapped into his death chair. As morning faded and the sun rose higher in the noon sky, his rants turned to threats. He ordered more and more uniformed squads into the streets and peppered the InComs with dire warnings of what was to come. He screamed about collaborators and traitors, about filling the camps and meting out harsher treatment than had ever been administered, about ordering the camp guards to squeeze their existing populations into tighter quarters in preparation for an enormous influx of new "workers."

Since there was no controlling him, Huston said he was going to personally supervise The Perimeters. He left the Overseers to mill around and carry out the flood of orders the Premier would continue to unleash all day.

When Huston left they were taping a series of personal messages to be broadcast over the InCom. Messages vilifying Niko as a traitor and accusing El of bewitching the winning racer into betraying his duty to the people and The Race, messages designed not only to distract people but to work them into a frenzy. Indeed, there was always a certain segment that would reply to hate with deeper hate, to violence with more violence, to irrational threats with their own irrational threats. Some people, when whipped into a frenzy, lose all humanity and act as a mob with one dysfunctional brain.

Huston had other priorities. He foresaw the chaos in the city's immediate future and tried to figure out where Niko would go to get help.

Huston ordered his car and instructed the driver to take him to a house high on a hill at the northernmost quadrant of The Compound. It was a rambling house in a hacienda style, with arches and an inner courtyard with a fountain. A high wall surrounded it with bougainvillea so thick the wall was completely obscured. On the iron gate that stood closed to intruders, a heart surrounded by roses had been welded into the middle. When the gate opened, the heart separated into two halves.

Huston got out of the car and pressed the intercom buzzer. A voice asked who it was, and he leaned into the microphone and quietly said his name. The gate slowly opened. Huston got back in the car and drove forward. The gate closed with a clank.

"Wait here," he told his driver. This loyal man had been with Huston since the beginning. "Don't get out of the car."

The driver nodded. "Yes, sir," was all he said. His face, as always, was impassive. If Huston spoke more than a few words to him, he prefaced them with the man's name, Zeke. He was a big man with rocklike hands who always wore a navy-blue suit and red tie. His hair was cropped close, and there was a visible scar at the back of his head down to his neck. He never turned on the car radio or spoke to Huston unless spoken to first.

Only once had he ignored a directive from his employer and left the car to protect Huston. It was on one of those nights when Huston had some business to conduct on a dark street beyond

The Hovels. It had only taken one well-placed blow. Huston never mentioned it afterwards, but a month later, a box filled with cash appeared in Zeke's apartment. More money than he had ever seen. There was no note. Now he watched Huston walk to the front door, which opened before he could pull the chain of an old-fashioned bell hanging from a hand-hammered brass hook.

A small woman in a white domestic's uniform swung the door aside to let Huston enter. Then the door shut with a soft *thunk*. Without speaking, she led him down a hall to a room with one glass wall overlooking a courtyard. To one side was a garden full of blooming plants and butterflies darting from flower to flower. Hummingbirds fed at hanging tubes of sugar water. They chased each other away or hovered, awaiting a turn. The garden was, in reality, a screened enclosure designed to imprison these delicate creatures who spent their entire lives without ever reaching the world beyond.

Huston stood at the entry to this room as the uniformed woman hung back to let him enter. Seated in a wingback chair covered in flowered chintz, a woman sat with her hands folded in her lap. A small matching couch and another wingback chair were placed with a marble coffee table in the middle, forming an intimate seating area. There was an antique rug on the marble-tiled floor and a European-style crystal chandelier hanging from the middle of an ornately inlaid ceiling. Old oil paintings on two walls had a vaguely familiar look, as if one might have seen them in a museum. The remaining wall housed books floor to ceiling, many in heavy leather bindings.

The woman wore a soft gray dress and an off-white silk blouse with a diamond pin at the collar. It sparkled in the afternoon light, as did the rather large diamond ring on her left ring finger. Her hair was carefully braided and coiled into a circle around her head. It had two elegant gray streaks at her temples but was mostly a dark reddish brown. She wore little makeup, but what she did wear enhanced her eyes and mouth in a way that made Huston remember another time and place. The scene seemed to him like a set in a 1930s movie he had once seen. The woman could have been the actress playing that part of a genteel woman who had become embroiled in an unsavory situation and was now trying desperately to hold onto her aristocratic status and remain above the dishonor that had been thrust upon her.

When Huston appeared in the open double French doorway, she looked up from a book in her lap. She did not smile but nodded slightly to the servant, who slipped away. Huston closed the French doors behind him and walked down the few shallow steps into the pleasant, sunny room.

Standing in front of her, he leaned down and took her right hand in his, lifted it, put it to his lips, and kissed it lightly.

"You never change," he said slowly, quietly, as if in a church.

"Won't you sit down?" She motioned to the couch, but he took the other wingback chair closer to her.

She knew he would tell her the reason for his visit. But he wasn't ready yet because this was a place where he might allow himself to ponder "what if." And to remember what used to be, when he had been much younger. Before he had turned himself into what he was determined to become. So he let his mind wander back in time to that beautiful night, hours filled with a thoughtless freedom when each moment seemed an hour. How her body had answered every one of his commands and her murmuring voice had led him further and further still. He could still see her long hair spread out behind her in a soft, loose cascade.

"I'm surprised you still remember," she said. And snapped the book closed.

"You always knew what I was thinking."

"Not always. Not when it mattered most."

"It's much too late for recriminations now."

"And yet you've come to my home. To my hideaway. To my prison."

"I need your help."

"Ahh." She nodded. "Money, I suppose." She looked around at the walls. "I wonder what these paintings would have brought in Paris or London. Too late now."

"No. Not money."

"What else then? I have nothing to offer. Nothing you can't get from *him*." She said the word "him" with great disdain.

"You have information."

The French doors opened and the servant woman entered, carrying a tray with an elegant silver tea service: cups, cakes, and little sandwiches. These she set up on the coffee table and then stood and looked at her mistress for further instructions. The woman told her in sign language that would be all and thanked her. The servant bowed and withdrew, closing the doors behind her.

"She came from one of the camps," the woman explained. "They cut out her tongue. So she couldn't scream when they took turns raping her. Fever took her hearing. They cast her out into the mud, and she crawled for weeks until she was found almost dead by the nuns."

Huston shuddered and then felt enormous shame. "I'm sorry. It's all barbaric."

"Tea?" she asked, and began to pour for both of them.

"You blame me. I understand. But we still have something to do."

She looked up at him, and what he saw was the only woman who had ever meant anything to him, the woman he'd had to give up to save her. The woman who hated him for it.

"You're wrong, Lawrence."

She'd said his name. His hand began to shake, and the teacup clattered in its saucer. He put it down. Before he could say anything, she spoke again.

"I understand everything that happened. You had no other choice at the time. You did save me and allowed me to save Father. But for what?"

Even in her circumscribed life, the tone of her voice, her bearing, the way she still served tea in the afternoon, it all reminded Huston of the difference that had always been between them. Even now, with all his power and influence and classes reduced to almost nothing but those in control and those controlled, she could make him feel like a poor boy from the other side of town. The wrong side. If only he'd been able to accomplish more, to make her proud of what he'd done. But such thoughts only led him to dead ends. It was all too late for that now. And, yet . . . he couldn't keep from wondering and had to ask.

"If I could change the whole system and completely topple it and come out alive, could you . . ." He stopped. She must know what he meant.

She sipped her tea and looked over the cup to the garden outside.

"I'm like those butterflies," she said. "I can flit from one place to another, but I can never go far."

"And yet," he said, "you do go far."

She turned away from the garden to study him.

"You surprise me, Lawrence."

"Still?"

"So you keep tabs on me?"

"I have to know everything. All the time. For instance, I know where funding for the convent came from."

"Do you? Oh, well, that's not so surprising."

"I also know about late-night visits here." He looked up at a cross hanging on one wall, at the small shelf below it, and the half-burned candles in silver holders. "I know, for instance, that you're the only one who has no InCom and who, shall we say, is allowed certain liberties."

"Like prayer?"

Huston nodded.

"And confession?"

He nodded again.

"I don't suppose you've ever confessed."

Huston stood up and walked to where the cross hung. He put his hands in his pockets and tilted his head as he regarded the swathed figure, the mock nails, the painted blood.

"I've never understood the symbol or the practice. What good has religion done? I've read all the arguments for it. The only one that makes any sense at all is how much worse humanity would be without it. Infinius is proof of that, I suppose. But power and might will always win for a time, no matter what god is displayed. Humans are basically corrupt. And the few who aren't maintain a tenuous balance that is always in a state of disequilibrium about to be subsumed by countervailing evil.

"If I wanted to seduce you again, I know this isn't the way to do it. I could make a flowery speech about how I've come to understand the righteous path of good. But I think you would know I wasn't being honest. And I was always, no matter what else I've been or done, honest with you. I loved you. I love you still. I will always love you. Perhaps that is my religion, and it is the hope I cling to when I look in the mirror and see who I really am.

"I was this man when you loved me all those years ago. I've not changed. I'm still the bastard I was. Everything I've done I would do again given the same circumstances and choices. If we had found each other in a different time and place, things would have been different for us. But we were thrust into this time.

"I could have fought him. And I would be dead now. There was no fighting that wave of hate and destruction followed by vile solutions and despicable acts. One has to live through the fever. Well, now it is almost over. And its aftermath will be brutal, too.

"I've come here to ask for your help, but also to help you survive what is surely to come. Will you help me? Will you let me save you, Saskia?"

Her name, softly spoken, was for him a prayer. He hadn't allowed himself to say that name in eighteen years. It would have been too painful. Still staring at the cross, tears came to his eyes. She couldn't see that, and he waited to turn back to her until, like his words, they had evaporated.

He didn't hear the soft rustle of her skirt as she stood. Or the footsteps as she came to his side.

"You cannot save me," she said, and took his hand in hers. "I died long ago. Only my body remains. That, and whatever good I have done these eighteen years."

As he turned to her, a sob broke in his throat.

"I did what I thought was best at the time," he mumbled. "I should have taken you and fled."

"And where was there to flee?" she asked, and kissed the tips of his fingers. "I had to save Father. And you had to save yourself and my baby. And if you had known then . . ."

"I've watched him. At least I've done that. And protected him the best I could."

He raised his hand, still in hers, to his own lips and kissed her palm.

"You're still so beautiful. You make me ache for you."

She pulled her hand away and returned to her chair as if it were a throne upon which she was obligated to remain.

"You want to know who is helping him. And how," she said. Gone was the tender note in her voice and the look of compassion—even love—in her face.

A deep sigh escaped Huston's chest like a great wind that had collapsed from inside his body. He walked back and sat down.

"Yes."

What else was there to say? The moment of possibility had passed between them and flown away like one of those fluttering butterflies outside the glass.

"I have a personal guard unit, loyal only to me," he said. "I'll post them outside your house. They'll protect you. The rest of the city will be in peril. If it comes to that, they'll take you to a safe place I've set up. Pack whatever is most important to you and be ready. She can go with you, too, if the time comes." He nodded toward the door where the servant woman had come and gone.

"It's Father Ignatius," she told him. "His base is a warehouse where he's been training youths to prepare for the takeover. They were as surprised as everyone else by what happened at The Race. They weren't expecting it to happen so fast."

"Serves me right for being such a heathen." Huston smiled for the first time, but it didn't last more than a few seconds. "I should have guessed it."

"They're leaving the convent. Probably gone already."

"Convent? That old converted garage?"

"Yes. I supported them until the last nun died."

"And the girl?"

"I didn't know her."

"Is she worthy of him?"

"I don't know, but I gave all my father's gold to the priests, and they stored it in the convent somewhere. The girl may know where it is. Or Father Ignatius. It's a fortune."

"Enough to buy a lot of ammunition," Huston mused. "Or information."

Gruen interrupted Fuller as Shag was in the middle of bathing him. It was quite an operation. Fuller now weighed well over four hundred pounds and was gaining week by week.

Constructed of aluminum sides and bottom from a deconstructed water tank, they had welded and bolted together a large oval tub like affair in the only bedroom. Hanging over the side was a hose for siphoning water either into or out of the tub. With nothing else in the room, there was a bit of extra space to move around it. Shag was a strong boy, so he could help Fuller get from the bed to the bath without too much trouble. Once in the bath, with a second hose, Shag siphoned warm water from pots on a makeshift electric stove using stolen power from the grid outside.

The water never covered Fuller's entire body, so he had to slosh around to clean all his parts. Folds of fat, looking like fleshy tubes around his body, glistened in the dim light from one naked overhead bulb. Fuller was soaping his elephantine thighs when Gruen appeared in the doorway.

"Holy shit!" he exclaimed, coming upon this scene.

"What are you doing here?" Fuller growled, making no attempt to cover any of his body.

"I brought what you need." Gruen took two steps into the room.

"Good. Then you can wait until I finish my toilette and then help dry me off and get me back to my bed."

"Fuck I will," Gruen spat back.

"Shag," Fuller spoke sweetly to the boy. "Take Mr. Gruen here to help change my sheets while I wash my dick."

"Funny." Gruen smirked. "I ain't no chambermaid. The boy can do whatever on his own."

"You want my help? You do what I need."

Gruen considered walking away. It was tempting. He had never liked being put in a position with no options. And Fuller was such a prick. But he'd come this far. And if he didn't complete his task, he was liable to be ratted out. They might tell someone else about the plan. So while Fuller continued to bathe himself with a great show of mock elegance, Gruen followed the boy to the living room and the huge bed.

"Why do you put up with him?" Gruen asked the boy.

"He pays me. And doesn't expect anything weird."

They stripped the bed and put on clean sheets.

"Besides," Shag said as he tucked in the last sheet, "the guy's some kinda wizard, and he's teaching me a lot of shit."

"How sweet." Fuller stood at the door, wrapped in a bed quilt, which was the only thing big enough to dry his whole body at one time. "I'm so glad you boys are bonding."

To Shag he said, "Empty the bathwater and leave us alone."

Fuller lowered himself onto the bed and arranged the pillows. He spread the quilt over himself and leaned back.

"So? Did you get everything?"

Gruen went to the door and picked up the roll of papers. He brought them to the bed and spread them out on the floor. They wanted to curl up at the corners, so Gruen grabbed some books and plates and whatever he could find nearby to hold them flat. The plates had bits of old food stuck to them. Meanwhile, Fuller studied the plans carefully. He seemed to be ticking off things in his head. He nodded and rocked back and forth. Finally, he swung his heavy legs over the bed so he could lean over and see the far-thest papers more closely. He looked up at Gruen, squinting at him. He put a finger to his lips.

"Are you done in there, boy?" he called to Shag.

"Almost."

"Well, finish it up later and go get my dinner now. I'm hungry."

"Yessir."

They heard him open the door and then heard it close.

LB Gschwandtner

"Do you know what you've got here?" Fuller asked, gazing up at Gruen with a smile. He shook his head slightly. "You're so dumb you probably don't."

"Hey, I'm smart enough to get it for you, ain't I?"

"Indeed you are, my good man. Indeed you are. Well, let's just say, for the moment anyway, that these papers are the keys to the kingdom. What I want to know is: What is the end game? Who is going to end up on the throne? Hmmm?"

"You seen The Race?"

"Oh, of course. I wouldn't miss one of those for the world. Young tads hurling themselves off a high-rise? Who could resist such wholesome drama? So what?"

"So it was the beginning. And those sounds you been hearing all day . . . they're driving the Detainers and squads into the streets all over the place. They don't know where it's gonna hit next. And it'll get worse and worse. It's all gonna collapse. And then you'll be right up there with them waiting to take over."

"And who's 'them'?"

Gruen smiled. "I can't say all of them for sure. But you'll be right there in the inner circle. And what's there now will be gone or dead. Or both."

"You're asking me to subvert the whole InCom system and send the electrical grid into a giant spasm. And you want me to believe that you alone are going to secure my position in the new order of things?"

Gruen nodded. And smiled. "I guarantee it."

"Where's the money? The inner circle holds little appeal to me. There are places in this world that beckon, and it takes money to get myself there."

"First, you do your thing. Here's something on account." Gruen pulled out a small bag and tossed it on the bed. "And when it's done, you'll have enough to go anywhere for the rest of your sorry life."

Fuller pulled the cord open and peered inside the bag. He seemed satisfied and studied the papers again. "Since my sorry life is about to make you a rich bastard, let's cut out the insults, shall we? That is, if you can twist your brain into an operationally functional organ for just a few moments. Once I gain control of these two grids, which shouldn't be too difficult, may I also assume there is some sort of plan in place for what to do with that control? Not that you've outlined such a plan. But someone has?"

Gruen thought about punching this bedridden blob in the face but held himself back. He was right. There was a great deal of money at stake. Gruen had never fallen into such a sweet pit, and he had at least enough control of his aggressive instincts not to forfeit this big chance.

"Yeah," he said. "Now that you mention it, there is a plan. When the InCom goes out, I'll be back with the rest of your share and instructions for what to blast out when the time comes. The InCom should go out at exactly ten tonight. And the electric grid at exactly eleven. Can you do that?"

Fuller pointed to a robe on the floor.

"Hand me that. I must dress properly for this assignment." He laughed at his joke and waved Gruen out of the apartment as he struggled to rid himself of the quilt and slide, first one doughy arm and then the other, into a huge cherry-red chenille robe that promised to cover his bulk.

Old Merrie sang softly, pushing the ponderous cart along, trying to find the smoothest route both for herself and her cargo. She could have gone a shorter way, but with all the commotion everywhere, she stuck to the less traveled alleys and cross streets. She knew where she was at all times and even stopped when someone approached to buy a piece of fruit or a canned drink. At such times she kept up a steady patter of casual commentary, avoiding any talk of the disruption. For her it was just another day of street selling. Or so she portrayed herself. And she was good at it. After all, no one really ever wanted to know Old Merrie except for what she could offer them. And then they went on their way. She was a cloud on the horizon. A well-known fixture that was, at the same time, invisible, melting into nothing, which made her the perfect conduit for an escape.

Toward the end of the lunch break, a group of Detainers stopped her.

"Whatchya got today, Merrie?" asked one of them, a skinny, dark-skinned man with stripes on his sleeve indicating he was an officer. "I'm thirsty."

"Got some cold lemonade in here." She pointed to the top compartment, the one that kept ice cold. "Want some? I'm almost out. Been busy today what with all the people out and about."

"Yeah. And one for the boys here, too."

Old Merrie grinned and pulled out four cans of lemonade. "I'll give you a discount on account of you keeping the peace and all, General." She held up two fingers and they all laughed.

They wandered off, guns slung over their shoulders, drinking from the cans. Old Merrie pushed on. As she got farther from them, she heard a gun go off and then laughter. And the sound of cans hitting the street. She didn't look around. Just tapped the cart's side door to let Niko know everything was okay.

As they were coming out of The Hovels and entering The Shanty Alleys, streets devolved into rutted dirt tracks with, every so often, a patch of cracked concrete where once the roads even in the poorer sections had been maintained. Now no one paid them any mind. In fact, few people were out even though, at this hour, people usually milled about, swapping stories or looking for a bit of extra food for their hungry families. Ordinarily Old Merrie might have been wary of this part of town, especially with her cart full of food and money deep in her pockets. But she had long since determined that her fate would befall her when it was ready. So, with her hidden cargo, she forged ahead.

They came to the beginning of The Shanty Alleys, where thousands of slapped-together shelters stood precariously side by side, each supporting the other in what, if seen from high above, would look more like a cavernous community of insects than any habitation for humans. Such disarray was the perfect place to disappear. With no streets or alleys with names, and no development system, to enter anywhere was to enter everywhere. Even Old Merrie had no bearings in The Shanty Alleys. But she plodded on until, after what could have been an hour or five minutes, she came to a pipe from which water dribbled next to a shed.

Here she stopped. There were noises not far away, but in here, there were no InComs. The last ones had been attached to a stanchion just before entering. They showed a picture of Niko where (although it didn't make any sense) he was taking El by the hand after The Race as his prize.

The dusty pathways in The Shanty Alleys were flat but pitted, and if there had been a hard rain, they would turn to mud soup. The shed next to where she had stopped was falling apart. It had no roof, and of its three remaining sides, one leaned precariously inward. Old floorboards had been hacked apart, and what had been left were rotted out amid a dirt floor. In one corner, a battered crib from some long-gone baby lay on its side, its pickets broken.

After looking around to make sure she hadn't been followed, Old Merrie pushed her cart inside.

"You better come out now. Get some air. Stretch those legs," she said in a low voice, leaning down to unlatch the cart doors.

She reached in to help El unfold herself enough to stick out one leg and then the other. Niko maneuvered himself out first and stood unsteadily.

"Best you rest here before we go any further. No one gonna come up in these Shanty Alleys no way. Nothing to steal here and don't never bother arresting no one neither. Here." She handed Niko a cold lemonade can and then gave one to El as she emerged slowly from the cart.

"You doing all right?" she asked El. "Close and hot in there. We still got a ways to go, but not till this sun sets himself down for the night."

Niko slipped outside, and they heard him peeing against the shaky wall.

"That's mens for you. Easy for them. You gotta go, honey?"

El nodded. She drank the lemonade almost in one gulp. "So thirsty," she gasped. "I thought I would never get out of there."

Old Merrie shook her head in sympathy. "I know. Ain't the best conveyance. But nobody's done bothered you. See? We get you to The Perimeters, I don't know what to think. Don't do no good to even imagine. We'll just push on and meet whatever comes."

Niko came back inside, and Old Merrie nodded to El. "You go on," she said. "Ain't nobody gonna bother you out back behind here."

El slipped out, and Niko sat against the old, broken crib. He tossed a small rock up and caught it in his palm, then repeated this again and again like a game.

"Don't do you no good to worry," Old Merrie told him. She reached into the cold compartment and pulled out a sandwich and another can of lemonade. Bringing them over to Niko, she grinned at him. "You troubled. I can see that, boy. Whatchyou got on your mind?"

"Ha," he laughed a humorless burst in spite of himself. He bit into the sandwich and drank from the can.

"Oh, nothing much," he said between bites. "The whole city's after me. Villinkash wants to hang me on TV. El hates me. And I shouldn't be running out on everyone like a rabbit. Other than that . . ." He continued eating the sandwich and stared at the dirt floor.

"I never pictured myself a hero," he mused, and looked up at the old woman, an unlikely rescuer. "I always just thought about staying alive. Living for the next day. Now . . ." He finished the sandwich and tossed the paper wrapping onto the dirt floor. "Now I think I have a duty to all those people out there risking their lives on account of me."

El appeared at the open wall, and when Old Merrie handed her a sandwich and drink, she took them as far from Niko as she could in that small space and squatted down to eat. Far off they could hear explosions that seemed to be coming more often. The sun had set, and dusk had crept in while they waited. Old Merrie leaned against her cart and hummed softly.

"Seem to me like you youngsters is joined at the hip for a while to come. I don't know what you gonna face on the other side. It ain't gonna be easy, but I 'spect it gonna be different. You got a whole mountain to get over if you heading for the Glimmer. And you gonna need each other. Wish't I could be there alongside you. To see it up close. To really be in Zamora.

"The people out there . . ."—she motioned toward the missing wall and the sound of explosions—"they doin' what they want to do for theirselves. They not thinking so much of you . . ."—she looked back at Niko—"or you . . ."—she pointed at El—"but of they own lives—of what they missin' and what they need, about they own hopes and about what's right and what's wrong. People can only put up with so much meanness, and when they reaches they boiling point, up the kettle top goes. That's right. These people out here, the ones blowing the lid off, they was ready to do what they doin'. What you done . . . you,"—she pointed to Niko—"and you . . ."—she nodded to El—"was just the instrument waiting be played by that orchestral band out there. Don't you go pay no mind to thoughts about you supposed to be a hero because that time might come and might not. People always say they want a hero. A great leader to take them to the promised land. But everything comes in its own time. And that promised land ain't noways here yet. Goin' to be a whole lotta destructions before that come to pass. Won't do nobody no good if you two was to be sucked up into the maw of that destructive beast. No, sir. Besides, didn't Jesus go into the wilderness and disappear for a time? You not the first to ponder what for you put on this Earth.

"Well, look like darkness comin' on soon, so we best get goin'. You ready to climb back in here?" She pushed the cart to the missing wall.

Huston gave his driver the night off, then sneaked into the garage situated two stories beneath his house and revved up a motorcycle he hadn't ridden in a year. With a helmet and jacket emblazoned with the insignias of a high-ranking officer of the Detectors Corps, he'd be regarded with fear by any Detainers he happened to meet and able to intimidate and arrest street people at random.

His plan was simple. If it worked.

After careening up the ramp from his underground hideaway, he made two stops on his way to The Perimeters. At the first, a storage depot controlled by the Regime, he collected plastic explosives and blasting caps. The guards didn't question him, because of the insignias, and gave him whatever he had requisitioned. He stored the caps and explosives in a pouch behind his seat. His second stop was the converted garage now boarded up and seemingly abandoned.

It was dark by then, and the explosions came more frequently. Sirens wailed in the distance, and no one was out on the streets. People who didn't have to be outside only wanted to hide until the mayhem subsided. The InCom screens continued to proclaim impossible numbers of arrests, but nobody believed them as none of their neighbors had been taken. They surmised it was all coming from The Shanty Alleys or The Hovels. Those people lived like animals anyway. The InCom also announced threats to "insurgents" and their families, although the Regime still had no idea who the insurgents were or how they managed to evaporate after each explosion.

By now, piles of rubble were strewn everywhere, even in The Ring, and from the roof of the Tower, huge balls of fiery debris rained down from time to time, lighting the night sky like hot orange meteors. Detainers were dispatched to climb all twenty-three floors to arrest the bombarders, but the perpetrators escaped, so instead they harassed the Tower's squatters.

Huston guided his motorcycle through the fence gap, being careful not to tear his jacket. Once in the backyard he went to the obvious door, not knowing about the secret entrance El had used. A deadbolt didn't thwart him. He took two hairpins from an inside jacket pocket, and with a few turns, while he listened closely to the sound of the tumblers inside the lock and applied just the right pressure, the bolt slid back. He was in. He squinted in the dark until he found candles and matches.

Of course, he thought as he struck a match, nuns would have candles. He looked up, and the first thing he saw was the hand-carved cross on a wall in front of him. Next he looked for an InCom, but he saw there was none in that room. The long table, the kitchen with its old porcelain sink, cupboards, simple wooden furniture, and only one rug under the table. This looked like a good place to start.

He carried one candle over to the rug, which was placed in an odd position toward one side of the large room and not centered under the table. And then he remembered: this used to be a garage. This must be it. He hurriedly walked over and, setting the candle on the floor, lifted the end of the table and moved it over. Then he pulled at one corner of the rug and hurled it back to reveal the door to a pit. He felt around with his fingertips, located a space between the boards, and there were the steep stairs down.

With light from the candle, he spotted the trunk, its lock already open, as if awaiting Huston's arrival. He couldn't believe it. Nothing was ever this easy. His foot grazed something hard: the crowbar Niko had used to pry the lock.

So, someone has been here. He opened the trunk and held the candle above it. There were a few empty bags and some papers in one corner. Pushing these aside, he spotted one bag, still tied shut. He pulled at it and set the candle by first tilting it to make a puddle of hot wax and then sticking the bottom of the candle into its middle until it hardened. It gave off a soft glow, and his eyes became accustomed to the soft light.

He pulled at the knot with his teeth, and it soon gave way enough that he could take it apart with his fingertips. And then, yes, it yielded to his touch. He placed it on the ground and sat down with it directly in front of him. Then he peeled back the top of the bag, and there, in the candle's light, the gold coins gleamed.

Huston dipped his hand in and pulled out a few of the coins. He held one close to the candle to look at its markings. He squinted at the image of Franz Josef and held it even closer to the light, turning it until he could make out the details on the back.

The Austrian Royal Crest and then *C Coronae MDCCCCXV 100 Corona*

Huston whistled softly and then turned the bag over to release all the coins in a heap, which he proceeded to count until he reached the last one. There were seventy-five in all, a small fortune in just this one bag. How many more bags had there been, and who had them now?

He dropped the coins back into the bag, stood and shut the trunk, took both candle and bag, and made his way back up the steps to the main room. After restoring the room to the way he'd found it, Huston sat down at the big table where El had eaten all her meals for fifteen years, where the sisters had nourished lost children and carved warm-from-the-oven homemade bread and spread hand-collected honey from their own hive, where tea had been brewed and prayers had been offered. Huston placed the bag of gold on that same table and allowed his mind to wander and wonder. It wasn't something he was accustomed to doing, so it felt foreign to him while, at the same time, soothing like some untapped undercurrent in his soul.

His mind went first to Saskia and how he had known her when he was a younger man. How lovely she had been. In his memory she was alluring and full of joy and excitement when first they had met. That first time—exactly how long ago was it?—in the garden of a friend's home, where she stood under a tabebuia tree in full bloom, her hair lit by the sun, a filmy skirt billowing like a silk sail about her legs, her head tilted back in laughter, her gold bracelets clinking each other. She had been like a beautiful bird surrounded by green and gold. He'd fallen in love in a way that surprised him. He'd always been the ruthless driver, always pushing and maneuvering, climbing to reach the next level, the next score, the better position, the greater wealth, the influence he craved, the importance he needed. And he had almost reached it on that day he saw Saskia, that day she lit up his life.

An older woman he'd had an affair with as a stepping stone to important connections, one of many in those years, noticed him staring and said, "She'll never tumble for you, dear."

"Why not?" he'd asked.

She'd wrinkled her nose and pointed to the sky. "She's way

up there. The daughter of the wealthiest old family in the city. I'd have thought you of all people would know that."

"I've never seen or heard of her. Why is that?" he'd asked because he'd always made it his business to get close to anyone who mattered.

"Her mother died in childbirth. Long ago she was sent away to a girls' school far away in some remote mountains. She's only just graduated. Her father wants her to marry well and preserve the family name and fortune."

"I see," he'd said.

"Rumor is he's fallen on hard times," she'd whispered. "And his money all came from the wife who died and left it all in trust to her daughter. Her family was in mining, you know. And that girl you're making goo-goo eyes at may just have inherited a fortune. So don't make a fool of yourself. Stay on your own side of the fence. You'll be better off that way."

But he pursued her anyway, almost as if her beauty was only part of the challenge. He wanted to capture her the way a hunter longs to capture a cheetah. It lured him not just for its beauty but for its speed in avoiding that capture. He may not have had the pedigree or the money at that time, but he had something just as valuable: determination. And no woman had ever gotten away once he'd decided he wanted her.

Thinking back on it now, he wondered if she had really been as reluctant as she seemed to be then. She had spurned him many times, but he wasn't deterred. And finally, she agreed to see him one night, just for a drink and dinner before she would let him down with a final thud. Yet he was still intent on winning her over, especially knowing she had no intention of seeing him a second time.

He held one gold coin between thumb and forefinger, turning it over and over as he allowed his memories to roam. He'd rented a fancy car for their date. Not to impress her so much as to make himself feel more important. When he knocked on her door, a uniformed maid opened it after looking through a peephole. She allowed him in and told him to wait while she informed Miss Saskia that she had a guest.

In the car, as they reached the end of the long winding driveway of her family estate, he'd stopped before advancing onto the road and said, "I don't think your maid approved of me."

Saskia turned to look at him, smiling. She was so beautiful in a simple sleeveless white silk blouse and a loose pale-blue skirt that rested lightly against her legs. Huston had the impression she'd just stepped out of one of those classical paintings in the city's museum, like someone had conjured her and she couldn't be real. A portrait of a princess too ethereal to touch.

"Should she approve of you?" she asked in a soft voice. She had a slight accent, from all those years in the girls' school, and around her neck she wore a slender gold chain with a matching gold cross.

He blurted without thinking, which was unlike him, "I suppose not."

He tilted his head as if listening for an argument or agreement, but all she said was, "I guess we'll see."

She perplexed him, and he drove on in silence. Once they were seated in the restaurant he cleared his throat as if to make a declaration. She giggled and unfolded her napkin.

"Are you nervous?" she asked.

He shook his head but said, "I've asked you out so many times. Why did you finally say yes?"

She fingered the cross for reassurance and said, "I'm not really sure. For one thing, I don't know very many people here. I've been away so long. And I was curious." She smiled and the waiter brought their drinks.

"Curious about what?"

"About whether you were as dangerous as they say you are."

"Who says I'm dangerous?" Now he was smiling.

"People."

"Oh, them. Do you think I'm dangerous?"

"I don't know yet. So far you don't seem to be."

"And what if I was? Would you run?"

She drank from her glass. "This is quite sweet. What is it?"

"Just something with a little rum in it. It's good for the appetite."

She drank again, then put the glass down. "I don't think I'd run. I don't scare easily. But since this is going to be our only meeting, I don't have to worry about being scared."

The dinner came. They ate and talked about the food. He ordered a bottle of wine, and they drank most of it. When they had finished and he had paid, he stood and pulled out her chair, acting as gentlemanly as he could. As she stood, his hand brushed her naked arm. It rested there a little longer than by accident but not long enough to be on purpose for certain. Then she turned briefly to look at him. He ignored it, though he'd felt a particular current at the touch of her skin.

As they returned to the street, he said, "Would you like to see my favorite spot for viewing the ocean at night? Since you've been living in the mountains for all these years, the ocean should be a treat for you, especially when there's such a big moon."

"How far is it?"

"Not far at all. Five minutes. It's just up that hill and around a few curves."

"All right." She smiled at him, and it seemed as if she had softened.

He took her arm then, firmly so she wouldn't think it was an accident this time, and walked her to the car and helped her in. He had no idea what was going on inside her at that moment, but he was sure he didn't want this evening to end. Not yet.

The coin dropped from his fingers and snapped him back to the table and the bag of gold and all that had happened since that night.

Gruen showed up at the address Fuller had given him and knocked twice on an old, rusted metal door. Someone opened it a crack.

"Jake?" Gruen asked.

"Yeah, what d'you want?"

"I came with something for Fuller."

The door swung wide and there was Shag with Jake, a rumpled guy in baggy pants and a dirty work shirt. His fingernails were black with grime, and in the farthest part of the room, Gruen could see motorcycles. It was illegal to be working on them outside the official factory, Gruen knew, so something was going on in there that shouldn't have been. Probably more than one thing.

Shag held out his hand, and Gruen gave him two heavy bags.

"I'm supposed to count it," he said.

"Go ahead. I don't give a shit what you do. But the job has to be done exactly at eleven, so you'd better haul ass and get back to your boss." He sneered at the word "boss."

Shag took the bag to a round table and opened it up. He dumped the coins, and Jake came to stand next to him.

"We could just kill this Scrounger and keep the gold," he said to Shag.

"Yeah, we could. But we won't, because Fuller's got some powerful allies, and they're the kind that like to hurt."

He finished counting, gave Jake his share, and went with Gruen to the door.

"Okay. I'll be at Fuller's in ten minutes, and the job will be done at eleven. Then we all better lay low."

"What time is it?"

"Don't worry. It'll all go off at eleven. And Fuller's got a closet with a huge battery backup, so he can keep going no matter what."

"I just want to know: Can they trace the power outage and the InCom change back to Fuller?"

"They can try. But Fuller says they'll be tracing right back to themselves and their own tracer in an endless futile loop," Shag said. He shook his head. "He's a genius with this stuff."

Huston roused himself from his musings and memories. The past was over. Yes, Saskia was still beautiful, but she wasn't here with him. She never would be. Her fate had been determined before that one night together when she'd given in to him with pleasure and they'd made love under the stars, facing the ocean that in those days still glittered with a million tiny sparkles and bright slashes of white under the moonlight.

He could barely believe it when she suggested they get out of the car to look down at the ocean. The flat rock ledge high above the water was better suited to eagles, but she showed no fear and laughed at the freedom of their perch.

"We could just take off from here and fly to the edge of the world," she'd said.

She'd raised her lovely bare arms. The bracelets clinked as they slid down, and she spun around like a dervish.

He'd been afraid she would fall, so he reached out for her without thinking, in what was his first unpremeditated act of the night. Because she was spinning so fast, his hands clasped her breasts instead of taking her at the waist, and he pulled her away from the rocky edge into his arms.

She'd tilted her head back and laughed again.

"Don't you want me to fly away?" she'd asked with a smile, her breath scented with wine.

"Never," he'd said, and leaned down to kiss her.

In spite of himself, knowing he had to get to The Protections before *they* did, Huston stood at the table, his hand covering the bag of gold coins, and remembered every delicious detail of that night. How she'd bent her body away from him for just a few seconds. And then how she'd let him kiss her. It was more than he'd dared hope. And what happened next astonished him. And then he forgot any plan he'd had. In a moment they were on the rock— she with her silk blouse unbuttoned and her skirt up around her waist, telling him to go ahead, to make love to her.

He'd done it quickly, so she wouldn't change her mind, so she wouldn't push him away. He'd laid his jacket under her body and taken off his trousers.

"Your shirt too," she'd said. "I want to feel your skin against mine."

Then their bodies were entwined, moving quickly, and she was so responsive that he had to hold himself back until she was ready, fully ready, and they reached their peak together.

When it was over, and her head rested on his bare chest, and they could hear waves crashing far below them, she'd asked, "Do you love me?"

"Yes," he'd said.

"Tell me," she'd said.

"I love you." It was the only time in his life he said those words.

"Then show me again."

They made love again, slowly this time.

But she never said those words to him. And how she really felt would remain a mystery to him. One month later, she was married. It was rumored they lived apart from the beginning and her new husband, Villinkash, gained control of a great portion of her money with the marriage and took over the city in a corrupt, prearranged, bloodless coup.

When the electricity and InComs cut off, the city erupted like a volcano. The only light came from constant blasts. These were bigger ones that rocked the streets. Chunks of cement flew and glass windows shattered, spiked shards crashing to the ground like hail. The frightening noise woke people from their sleep; children huddled and babies screamed. In the Tower of David, people came to the gaping openings where windows had once been to stare at the city that seemed to be descending into hell. If it was war, who were the factions fighting each other, they wondered. Rumors spread like smoke blowing on a wind that wasn't there at all, so still was the night except for the turmoil. Rumors said it was Villinkash blowing up the city to find Niko and El. But no one knew where they were.

Then, at exactly midnight, the InComs sprang back to life with Niko's face and a voiceover. The message that played over and over said:

"Resist!"

"Take back your city."

"Do not be afraid."

"The city belongs to the people."

They barely had time to say goodbye. Just as Niko and El turned to Old Merrie, there was an enormous explosion way beyond the main guard tower, and they could see all the guards streaming out of the towers toward the noise and fire that followed it. It was just one more explosion during a night of blasts going off all over the city.

El grabbed Old Merrie by the hands. They looked into each other's eyes.

"I may never see you again," she said. "Thank you for helping us and for showing me the Glimmer that day on the roof. I'll never forget you."

"Here." Niko saw Old Merrie pressed something hard and flat

into El's hand. "If I'd had a daughter, I'd'a given this to her. You take care out there."

Niko touched El's arm. "Come on, we have to run like hell now." He waved to Old Merrie and mouthed a thank you, and they took off for the tunnel.

Before they climbed down into it, Niko looked back along the barbed wire. A lone figure, Huston, stood by a motorcycle down near the first guard tower. It was not so far away, and, although maybe it was just a trick of the emergency spotlights playing on his face, to Niko Huston seemed to be smiling. Niko raised his hand to wave and then it occurred to him that Huston had set the explosion and, once again, Niko wondered at this crafty, improbable rescuer.

"Come on, Niko," El called from inside the tunnel. "It's so dark in here."

So Niko turned away and climbed down into the tunnel. Just before he disappeared from sight, he looked one last time. Huston had raised his arm in a salute. He just stood there, his shadow wavy on the ground from the spotlight. And then his hand snapped down, and Niko descended to the bottom where El was waiting.

He reached for her in the utter darkness and, finding her hand, took it in his and began to feel his way forward, leading El as one would a small child.

"Don't be afraid," he said, and they stumbled along, unable to stand upright. The dark closed like deep waters around them.

Old Merrie shut the doors on her cart. She stood and watched the horizon as if trying to gaze into the future, but all she could see were lines upon lines of barbed wire and sporadically placed gun stands where no sentries stood guard. These were strange days. She had been out here a few times before. Always there had been guards, ominous and ever-present. But she'd gotten them to come down off their stands, one by one, for special treats she'd managed to cadge. One time, she had cigars. Another time, bottles of icy cold beer. So when she heard footsteps at her back, she didn't flinch or even turn. Just kept staring as far as she could see.

"What're you up to, Old Merrie? Out here late at night like this?"

Huston's voice was gruff but somehow familiar. Maybe she'd done business with him before. Turning slowly with a big grin on her face, she said, "I got to make my living, don't I? Don't matter none to me what's happenin' on the street from day to day." She hummed a little. "You know that song? Keeps coming back to mind now and again."

"No, I don't know your song. And you'd better get on home before someone hauls your old ass in for questioning." He sounded rough, but she saw a tiny smile at the corners of his mouth. Or was it those strange lights, glaring and yet not completely illuminating? This light could fool you if you weren't careful.

Old Merrie bent over her cart and opened one door.

"I got pineapples today." She put a finger to her lips. "Give you a special price." She had to keep him occupied so he wouldn't see when Niko and El came out of the tunnel and had to get through the last two courses of barbed wire. "Are there others?" Now that he had spotted her, maybe he wasn't alone.

"They all got called away to deal with that big explosion. All hell's breaking loose over there since the lights went out." He came around to the cart and peered into the dark cavity. "What else you hiding in here?"

"I got a few yams left. Was goin' to cook 'em for my dinner, but if you want those too . . ."

He looked her up and down, looked all around The Perimeters, looked up at the guard stand, which was empty. "Anyone else would haul you in, anyway. Did you come all the way out here just on the chance someone wanted to buy some yams?"

It wasn't the usual way a guard would question a person. Something about him was different.

Old Merrie had been around a lot longer than the guards, a lot longer than most of the inhabitants of Infinius. She knew what they were capable of, what the Regime could do to a person. The thought ran through her mind that she could lean down as if to pull out a pineapple, grab the carving knife she kept in her cart, and slit this man's throat with one quick swipe. She could cut him up and dump his body parts all over the city, and no one would ever know. Yes, she could. It was just the two of them standing by The Perimeters. Just two people, each with a weapon, each with a need.

But having butchered pigs and steers in her earlier years, she knew how much blood there would be, and besides, she was no killer. She chuckled at herself, at him, at the situation.

"You bring me in, they goin' to laugh you right outta that place, honey. Best you take a pineapple and a yam home for supper and we both call it a day. What you say?" She grinned at him and leaned down to pull out the food. "Oh look, what else I got me in here."

She wrapped her stubby fingers around the neck of a bottle and lifted it up.

"Rum?" he asked.

Old Merrie winked at him. "I guess this'd make a nice punch for after working hours. What'd you think of that?"

"How much?" he asked.

For a second, she thought of giving him both the bottle and the pineapple, but she immediately thought that might look like a bribe and make him suspicious again. So instead she upped the price.

"Twenty-five." She said it fast and in a definite voice.

"Too much."

He'd taken the bait. She was almost giddy. She stared out past the barbed wires and saw, far in the distance, two small dots on the horizon. It looked like they were crawling on the ground, slowly, stopping now and then. She figured they must be cutting their way through the barbed wire, so she would have to drag out this negotiation.

"But this is a rare, special rum. I won't never have this bottle again. Been saving it for some higher-up one day who wants something he can't get nowhere. And here you are."

"I'll give you fifteen and no more."

"Well, but it's two—no, *four*—for the pineapple. It's the last one I got."

"Okay, then, fifteen plus two. Seventeen."

"No, I won't sell it at all. I should save it." She tilted her head and squinted at the barbed wires again as if considering her options. She knew he could just swipe it out of her hands. But something held both of them from moving out of this moment.

"Old Merrie, you're one mean old woman."

"No, I ain't. Just an old woman got to make a living with whatever I can."

They had disappeared over a rise. She knew those fences went on a long way, but with them out of sight, she could finish this up.

"I'll give you twenty and not one more."

"Twenty-two and they're both yours."

He fished in his pants pocket and pulled out some bills, handed them to her, and reached for the bottle. Old Merrie stuffed the bills into her skirt pocket, took out a pineapple, and wrapped it in an old piece of brown paper.

"There you are. You gonna enjoy your supper tonight."

She shut the bin door and turned her cart back to the dusty

path. It was much easier to push now. She bumped along after raising her hand in a backward wave at the man and the others who were now too far beyond The Perimeters to see her.

Huston watched two tiny dots moving slowly out beyond the most distant barbed wire. He would go back to Villinkash and report that The Perimeters were secure, that no one knew where the two of them were hiding. He would make a great show of anger and frustration. He would get his lieutenant to fix the barbed wire and then give him safe passage with his family out of the city on a boat leaving for a place so far away he would never come back to tell what he'd been instructed to do.

Huston had no way of knowing what would happen to Villinkash and the rest of them, but he was determined to survive this as he'd survived everything else. He was as sure of that as he was of the bag of gold hidden in the pouch behind his seat as he gunned the engine and climbed the hills that led back to her house. He grinned as he thought of those two dots in the dark landscape heading for some promised land to find the love that had escaped him eighteen years ago.

He made the last swerve to her drive fast, too fast, but he didn't care. He was high on the changes happening on this darkest night, on the heat and the smell of explosions and fires hanging in the air. He was high on their escape and on his own sense of adventure. Indeed, he thought, when there is chaos, there is opportunity. You can hide a lot in chaos. You can change minds and affect outcomes. He hadn't started this uprising, but he'd known it would come at some point. He was glad it was here.

He roared into her driveway and sped along until he arrived at the house, skidded to a stop, and fairly jumped off the bike. It was like being a kid again. Free and careless and bold.

He pounded on the door and saw a sliver of light at the bottom growing stronger. Then the door opened a crack, so he pushed it wide. The same servant stood there in a bathrobe and slippers, holding an oil lamp. She looked confused. And then afraid.

"Where is she?" he barked at her.

Before the servant could answer, he saw Saskia behind her.

She hand-signed to the servant, "It's all right, Nora, let him come in."

He brushed past the old woman. And there was Saskia in a soft sleeveless silk robe over matching pajamas, her hair down around her shoulders in curls like waves on the sea. She held a candle to light her path. Her feet looked like fluffy birds, all pink and frothy. For a moment, Huston hesitated.

"Follow me," she said, and turned.

She led him to a sort of den with a desk and couch and stuffed velvet chairs, bookcases and lamps, and a small serving trolley on wheels with glasses and bottles of liquor. She put down the candle and lit two others so the room was infused with the intimate, old-fashioned light of a Vermeer painting.

She shut the door and went to the trolley.

"Drink?" she asked.

He shook his head.

"Tell me about your wedding. Was the marriage consummated?" he asked, his voice low.

"You've turned obvious over these years," she answered him.

"I was always obvious," he said. "Isn't that what you saw in me?"

"What makes you think I ever saw anything in you?"

Even after all that had happened, she could still make him feel like a boy from the wrong side of town. "Was it?" he asked again.

"Why do you care?"

"Because I have to know. Did you marry him for the power, for the position?"

"To ask me such a question is to demean yourself, not me."

"Answer me. Did he fuck you?" Now his voice was louder. More demanding.

"You mean the way you did?"

"I never did. We made love. There's a difference. You were more than willing. You wanted it. Now answer me or I'll . . ."

"You'll what? Strike me? Rape me? Kill me? I died long ago, except for one thing. One thing kept me alive all these years. And now I hear it's happening. And I'm happy. For the first time in all these years, I'm happy."

She poured herself a shot of vodka and drank it off.

"Why did you come here?"

"Because I have to know. Did he fuck you? Just answer me that one question."

"You men get so hung up on a woman's virginity. You think you were my first and then there was nothing for nineteen years? What is so important about a body, anyway? Just a bunch of water and some bones. And a little of this." She poured another drink and he was at her side, her wrist in his grasp as she held the glass.

"I'm not hung up, as you put it, on your body. I just want to know if you gave yourself to him the way you gave yourself to me."

"And what if I did? Or didn't? What difference does it make now?"

"It makes a difference. Now tell me. Did he fuck you after me? Did he?"

She stared at him, his fingers tight around her wrist. And something in her loosened, like a belt falling away. He let go of her hand, and she put down the glass.

"All these years, I've lived alone like a nun. Worse, I didn't even have God to love. Knowing you were out there, in the city, so close and so far. Me and Nora going about our daily lives, our little routines. You say you have to know about him. There is nothing to know about him that you don't already know. Did I love him? Did he love me? Did we share our lives? Am I invested in his power? How can you ask such things? And yet you do."

"Did he? I have to know."

"And you. Going to him. Always going where the power was. You at his side, helping him in all his degradation. More than helping him—*allowing* him and all that he did. I heard about it. Heard about everything you did. Saw the results."

He grabbed her wrist again and twisted it so her arm was pinned against her back, so hard he could have snapped it off.

She glared at him, defiant, knowing he could hurt her. Not caring. Then something in her softened.

"No, I never slept with him. The marriage was purely a monetary arrangement. He needed the prestige and the money, and I needed to save my father's life. Well, as it turned out, he died from grief and loss and whatever else you want to assign to what happened.

"So, are you satisfied? Now that you know?"

Huston picked up the glass of vodka and drank it in one gulp.

"I have something for you," he said. "It may not mean much to you. But I want you to have it. Will you wait here while I go to get it?"

He walked swiftly out to his bike, took the bag from behind the seat, and let the top of the pouch snap shut. Then he walked quickly through the dark house toward the soft light emanating from the room where he'd left her. He felt like every nerve in his body was on fire. His muscles taut and his eyes focused only on her, he entered the room and took her hand in his and led her to the couch. Then he placed the bag of gold into her hands and let go of her.

"It's all I could find, but there must be more."

She untied the bag and opened it slowly. Then she laughed. Threw her head back and howled with laughter until she struggled to breathe. When finally she could contain herself, she turned to look at him.

"What is this?" she asked. "Are you trying to buy me now? Do you think I'm for sale to the highest bidder? That I'm as corrupt as you?"

"Think whatever you want about me. You're right. I was ambitious. I would have done anything. And I did a lot that you would say was depraved, evil. I make no excuses. I was already on a trajectory when Villinkash showed up.

"But this . . . this is for Niko. Now I know for sure. For our son. Keep it for him. One day he'll need it. One day when he . . ."

"When he what?"

"I can't say now. Just keep it. I think there must be more somewhere in that convent, but there's no time for me to search now. I have other tasks to perform. And if I don't come out a success, then only you will know. But one day you'll understand that what I've done in the past, and what I'm about to do now, was all for him."

"Our son?" she asked, her voice soft now. "Is that why you wanted to know about . . ."

Huston nodded. He held back a sob.

"I'm glad you know."

"I suspected but was never sure."

Saskia reached up and touched his cheek with her fingertips and ran them down to his lips and then pressed one fingertip on his mouth.

He took her hand in his and said, "Don't. Not unless you mean it. Not unless you meant it years ago. I wanted to see you again, but you were closed off to me. And then . . . when I heard about the baby, I almost went crazy. So don't do this now. Not unless . . ."

She pressed her finger to his lips again.

"Shhh, Lawrence. Be quiet."

And he was. As her robe fell down from her shoulders and the buttons on her silk pajamas came undone and his hand caressed her breast and his lips found hers. He was quiet for all that and quiet as she gave herself to him again, and quiet as their bodies melted into each other, and quiet until the very last moment when she breathed, "Lawrence, you came back to me."

Niko was in bad shape. Getting through the last of the barricades after the tunnel, especially the barbed wire, had left him with deep cuts caked with blood and dirt. And there was that limp. Though it did not completely hinder him from walking or climbing, it was persistent. And it was getting worse. Since they had traveled at night, El didn't see the extent of the damage until they came out of the cave to the morning light. When she did see his battered arms and the gashes on his legs, she gasped.

"You can't travel yet," she told him.

"We have to get farther away. They'll be tracking us." But he sank down, exhausted, and laid his head against the side of a rocky ledge.

In the tunnel, El had been afraid.

"It's so dark," she'd said. "What if there are rats or snakes?"

"Here," Niko had told her. "Take my hand. I'll go first. Is your backpack okay? Is it too heavy?"

"No. I can handle it."

He took her hand and stepped in front of her. That way they fumbled along in the dark tunnel until they could feel outside air.

"I think we're coming to the end," Niko had said, and yes, there was the opening to a night with no moon or stars visible.

There were courses of barbed wire to get through, though, and Niko set to work cutting with a tool he'd managed to scrounge. El kept watch behind them. At any moment, motorcycles might come barreling up, but it was silent and the fire still burned from that huge explosion. They inched forward.

"It must have hit an ammunition pile," she told Niko. "Or maybe gasoline drums."

"Come on," he urged. "Go through this hole in the wire."

He held it apart, and El wedged herself through. Niko handed her the backpack and tossed his through the hole. Another big explosion shook the night, illuminating even them so far away, and they heard a siren. Niko rushed forward and flattened himself on the ground, scraping himself along some barbs. He held back from yelping with the sudden, searing pain, and lurched forward until he was through the hole.

And then they picked up their packs and ran. Ran, it seemed, forever. Stumbled and fell and picked themselves up and ran and ran until finally El fell down to her knees, panting, exhausted.

"Okay," Niko breathed, huffing for air, "let's rest for a minute."

"Water," El said, reaching out to him. Niko handed her an open canteen and she drank. Then he drank and closed it back up.

They stood and ran some more. They ran and ran, and finally, when they were sure no one was behind them, they walked. It seemed like they walked all night until they sank down in a field and fell asleep from exhaustion. Later they awoke and walked and walked on and on. The ground began to rise, and they realized they had begun to climb as the sun came up behind them. They climbed all day. At first the rising sun was at their backs, then overhead, then in front of them, and then they followed the stars as El had learned from the sisters in astronomy lessons.

That night the clouds cleared, and when the half-moon rose and the stars dimmed, it gave off enough light to see well-trodden animal paths up the mountain. It was easy to know they were ascending steadily because their breathing became more labored and their legs ached with the effort. By the time they happened upon a cave in a rock wall, they had long since used up all their water and food.

As they approached it, Niko cried out, a sharp cry of pain.

"What is it?"

"Nothing," he said. "Go on. Get in the cave."

At dawn El woke first. She glanced over at Niko and could just make out dried blood on his torn shirt shoulder.

She went to the cave opening and surveyed the area. How they'd found this cave was a miracle in itself. She could hear water running somewhere nearby. This was a good sign. An omen. She went back into the cave and looked through the knapsacks they had managed to carry with them. Ah! She found a small medical kit. It was one of those throwaway kits the nuns had kept in reserve for Scavengers who came to their door with wounds. They would treat the wounded and send them back out with these kits. She opened it and found everything she'd need.

"I'm going to find that water I hear," she told Niko, who by then had opened his eyes to take in the cave and their situation. El slung a mess kit over her shoulder. It held a plate, a cup, a one-piece silverware gadget, and she had also stuffed it with a small flat dish towel. "I wish I had a bucket," she added.

"Be careful."

She turned to him and said, "If I'd been careful I wouldn't be here in the first place, so it's a little late to warn me now."

"I only meant—" he began, but stopped and pointed to the canteens lying beside him.

El grabbed them and knelt down to make sure her boots were well tied. Finding water and food, fixing up Niko so he could travel again. These were what she faced now.

"Are you okay?" she asked. "Did something happen before we got to the cave? It sounded like you got hurt."

"No, no." He shook his head. "But I'm going to stay put for now. You go on out and see what's there."

Looking around she spotted a stout, straight branch, hip

height for her, and took it firmly in one hand. With this walking stick, the canteens, and mess kit, she headed off in the direction of the water sound and, in a short time, located its origin. Spilling over the ledge farther down from the cave, a waterfall's graceful arc greeted her. There was a wide ledge that stretched along a ravine to the left of the cave. This was where they had traversed at sunset to find the cave. But there was also a well-trodden animal track—probably deer or mountain goat—that went down along beside the ledge through the overhanging forest. That made sense. Animals would go to water. So, carefully picking her way down, using the stick to steady herself, she followed the path, and yes, saw deer hoof prints and what looked like possibly raccoon tracks as well. All this cheered her. Soon they would have water to drink, and if she made a fire, they could also cook with it.

Carefully following the path, she came to a spot where the waterfall reached a rock platform with hollows from eons of water pressure. Water filled pools before continuing to spill farther down the mountainside. From where she stood she could not tell how far. The morning sun peeked in speckled patterns through the tree canopy, and a gentle breeze fluttered the leaves so El felt herself like a person in a biblical Eden. If only she weren't a renegade she would have been completely at peace. Birds twittered and sang all around her. Mist from the falls dampened her skin. She lifted her face to the canopy of green. This was so different from the stagnant heat of the city. Air so pure it felt like medicine to breathe it in.

She sat down and put her walking stick, canteens, and kit to her side on a flat rock. In front of her a clear pool of water plunged into and out of a wide, smooth depression in the granite rock, carved like the others from the waterfall. It looked to be about three feet deep at the center. She watched it in wonder, transfixed by its endless motion and hypnotic sound. She could stay here forever and never miss anything she had known. Why was life so hard? What had she ever done to deserve the punishments meted out to her?

She lay back on the rock and listened to the forest. Turning her head, she noticed something red and small to her right. Berries! Yes, wild strawberries covering the ground in a delicate profusion. And blackberries, too, growing on purple-green canes that arched above the ground reaching for the sun. She scrambled over and picked handfuls of the juicy berries, cramming them into her mouth in bunches. Purple juice ran down her arms and covered her hands, but she persisted. Never had she been so unaware of her own hunger until the sweetness of those berries reached her parched tongue.

After she'd had her fill, she looked around for some extra-large leaves, which she found not far off. She had to push the blackberry canes with her stick to avoid being scratched, but she made it to what looked like a poplar tree. It had wide, three-lobed leaves, perfect for her purpose. She pulled off four of them and also found a few slender, pliable young branches, which she pulled off at their growing points. Out of these she would make leaf cups by folding the leaves—two points to each other and the third point up and above to fill in the open space, then weaving the slender branches into the seams.

When done, she filled two cups with blackberries, and for the other two, she set about gathering wild strawberries. It would have taken a long time to fill if the berries hadn't been so plentiful, but the waterfall's mist combined with the altitude seemed to perfectly suit them as if cultivated in a garden. She ate some, collected some, ate some more, and finally filled the cups to the very top.

Back at the rock, she found a young vine, and with the knife part of the mess kit's cutlery tool, she cut a slender length and looped this through the cups of berries. Thus she could carry her harvest back to the cave. Now that she'd eaten and prepared for later, she realized she was caked with dust and dirt from the escape. The pools looked so inviting, and the air had grown warmer as the sun rose farther in the sky. So El decided to take a few moments for herself.

Carefully she looked around her in all directions, which seemed foolish since who could have seen her? Still, habits are difficult if not impossible to change, and when she was confident of her solitude, she removed her pants and shirt, bra and underpants. At least she hadn't been cursed with her period so far. But that would come, and she'd have to deal with it. She crouched down to untie her boots and remove the socks that now stuck to her feet.

Ahhh, the air was cool. The mist refreshing, the forest scents sweet. She dipped her toes into the pool, then extended her legs farther down. Icy cold water set her skin tingling. No time to waste, no time to dawdle, and thinking about Niko waiting atop the ledge for her to return, she dipped her body into the water and laid her back against the cold rock beneath her. Every nerve ending stood at attention, so cold was it, and yet so delicious. There was only one thing left to do. She let her head sink backwards into the water far below the waterline. She shook her head so all her hair was soaked in water, and with her hands, she rubbed the dirt from her face and ears and neck.

She stood quickly and steadied herself on the ledge, then climbed out to stand naked and dripping in the sun and breeze. Taking her underthings, pants, shirt, and socks in hand, she doused them under water rushing from above the pool to wash out the dirt and sweat of their escape. Afterwards, she wrung them out as best she could and laid them on a rock to dry in a sunny spot that appeared as if on command. Finally, she dipped the two canteens into the clear water, until they were filled to the brim, and screwed the tops on tightly. With all her chores finished, El settled herself naked on the warm rock and fell into a deep sleep, caressed by the midday updrafts from the canyon floor far below.

The raucous cry of a crow wakened her, and she hastened to dress. Miracle of miracles, her clothes were nearly dry and now smelled of the waterfall. She could begin the climb back to where she'd left Niko at the cave. A glance at the sun overhead told her it was past noon but still early.

Going back was more difficult, but not impossible. It was slower, and she had to be more careful as she was carrying so many more items. But she made it and, rounding the corner, spotted Niko right away. He stood with his weight resting on one leg, the other bent at the knee. He leaned on a tree branch with a crotch where it had branched off, using it like a crutch, and watched with narrowed eyes toward the dense forest. He had made a circle of stones and gathered dry kindling, stacked it in a fashion to allow air to circulate, and stuck it through with dried pine needles and leaves. Next to the circle he had stacked dry wood.

"So you hurt your leg?"

"It's the ankle. I must have turned it wrong last night."

"Can you put weight on it?"

Niko shook his head. He looked disgusted with himself. "This isn't going to help us get anywhere. Maybe you should go on alone."

"No. That doesn't make any sense at all. Here, I've got some food." She handed him the cups strung together with the piece of vine. "I think there might be fish if I could get to a calmer pool of water."

He took the vine and poured the berries from each leaf cup straight into his mouth as if he'd never had a meal.

"Where did you find them?" he asked between mouthfuls.

"Not far. There's a waterfall. Here." She handed him one of the canteens, and he drank his fill.

"Are there more?"

"Plenty. What's this?" She pointed to the stone circle at the mouth of the cave.

He shook his head until he'd swallowed. "I thought about making a fire. Do you think they'd be able to spot it way up here?"

This was a question that had been on El's mind too. How much could they trust the dense forest to hide them? And if they made a fire, would it be obvious from the ground? Did the Regime have flying craft to hover above them? Had they begun searching outside the city Protections? There was no way to know the answers for sure. She had never seen anything but a blimp. And she'd never heard of anything else. They seemed only to have developed the few technologies they needed to keep the city population subservient and cowed.

"Is the wood very dry?"

"Yes. I don't think it'll make much smoke. But fires can be tricky. Maybe we won't see smoke but . . ." There was still the smell of it, depending on the wind direction.

"I wonder how far we came from the Protections."

Niko shifted his weight a little. "Let's see, we traveled all night and one day. And we climbed for a lot of that. We seem to be facing west." He was quiet.

"You're thinking about it, aren't you?"

Niko nodded, afraid to say the name out loud. Afraid they might never find it, that it didn't really exist, that they'd come all this way for what?

"Do you think it's a myth?"

He shrugged. "Who am I to say yes or no?"

"Well, there's no reason to make a fire if we have nothing to cook on it. And we need to get your wounds cleaned up. Can you still walk?"

"I think so. I've been hobbling around up here anyway. And I have this." He pointed to the tree crutch with his free hand. "I used my hunting knife to cut it to size."

It was slow going down to the pools at the waterfall, but they made it. At times Niko had to lean on El for support. They had never truly made peace, but in their situation, with the storm at their back and the hope of salvation ahead, they took their reliance on each other for granted in a tacit, if not specified, peace treaty. At one point El looked up to a narrow rock ledge across from the falls to see a mountain goat perfectly balanced on what looked to be three inches of rock outcropping. It watched them with steady eyes from what appeared a precarious perch but the goat seemed unconcerned for its welfare up there. El took that as another sign that they were safe, positioned as they were closer to the clouds than the plains, at least for the moment.

They carried with them the medical kit, a towel, a mess kit, and both canteens. Also, although it was more of a burden, they had brought a knapsack with supplies that might be useful.

"Wow." Niko whistled as the waterfall came into sight. "Never seen anything like this."

"We're headed for those pools below." El pointed to where she had bathed and washed her clothing. "I think farther down in the quieter pools there could be fish."

They made their way farther down until they came to the depressions in the rock cliff. Niko sat down, worn from the descent. He let the crutch fall by his side and just sat there, watching the endless cascading water and listening to its reverberating rush. Mist clung to his face and arms, and spots of sun lit glistening droplets of water as they splashed off the rocks.

"Come on," said El. "You need to take off your shirt and pants."

She set about the business of a nurse, unpacked the medical kit, and found it had everything she'd need.

Niko unbuttoned his shirt, slowly slid one arm off, and tried to do the other but winced in pain, as it was stuck to some cuts.

"We need warm water," said El. She opened the knapsack and, in an inside pocket, found a lighter. "We can make a fire on the rock here. We'll just have to chance it. Take off your shoes so I can look at what's causing you to limp."

Niko tried to bend his knee to reach his boot, but he couldn't manage it and again winced with pain.

"Let me take it off for you." She knelt down on the flat rock and unlaced the boot, then pulled its sides as wide as she could to relieve any pressure when she pulled it off.

"Owwww," he breathed as she unleashed it from his foot.

"Now the sock," she said, and seeing the foot for the first time, she could tell something was drastically wrong. The ankle was swollen to the size of a grapefruit. "Hopefully it's just a sprain and nothing's broken. I can't tell until . . ." She began to work the sock as gently as she could, trying not to put pressure on the ankle.

"Go ahead," he said. "Just yank it off."

"No, I can do it this way." Inch by careful inch she managed to slide it down until it was over the most swollen part. She stopped and grabbed the canteen, which she had filled in the icy water of a pool. Then she poured the whole thing over his ankle, soaking the sock. This made it easier to stretch over the swelling, and little by little, she worked it down past his heel until she could pull off the whole thing.

Niko let out a long breath and closed his eyes. "How bad is it?"

"I don't think it's broken. There's no blood, nothing sticking out. Just a really bad sprain, I think. Drop your foot in that water pool and let it get cold. I'll try to find something to bind it with."

Before she did that, she went about gathering stones to make the kind of circle Niko had made up at the cave. Then she gathered sticks and leaves and larger pieces of wood for a fire. She raised her face to the breeze to feel which way it was blowing and built a small fire downwind of where they had stationed themselves. She made some more leaf cups and gathered berries and found a patch of large fiddleheads that hadn't yet opened to fronds. These she cut off at their base with the small knife from the mess kit.

Nurtured by the shade and mist, there were also pale-gray and beige morels growing in abundance nearby. She brought all this back and laid it on the rock. Afterwards she looked for a flat rock to rest above the fire on the circle. This would make her pan. She washed this rock in a pool and then made the circle so this flat rock would balance across it. Once the sticks and kindling were in place, the larger pieces of wood rested atop and the flat rock above that. She lit the kindling with the lighter, and it sprang to life right away, so dry was the kindling and wood.

"Here." She handed the berry cups to Niko and kept one for herself.

She filled the metal canteen again and secured the top firmly, then laid it flat on its side on the rock, which was already warming from the fire. It wouldn't take long before they had warm water, but first she had to bind that ankle to get the swelling down.

"I need your knife," she told Niko.

It was still in its leather sheath strapped to his leg. He looked at her for a moment, and his fingers went unconsciously to where the scar was hardening on his cheek.

"I have to cut some vines to make a tight wrap around your ankle." She took the flat towel out and held it up.

Niko slid the knife out and handed it to her.

"I'll be back soon. But I think we can get your shirt off now with warm water." She touched the canteen and it felt warm, so she picked it up and unscrewed the top. "Lift up your arm if you can."

Niko held out the arm with the sleeve stuck with caked blood. El slowly dribbled warm water over the bloodied part. As she poured with one hand, she carefully released the fabric starting at the outer edges. As she continued, the shirt did begin to release until it came to the middle where the wound was deepest.

"This may hurt," she told Niko.

"I'm okay," he said. "Go ahead. Rip it off."

"No. I don't want it to start bleeding again." She dribbled more warm water on it and painstakingly released it a tiny bit at a time until, all of a sudden, it came away, leaving the gash exposed to the air.

"Well," she said. "That's it." Putting the shirt aside, she reached for the medical kit and rummaged through it until she found peroxide and bandages. She set about tending the wound but didn't apply a bandage yet. "I'll wait for that," she told Niko. "We have to get your pants off so you can bathe first. Then we'll dress all the wounds."

Niko nodded. "I'll do that while you're cutting vines."

El refilled the canteen and laid it on the hot rock and added a few pieces of wood to the fire underneath. Then she disappeared into the forest.

Niko managed to get his other shoe and sock off and slowly slid his pants off one leg at a time. He couldn't get the last leg past his swollen ankle, so he left his pants and underwear hanging half-off and slid into the cold pool. Immediately his skin tingled, and he felt as if he'd been submerged into an iced drink. The days were still long, and the sun shone in the west above the trees.

He rubbed the dirt off his face and neck, ducked his head below the frigid water, and came up gasping but with an exhilaration he'd never felt before. He wanted to get right under the falls, let them wash over him to wash away the taint of The Race and everything that had happened after it except for the past few days with El. Those he would always keep close, untouched. That was what mattered now. To be the man who deserved her love.

He reached out of the water to pull his shirt in so he could wash all his clothes in the clear running water. His cuts and the gash on his arm hurt, but the frigid water had a slight numbing effect that allowed him to move more freely. Soon he felt clean and dragged himself up onto the flat rock. He laid his clothes out to dry. His one pant leg and underwear were still attached at the ankle. Then he lowered himself down on his back.

Staring at the sky through rustling leaves, he thought back on all that El had done for him since they'd reached the cave and the falls. He would find a way to repay her, to make up for what he'd done, to show her what was truly in his heart.

As these thoughts ran through his mind, he relaxed and sleep overtook him. The sleep of someone tired in mind and body. A sleep of contentment in the moment.

When he woke, El was still not back. His underwear and pants were dry enough to struggle back into them. He left the shirt off and, for the first time, noticed that the cuts ran through one of the first tats he'd gotten when he'd joined a gang. Most of those people were dead now, and the gang had morphed long ago into something alien to him.

He pondered these life changes, thinking about what he'd done to stay alive and how he'd come to this remote spot with nothing familiar around him. Nothing from the old life except El. And his memories.

El didn't have to go far to find slender, strong vines. Using Niko's knife, she began right away. She cut them near the ground, then pulled as hard as she could to release their hold on the branches above. Some swirled down easily, while others hung up higher in the trees. These she pulled as far as she could and cut them off, then moved to others until there was a pile of curling vines all around her. Most were wild grape, but a few she couldn't identify. After trimming the leaves off she wound them into circles like ropes, left them hanging from a low branch, and moved farther into the forest to repeat the procedure. With enough vines, she could make any number of useful items.

After gathering all the circles and hanging them from her shoulders, she followed her path back to the falls and found Niko sitting up, tending the fire, with morels and fiddleheads cut and lined up on the rock next to the fire, ready to cook. He had propped his foot up on a large branch he'd dragged over.

El dropped the vines and examined his ankle.

"Can you reach that knapsack?" She pointed to the one she'd carried down from the cave.

"What are you going to do?" Niko asked, and handed it to her.

"You'll see. Hopefully this will work."

She pulled the flat towel out of the bag. It was the thinnest piece of cloth they had except for their shirts. With the knife, she cut a long strip of the thinnest vine. She moved the log where Niko had elevated his foot so only the ball of his foot was on it, leaving the ankle with room around it. Then she wound the towel around it a couple of times so the ankle was completely covered. Holding the end of the vine at the very bottom of the wrap and on the outside of his ankle, she made a loop at the top. Then, holding the loop and starting at the top, first she threaded the other end of the piece of vine through the loop, then wound the vine over this loop as tightly as she could around the ankle, making sure the vine rings butted close against each other to almost completely cover the towel, putting pressure on the ankle as she went.

When she reached the bottom of the towel, she slid the remaining extra vine at the bottom back up into the top loop. The last step was to pull on the bottom piece of vine she had left untouched at the beginning down under the rings to about the middle, thus letting the pressure of the rings hold the whole thing in place.

"That should help reduce the swelling," she told Niko, and sat back to look at it. "But I wouldn't walk on it. Use that crutch until the swelling goes down."

"How did you come up with this?" Niko asked, inspecting the contraption on his ankle.

El shrugged. It was one of the things Father Ignatius had taught them. But he'd used it to show them how sailors kept rope ends tight. "It's called 'whipping.' For ropes on boats. To keep the ends from fraying."

She cut more vines in strips of the same length.

"What now?" Niko asked, watching her closely.

"We need to make some nets. To catch fish."

"Hand me some of those vines. I can do that if you show me how."

El taught him how to loop the vine ends and weave them in and out to make a slightly concave circle. When done she showed him how to weave another vine through all the end loops and pull it together so the top was a bit smaller than the rest, leaving a good length of vine as a sort of rope handle. He added two more vines as ropes to make an even three-rope system for holding the net steady.

El made her way with the first net down to a flat rock over-hanging a large pool. The afternoon sun shone on the water, and she could see a fat trout facing against the current, lulled into slumber. Carefully she lowered her vine-woven net behind and under the fish. Then, imperceptibly, she moved it directly beneath him and tilted it up at the front. The trout realized something was nearby, and as it suddenly thrashed sideways, the net was wide enough to thwart its escape and—wham!—she yanked it up. In an instant it was out of the water and the trout had been caught.

He flopped and struggled for a short time, then stopped. She laid him out on the ground and found another rock. She repeated the process until she had four good-sized fish. These she placed in the vine net and retreated to where Niko sat next to the fire, weaving nets. She handed him the fish, and he set about scraping the scales off while El collected large leaves to wrap them in.

She used one of the nets Niko had made as a pan, wrapped each fish with a generous amount of the morels and fiddleheads, and even threw in some berries before sealing each packet in more leaves and lining them up in the net. She placed this on the rock that was now hot from the fire beneath it. As the vine heated up and shriveled, the leaves inside began to steam. Soon the air carried an aroma so enticing that both El and Niko could hardly wait.

"I've never been so hungry," Niko said. He pulled out the mess kits and opened them up. "I guess we could have used these metal plates for pans."

"Probably." El nodded. "But I think this will work." Suddenly all she had done since the trek up the mountain, the climbing and foraging, weighed on her. With still a few hours of daylight left, she felt as if this day had lasted a week. And the last week had been a month. She looked at her hands. Callouses were starting to form, and there were scratches all over her forearms. She went to the pool again and cleaned her hands and arms, dangling them in the icy water to soothe the muscles and skin. When she turned back, Niko had arranged a place for them to eat.

With two forks he slid what was left of the net to the edge of the rock and opened it. Steam rose in a cloud, filling the air with a sweet scent of fresh fish and a nutty aroma of cooked morels. Niko slid two of the leaves onto one plate and handed it to El. She brought the canteens over and sat down by the warm fire. They pulled the leaves apart and ate the supper they'd worked so hard to create.

After finishing, they discarded whatever scraps were left of the meal by tossing it all as far down the waterfall as possible. Then they splashed water a number of times from their canteens to clean the area and buried the fire without wetting it. Tomorrow they would rebuild and cook again. But it was best not to encourage animals to poke around by leaving food scraps near their campsite.

With his crutch on one side and El on the other for support, they made their way back up to the cave. It was not as daunting as the hike down, and the compression wrap El had made seemed to help. The throbbing had stopped, and after a few days, he would be able to put weight on it once again.

The last chore before they could fall asleep was to make some sort of bed inside the shallow cave.

El gathered sheets of thick moss and laid them out on the cave floor. She covered these with branches of hemlocks that had fine, feathery needles. Then she gathered the biggest leaves she could find and laid them over the hemlock branches. When she was done, Niko crawled over to try it out.

"It's perfect," he said. Before he could say another word, his eyes closed and he was asleep.

El stretched out next to him. Although just a few days before she had wanted to kill him, she felt no fear now. There was left only a deep, empty fatigue that sleep could fill. She breathed deeply and sighed.

The forest was waking up outside the cave. Night sounds came to her. Katydids screeching in the trees. The rushing of wind through leaves, an owl hooting far off and dimly, the waterfall behind it all. Soon her eyelids felt heavy. One arm twitched.

Her leg muscles relaxed, and she gave in to a restful sleep that had eluded her for too long.

El marked their days in the cave with one line for each night. She drew the lines with a sharp rock on the cave wall. There was plenty of food. She even found edible beautyberries and wild cherries. She stole eggs from birds' nests. Niko's ankle improved with the pressure bandage El had made, and he soaked it in the frigid waterfall as often as he could. After the swelling subsided, he began to exercise it. By the seventh day, he could put some weight on it.

"We can't stay here forever," he said to El after their first week at the cave.

"I know. I wish we could. It's so peaceful."

"But the weather's sure to change. And if it gets cold, what will we do? There won't be berries and fronds. The fish will go deeper. And it might snow."

"I've never seen snow," El said.

"I haven't either. But in the mountains, if it gets cold enough, rain becomes snow. We'd freeze."

"Do you think you can walk yet?"

"I'm going to try without the crutch today. It doesn't hurt anymore. I think I'll be fine. And the shoulder cuts are all healing."

"Do you think Zamora really exists?" El asked, almost to herself.

"I hope it does. We have to be heading somewhere."

They were both browned. Their legs and arms trim and firm from being outside all day, from swimming in the pool beneath the waterfall, and collecting food and wood for the fire, which had burned steadily since they'd first started it.

Finally, after two weeks at the cave, it was time to leave. They packed what was left in their knapsacks, filled their canteens, gathered as many berries as they could pack, and rolled up cooked trout in wide leaves. They figured they could gather more food as they descended the other side of the mountain. But first they had to reach the summit. They took their walking sticks, tied their boots, finished their breakfast, buried the fire, and took off for Zamora as soft amber light spread over a new day.

It didn't take long to reach the summit. They followed goat and deer tracks almost the whole way up. They didn't have to traverse any ledges or cut through branches of felled trees. At one point they stopped to rest and drink some water, and found blueberries growing in profusion, so they gobbled as many as they could hold and then sat for a while to digest.

While resting quietly, a twelve-point buck appeared in a small clearing. One front hoof raised, it stared at them. Neither the buck nor Niko or El moved, and the buck finally wandered off.

And so they reached the very summit of the mountain. Although neither of them had ever been to a mountain, much less to the very top of one, there was no question they had arrived, for the view was all around and everywhere. They could see where they'd left Infinius and, to the north of it, an arid plain; to the east, the sea which, from way up there, looked like a thin blue, far-off line. Below, to the south, was a forest canopy. From where they stood it looked dense and impenetrable. And there, to the west, there it was, as they had seen it once before, each of them separately and now together, able to confirm that their eyes hadn't deceived them.

Old Merrie's tale had been true.

The Glimmer.

It did exist. Closer now and more vibrant, beckoning them onward. They looked and looked, unable or unwilling to give up the sight of that place where anything might be possible.

"We'd better go," Niko finally said.

"How long do you think it will take to reach it?"

"That?" He pointed to the Glimmer, and El nodded.

"I'm still not sure if it exists or what it is. It can't be Zamora because it just looks like light and color."

"Maybe that's what Zamora is," said El.

"No. It can't be only that. There must be people and buildings and . . ."

"And what?" El asked. "What do you think Zamora will be like?"

"Different," said Niko. "Not like Infinius. Not like anything we know."

They started down the mountain. It didn't take nearly as long as the ascent had so many days ago. They made some hairpin turns and scrambled over rocks and fallen trees. Soon it wasn't so steep anymore. Breathing was easier, and they came to a shady glen where the land flattened out with rolling hills and smaller vegetation. They kept walking west toward the Glimmer, which they couldn't see anymore, and the air had a sweet, wet scent.

They came to a large lake and walked around the edge of it on sand and pebbles until they came to a trail and followed it with the morning sun behind them until it was overhead. They stopped to eat and drink water. They did not talk. There was nothing to say now. They had only a desire to arrive. But where, they weren't sure. Not yet.

They walked until the sun was low in the sky. As it disappeared, a momentary red blaze was followed by pink and orange and lavender washing across the sky like chiffon veils.

El said, "We'll need to sleep somewhere. We can't walk at night."

In a little while, before them, spread out like a blooming sea, wildflowers waved in the evening breeze: something neither of them had ever seen before. Nor had they felt such a soft breeze caress their bodies. There was a sweet, fresh scent in the air as they wandered slowly into this endless field that now surrounded them.

Niko stopped. He brushed the tops of flowers near his fingers. He leaned down to breathe in their perfume.

"I never imagined there could be anything this beautiful. How is it possible that the city became so ugly, so stale?" He shook his head. "Are there other places like this in the world?"

"Look." El pointed to a slight rise with willow trees growing at its edges, their feathery branches grazing the ground like tresses. "Let's stay under those trees."

When they reached the rise, they saw, at one edge of it, a spring burbling to the surface from somewhere deep underground. Near it a rabbit nibbled at fresh green shoots. As they approached, it looked up, its nose twitching, its ears at attention, then went back to nibbling at the shoots. It sensed no danger in El and Niko.

They took the far side of the rise so as not to disturb the rabbit and, pushing aside the willow branches, found a small glen in the center surrounded by the weeping trees. Niko took out his hunting knife and cut some soft willow branches, laying them in a crisscross for bedding. El gathered wildflowers in her arms and spread them over the branches for cushioning, and soon they had made a place to bed down for the fast-approaching night.

They unwrapped their fish and berries, ate mushrooms, and drank all their water. Niko watched the rabbit hop away before he went to the spring to refill their canteens in the cool, fresh water.

There was a field of flowers where El could squat down and pee. When she came back, she, too, went to the spring with a towel and washed herself in the cold water bubbling up from somewhere deep in the earth. When she was finished, Niko did the same, and by the time he returned, El was lying on the bedding they'd made, staring up at the sky through slots in the willow leaves. Stars began to emerge, and slowly the day gave way to a dusting of stars scattered across a darkening sky.

As they lay on their backs next to each other in silence, the night noises began all around them. They heard a musical din of tree frogs calling in high-pitched chirps, and crickets chirping a singsong. Then frogs, drawn to the water flowing from the spring, began low barumphs to each other. Bats, emerging from some-where, whirled and dove in silence. What had seemed like a placid landscape pulsed with life.

El knew she should have been tired. Indeed, her legs wanted rest. But her mind could not calm itself. She watched the end-less array of stars in the night, ever more of them emerging, and exclaimed when she saw a shooting star.

"Did you see that?"

"No, what?" Niko asked.

"A shooting star. It's a good omen."

"Do you think so?"

"Of course."

"Then you're happy being here? You think we did the right thing escaping?"

She was quiet for a few moments, waiting for another meteor to flash across the sky.

"I think we had no choice."

"And I think I should have stayed to fight them."

"Does that mean you're sorry to be here?"

"No," he said, and was quiet before speaking again more softly. "I'm happy to be here with you."

El turned her head to look at him. He was looking at her already, waiting for what she would say. But she didn't say anything.

"Why did you take care of me, El? When my ankle was bad

and I couldn't walk? You could have left me any time and gone on. You know how to take care of yourself. Better than I do out here. In the city, I knew how to get along. But this . . ." He waved one arm at the trees and sky. "I'm lost out here. I probably would've starved without you. Why did you do it?"

"I don't know. I never thought about leaving you behind. I don't know what's out there, either. It's like Old Merrie said: We're tied at the hip now."

"What about later? When we get there? Will we still be tied like this?"

"I don't know what will happen."

"Would you want to be? I mean, when we get there. Together . . . would you want to be together then?"

El turned away to look up at the sky.

"We're so small, aren't we? I wonder if we matter at all. If everything that happens matters or if we're just a dot in a blur of time. We think we're so important, and we're really not. Nothing that happens to us is permanent. We're like these willows, waving in the breeze."

Niko was very still. It seemed as if he'd fallen asleep until he asked, very softly, "Have you forgiven me?"

El's eyes had gotten used to the dark by then, and she could see where there would be a scar on his cheek after it healed. She reached out and touched it with the tip of her finger.

"We hurt each other. I'm sorry for that. I don't think we meant to. I think we were cornered and treated like things, not like humans, not like living creatures, but like something you use to get what you want. I don't know if I've forgiven you. What happened will always be with me. Like the scar will always be with you. But it doesn't have to be who I am or who I can become."

Niko was quiet again, thinking about what she had said.

"I wish I could take it back," he told her. "But I can't. I can't even forget it happened. I wish I could."

"I'm not afraid of you, Niko," El said. "I try not to blame you for what happened but it's not possible. I was shocked and very fearful , and then very angry. It was like someone had taken over for me and was living a nightmare inside me. All that hate and anger was like a sickness. But after I went back to the convent and took some time for myself, I remembered who I had been before. That helped me some. But I realize now I'm not the same. Something was stolen from me. Or maybe stolen is not the right word. I also remembered who you had been before. And that person wasn't the same one from the night of The Race. It was hard for me to separate those two people. The Niko I knew before, who was so sweet to me, and that other Niko. I think it must be hard for you to separate them too. But I think we have to forgive ourselves before we can forgive others."

She thought about taking his hand in hers but held back.

"I hope you can forgive yourself," she told him.

"I don't know what to say anymore," Niko said. "Am I sorry? Yes. Do I regret choosing you instead of one of those approved girls? I regret how it made you feel. I regret what has happened and how close I came to attacking you. I regret all the trouble I caused you. But I don't regret escaping from Infinius. And I hope that something better waits for us somewhere. You think that will be Zamora. I hope you're right. Perhaps, if you are right, then you'll be glad we escaped, too. Maybe you won't want to stay with me or even know me when we get there. I regret that. I can't imagine not wanting to be with you. I won't miss anything from my old life."

He paused for a moment and then added, "But at least there I knew where I stood and what to expect. Here I'm no one with nothing. I'm just a floating island. And you're the only thing that keeps me from disappearing into nothing. I don't know if I can forgive myself. But if you can forgive me, that's a place for me to start because this sense of floating in a sea of nothing, with nothing to fight against, nothing to scrounge for, nothing to fear, it's an alien existence. Not mine. Not anyone's."

They were quiet for a time until suddenly Niko said, "I've never kissed a girl."

When El didn't answer he said, "I always wondered what it would feel like. Just to kiss a girl."

"Do you want to kiss me?" El whispered.

"Would you mind?"

"I don't know. I've never kissed a boy."

"Then it would be the first time for both of us."

"What do you think it will be like?" she asked.

"A kiss?"

She shook her head.

"Zamora. I keep thinking about it. Haven't you wondered what it will be like?"

"I haven't let myself. Back there . . . back at Infinius . . . I knew who I was. I knew how my day would start and probably how it would end. I had confidence in myself back there. Now . . ."

"Now?"

"I don't know anything anymore. I only know that you're the only completely good thing that ever happened to me. And I ruined it."

Niko closed his eyes, but shutting out the sight of the night sky through the willow leaves couldn't close off his thoughts or the pain that engulfed him. Yes, they would get to Zamora, safe and alive, but what then? What was there for him in Zamora? El wouldn't need him there. He would be alone with no reason to be anywhere. It was terrible, this feeling of loneliness, terrible to feel completely detached.

And then, as the night air turned cooler and the breeze died away, and the branches of the willows stopped swaying and the night chorus became like a steady heartbeat, he felt El's lips on his and her fingers touching his face and her body so close that her warmth radiated over him.

Back in the city, the name *Niko* became a kind of myth. A myth that Villinkash couldn't extinguish. The myth grew, along with images of El. Her face was reproduced on walls and street corners, taped on paper over InCom screens, dropped from windows and raised in triumph like a battle flag. No matter how the Regime might try to stamp it out, the myth grew, and one day, one day soon, Niko and El would reappear.

The people believed in it, prayed over it, lived for that day.

Discussion Topics for Book Clubs

1. Was Niko justified in what he did to escape Child Holding Center Number Five?

2. If you were in Niko's situation, would you want to move to The Ring, knowing you might be selected for The Race?

3. How does the political system of Infinius dictate the ways people find to survive?

4. What happens when the political powers shut off free press and free speech?

5. Is Huston a "good" guy or a "bad" guy?

6. Why does Saskia still love Huston? Why was she drawn to him in the beginning?

7. How should El have dealt with Niko after he attacked her?

8. Is Father Ignatius still a religious leader?

9. Does El love Niko?

10. What do you think El and Niko will find in Zamora?

Acknowledgments

Thank you to all the wonderful support system at She Writes Press and SparkPress: Brooke, Shannon, Lauren, Julie, and everyone who had a hand in helping see this book over the finish line.

As well to all the writers at workshops who added helpful comments and critiques, my appreciation goes out to you: Erica, Ruth, Rebecca, Jessica, Tom, Mark, Paul, Paula, Rimas, Amy, Whitney, Ellen, Shannon, Lisa, Maria . . . we had such fun, didn't we? And Denny's incredible lunches, can we ever thank her enough?

To the writer-teachers Bob Bausch, Tom Zoellner, Dick Bausch, Joyce Maynard, Sue Levine, Lary Bloom, Wally Lamb, Fred Lebron, I say thank you for your own works and for sharing the process, and especially Jen Haupt, dear friend and wonderful reader.

I've been fortunate over the years to meet and mingle with many writers. I treasure those memories and value the experiences of reading their works and sharing in their growth.

SELECTED TITLES FROM SPARKPRESS

SparkPress is an independent boutique publisher
delivering high-quality, entertaining, and engaging
content that enhances readers' lives, with a special focus on
female-driven work. www.gosparkpress.com

Gatekeeper: Book One in the Daemon Collecting Series, Alison Levy, $16.95, 978-1-68463-057-8. Rachel Wilde—sent from another dimension to bring defective daemons in for repair —needs to locate two people: a woman whose ancestors held a destructive daemon at bay and a criminal trying to break dimensional barriers. Helped by a homeless man with unusual powers, she uncovers a rising shadow organization that's changing her world forever.

Sky of Water: Book Three of the Equal Night Trilogy, Stacey L. Tucker. $16.95, 978-1-68463-040-0. Having emerged triumphant from her trials in the Underworld, Skylar Southmartin is stronger and gutsier, and can handle anything that comes her way. In the gripping climax of the Equal Night Trilogy, she uncovers one last secret no one saw coming—one that Vivienne, the Great Mother of Water, hoped would stay buried for another 13,000 years.

Echoes of War: A Novel, Cheryl Campbell. $16.95, 978-1-68463-006-6. When Dani—one of many civilians living on the fringes to evade a war that's been raging between a faction of aliens and the remnants of Earth's military for decades—discovers that she's not human, her life is upended . . . and she's drawn into the very battle she's spent her whole life avoiding.

Pursuits Unknown: An Amy and Lars Novel, Ellen Clary. $16.95, 978-1-943006-86-1. Search-and-rescue agent Amy and her telepathic dog, Lars, locate a missing scientist who is reported to have an Alzheimer's-like disease—only to discover that someone wants to steal his research for potentially ominous purposes.

Deepest Blue: A Novel, Mindy Tarquini. $16.95, 978-1-943006-69-4. In Panduri, everyone's path is mapped, everyone's destiny determined, their lives charted at birth and steered by an unwavering star. Everything there has its place— until Matteo's older brother, Panduri's Heir, crosses out of their world without explanation, leaving Panduri's orbit in a spiral and Matteo's course on a skid. Forced to follow an unexpected path, Matteo is determined to rise, and he pursues the one future Panduri's star can never chart: a life of his own.

About the Author

L B Gschwandtner's short stories have been awarded prizes from two *Writer's Digest* writing competitions, The Lorian Hemingway Short Story Competition, and one of her stories was short-listed by the Tom Howard Short Story Contest. Her work has appeared in various journals including *Del Sol Review*. Her prose poem "In The Forest of My Dream" has been included in the anthology *Oil and Water*.

Her novel *The Other New Girl* was a USA Best Book Awards winner and received an honorable mention from Reader Views Literary Awards.

She lives in a house on stilts overlooking a tidal creek in Virginia where she sees bald eagles soar past her windows and perch in the trees.

Books by LB Gschwandtner:

The Other New Girl
The Naked Gardener
Shelly's Second Chance
Carla's Secret
Page Truly and The Journey to Nearandfar
Foxy's Tale
Maybelle's Revenge